CU01401645

A Dales Companion & Other Stories

Norman Harrison

Acknowledgments

My thanks to my editor, publisher and proof readers for all their efforts.

Any remaining failings are entirely my own.

First published in 2006

http://www.normanharrison.co.uk

ISBN on back cover

Contents

A Dales Companion

Introduction

This is a gentleman's account of an energetic and inspiring week spent in the wilds of the Yorkshire Dales. Each day is dealt with separately and honestly. My intention is not to conceal any details, even if occasionally they appear to place me in a less-than-favourable light. I do not claim that it will be easy; efforts must be made on both sides, but I feel sure that it will be obvious from reading the ensuing chapters that a great deal can be achieved in overcoming social barriers if one approaches the problem with an open mind and a willing heart. Talking of open minds, I've often been accused of being an anachronism in this day and age, quite mistakenly I believe. However, I do maintain that one's position in society, and I say this with all humility, carries with it a certain noblesse oblige. One has to set standards and lead the way, both figuratively and literally, much as I try to do on these mini-expeditions.

I do allow that springtime is rather early in the year to be spending a week in our country cottage, but summer holiday plans, we're going to the West Indies again with the Godfrey-Thornton's, by the way, mean we have to rearrange our timetable. The other factor is that the Little Lady is quite adamant that I lose at least two stones in weight before I can be seen in bathing trunks. In fact, to tell the truth, it was she who arranged this trip. We're here with our retainers; listed below, with a few pen-portraits:-

Partridge, excellent chap, served as my batman in the Regiment; now my man and chauffeur, loyal, a bit stolid, but strong as a donkey, possibly not quite as intelligent.

Cook, don't know her actual name, salt of the earth, knows her place, never seen out of it.

Snipe, local youth, peasant stock, bit of an attitude, helps Finch look after the cottage grounds.

Finch, head gardener and general factotum; one of father's old retainers, bluff, taciturn to the point of rudeness, needs watching.

You must wonder why I chose such unlikely raw material with which to attempt to weave a cohesive social fabric. Well for a start, it's like being in the army, one has to work with the material one has. Secondly, I really believe, that the more people know about each other and their respective lifestyles, the easier it is to form harmonious working relationships. With greater harmony comes greater efficiency and greater efficiency automatically means greater output. Follow my drift?

To really know people it is often necessary to share their lifestyle for a time. One should not be unduly deterred by this. Think in the long term! These initial sacrifices can be regarded as an investment, and who can say what the lasting and far-reaching benefits of sound investments might be?

Monday

The Celtic Wall, North Yorkshire (GR 802674)

I realised something special was afoot this morning when I found my Norfolk jacket, tweed plus-fours, a deerstalker hat and a stout pair of brogues laid out neatly at the side of the bed. I tackled Partridge about it when he came in with the breakfast tray,

"Begging your pardon Captain, but you did say yesterday evening that you'd like to get started straight away. I thought a nice brisk walk would be a good idea."

I do wish these retainers would mind their own business. They don't seem to understand that what is said over port in the evening, bears no resemblance to what one intends to do on the morrow.

"I've asked Cook to prepare a picnic lunch, Captain, and Snipe, the lad, will come along as well. I thought a stroll up the Happy Valley to see the Celtic Wall might be just what you needed, sir."

It looked as though I didn't have much choice; everything seemed to have been arranged. The Little Lady must have been working overtime. Fortunately it was a bright morning and it might not be a bad idea after all, I thought, as I selected my favourite walking stick, the long shepherd's crook.

Partridge parked the Range Rover in the car park in the village of Stainforth and we set off down the narrow lane to the river. I strode out in front and set the pace, as befits the expedition leader. Young Snipe followed with the blankets, the picnic table and the waterproofs, and Partridge brought up the rear with the picnic hamper. I crossed the delightful packhorse bridge over the Ribble and soon outdistanced my companions. I'd told Partridge he shouldn't have brought the largest hamper, and looking back I could see he was getting it wedged on the sides of the bridge.

"Use your head, man!" I shouted. Good God, you've even got to do their thinking for them.

Thirty minutes later at the top of a slope I had the first glimpse of the Celtic wall, prominent on the brow of the hill across the valley to my left. My team was nowhere in sight so I pushed on, eager to reach our objective. The wall had been built some 2000 years ago by people who could not even have imagined me, or my lifestyle; yet here was I on this sunny morning in the year 1995 AD. admiring their handiwork.

"Look on my works ye mighty and despair."

Breathless after the short climb I leaned on the wall, solidly built out of local limestone, and looked across the valley towards the dramatic cliffs of Smearsett Scar. Below me, in the valley bottom, I could see the tiny figures of my companions moving slowly along the green track towards me.

Whilst I was waiting for them to arrive I paced out the wall; just about the length of a decent cricket pitch! Five feet high and five feet in width at the base, much thicker and stronger than the usual field boundaries in the area.

It was nearly half an hour later before we sat down on the tartan blankets for a welcome lunch. The pâté, however, was a little too gamey for my taste. I must remember to tell Cook; she's too fond of patronising these new-fangled supermarkets for my liking.

Over lunch we exchanged views on the probable reason for this ancient structure we were using as a back-rest. Partridge was of the mind that it was some kind of defensive wall, built to protect a settlement in the valley below. Snipe, too pedantic by far for an under-gardener, maintained that it was probably used as a cover for a Celtic burial mound. I soon silenced them with my theories. It was, I told them, either a shooting butt for a dozen or so guns. And I explained how the beaters would have driven the birds up the valley onto the waiting guns or, I went on, before they could interrupt, it could have been a show wall. My companions were suitably stunned at this, and I had to explain that it was probably one of the very earliest forms of advertising. The Celts could have built this section of wall as a sample, to publicise their skills. Travellers coming up the valley would see it on the top of the hill and be tempted to order a similar one for their own particular village.

"There could even have been salesmen on the track below", I suggested. "You know, like those time-share Johnnies you get on Morecambe promenade - Order your wall here. As seen on yonder hill beyond Stainforth. You know, chaps," I went on after a moment's thought. "A man must carry knowledge with him, if he would bring home knowledge." That really subdued them. I find that the timely use of one of the good Doctor's epigrams is usually enough to demolish the opposition.

Leaning back against the wall with a blanket snugly around my knees, somnolent with the exercise and the post-prandial claret, I couldn't help daydreaming about those ancient Celts. I wondered just what delicacies those chappies would have had in their picnic baskets. After a short time, and feeling the chill of inactivity, I decided the lounge bar of the local hostelry was more conducive to serious contemplation than our present position. Leaving the men to strike camp I set off back down the valley. Happy Valley, to the right, is a misnomer nowadays; some miserable peasant has blocked off the route at the bottom. Don't these people realise that my forefathers, whose portraits hang on the wall of my drawing room to this very day, fought and died to preserve the freedom of this great country of ours?

I was feeling the self-satisfaction of a successful expedition leader and invigorated by a tough day in the mountains as I strode down the hillside. I soon reached the hamlet of Little Stainforth with its multifarious signs of curt negatives. No Parking, no access, no footpath...no this, no that and certainly none of the other. I made a short diversion across the field at the packhorse bridge to glance down into Stainforth Force. On this day resembling nothing so much as a raging torrent of draught Guinness frothing down the ravine.

Comfortably ensconced in the lounge bar of the Craven Heifer whilst waiting for the chaps to arrive I reflected on the day. In three hours or so we had travelled back in time 2000 years. It makes one feel somehow...rather humble. I mean, that ordinary members of the public like us, can, if we just make the effort, experience some of the hardships endured by our primitive ancestors.

An hour later wallowing in a hot bath, a brandy to hand on the washstand, the aches and pains of the day's efforts soon disappeared. One of cook's special gourmet dinners to look forward to this evening and I'm beginning to feel I could quite enjoy this rigorous country life for the rest of the week.

Tuesday

The Heights of Ingleborough, North Yorkshire, (GR 741745)

Up early today and away up the A65 to Clapham. Didn't see the Little Lady this morning but did notice rather a stack of unopened parcels in the drawing room before we left.

Now this village, Clapham, from which we start this expedition, is a place after my own heart. It's a picturesque little spot with a babbling brook neatly dividing the main street, grey-stoned cottages along each side, and the parish church solemnly overlooking the village from the top end. However, more important than these physical attributes, in my opinion, is the fact that the village has been almost entirely owned by the same family for hundreds of years. It is this sort of paternal feudalism which made the British Empire respected throughout the world, and I put my own successful business career, in large measure, down to a very similar approach. I think I can honestly say that each member of my office staff knows his, or even her, place in my organisation, and furthermore, I feel that I am not too remote in my boardroom if any of my underlings need help with any personal problems. All they have to do is make an appointment through my private secretary, Miss Grimside, and the matter can then be thrashed out. 'A contented staff is an efficient staff', has always been one of my mottoes.

Sorry about the diversion. Let's get back to the expedition. One of the beauties of walking in the countryside is that one can ruminate and reflect on one's ideas, without the constant interruption one gets in an executive position in the company. In mid–reverie, however, I became aware of a plaintive cry from the rear.

"For God's sake, what is it, Partridge?"

"We should have turned right there, sir. Through that gate and into the estate."

I'd left young Snipe behind on this trip and brought Old Finch, the head gardener and general factotum. Snipe had got on my nerves yesterday with his know-all attitude. He could do a bit of gardening today for a change, rotavating that soggy pasture would do a lot for his humility. These know-alls always seem desperately keen, somehow, to share their knowledge with everybody within earshot.

"I'm well aware of that, Partridge, thank you. Don't you start. This way, chaps, follow me, through this gate."

Now this was more like it. The Reginald Farrer Estate. A public benefactor and a man after my own heart. Travel abroad and bring as many plants back as you can carry and plant them on your own estate.

What a truly glorious walk through the woods; the lake below us to the right shimmering in the morning sunlight. I strode ahead. I imagined Reginald must have felt like this in south-east Asia as he strode along the jungle trails at the head of his team of porters. I raised my hand, "Halt!" I called. "We'll make camp here for a while and have a coffee break." Selecting a suitable patch of sheep-cropped turf near the stream I waited for Partridge to unpack the tartan rug and the folding chair.

"There you are, Captain....black, white or Capucinno?" he asked, producing a selection of flasks from the hamper when we were all settled.

"Oh, white, I think, er two sugars please, there's a good chap."

"Sorry, sir, her ladyship says you're only to have one sugar."

Drat the bloody woman, I do wish she wouldn't confide in the servants so much. I'll bet if Reginald had wanted two sugars in his coffee he'd have damned well got it without question. Probably shot the bearer if he'd answered back like that.

This was bliss, basking in the warm sun, listening to the rippling music of the beck. I felt fitter and more relaxed already. Pity about the profiteroles though, they're never quite the same when they've been squashed flat and some clumsy handyman's coarse fingers have attempted to reshape them. After thirty minutes rest I gave the order to move out.

"Prepare to strike camp," I said, still feeling very Reginald Farrerish. "I want to reach the summit before nightfall." I could tell from Partridge's face that he was somewhat disconcerted by that last remark and Finch looked none too happy either. When the peasant classes develop a sense of humour they might not need us to organise their affairs for them so much.

The large cave mouth at the foot of a limestone cliff attracted my attention. "Ingleborough Cavern," I announced, glancing at the notice board. "A show cave, many unusual formations. The public are admitted at certain times. Unfortunately, we don't have the time today."

"I've been in," muttered Finch.

"So have I," said Partridge.

I strode on. Perhaps I should have brought Snipe and left these two at home. We negotiated Trow Gill with some difficulty. I was perfectly all right, of course, but Finch made a meal of it with the hamper. Getting it caught on the overhanging rocks and muttering all the time about his bad knees. I had to lend a hand up the narrow staircase at the top, at great risk to my camera, I might add, which once or twice swung dangerously close to the rock face.

With some relief we emerged into the open and followed the wall up to the stile onto the open moor. Our destination lay ahead and I led off on the track across the moor. Passing a declivity on my left and feeling it my duty as leader to keep the men informed I said. "Gaping Gill on the left!"

"Bar Pot!" muttered Finch.

"Bar Pot?" I queried immediately, not liking the contradictory tone of his voice at all.

"Bar Pot," he repeated. "Gaping Gill's over there."

I consulted the map through its transparent cover, "Ah I see, perhaps you're right, there's a speck of dirt on the cover just there."

Old Finch snorted, but said nothing. Now I don't know whether he was snorting out of habit; he seemed to snort an awful lot. It wasn't a pleasant mannerism at all, but I suppose one had to make allowances for the elderly.

Standing on the rocky edge to Gaping Gill I experienced a profound feeling of discomfort. The surface of the rock was slippery and I found the unseen depths somewhat intimidating. I backed off a little way and called the men to me.

"Here Finch! Don't get too near the edge."

"It's all right, sir, I've been down before, many times," he added.

"Not without a rope though," I countered, rather pleased at my witticism, but somewhat disappointed at the lack of reaction from the men.

"You know, sir. The first man to get down to the bottom went down on a ladder, a Frenchman he were an' all."

"Don't be ridiculous, Finch." These primitive people believe any thing they're told; they probably think spirits live in the caves as well. "Where is there a ladder long enough to reach to the bottom of there? And how do you think they could carry it over the moors? It'd take at least fifty men to carry it on their shoulders. How could they get it up Trow Gill? You couldn't even get the hamper up."

There was that snort again. When we get back, the first thing I'm going to do is insist that Cook sees to it that Finch gets a medical check-up. His nasal membrane must be like a piece of raw liver.

On we went, me in the lead setting the pace. Up the muddy slopes and onto the shoulder of Little Ingleborough; a pause to let the men catch up and for me to catch my breath, probably the rarified air one gets at altitude. Now, with the wind whipping across our backs, we moved more quickly across the less strenuous ground towards the summit. What a great feeling of achievement I experienced as I surmounted the last little climb and emerged onto the summit plateau at the head of my party.

"This is it lads. Well done. We'll make for the shelter over there and have a rest and a bite to eat and decide on our route back." Heads down, buffeted by the wind we strode across the large plateau. Away to our left the sands of Morecambe Bay and the vast expanse of the Irish Sea were clearly visible. In front one looked over the valley towards Whernside, picking out the arches of the viaduct at Ribblehead, and then one's gaze swept over Kingsdale across to Gragareth. Beyond that the dark peaks of the Lake District loomed majestically on the horizon.

"Just look at that view, men," I exulted, when we were settled in one segment of the shelter. "Just look at that." I was overwhelmed, both by the amazing views, and the effort it had taken to reach this spot against the battering of the wind. A cup of coffee and a cucumber and salmon sandwich were the order of the day, and feeling refreshed and still excited about the success of our mission, I was prompted to share a few of my spiritual thoughts with the men.

"You know, men," I began, using my inspirational Henry the Fifth voice. "We belong to a very special group of people; men who have surmounted obstacles, overcome the heights. We are the few, the blessed few. People down there, never even dream of such places in the clouds; they do not know what summits can be reached with a little effort and self-belief." I must admit I was feeling almost God-like on this elevated platform looking down on the rest of the world and pitying the mundane day-to-day activities which absorbed their time so relentlessly. One even felt sorry for the Little Lady busily shopping away her soul in Harrogate; not even aware of the sublime joy I was sharing with my men at this very moment.

"They used to live up here."

Lost as I was in divine contemplation, I thought I'd misheard Finch's remark.

"I beg your pardon, Finch?"

"They used to live up here," he repeated.

"The Gods, you mean?" I queried, feeling that this was yet another example of primitive folklore. Although on this occasion I could quite well see the basis for it.

"Naw," he half-grunted, half-snorted. One was never sure whether the sound came from his mouth or his nose. "A bunch o' scruffy, dirty natives called the Brigantes used to live up here in the summer."

I just looked at him in utter contempt. The fool had completely overstepped the mark this time. One could excuse simple-minded ignorance but I will never condone, or accept, outright pig-headed stupidity.

"Don't be bloody ridiculous, man. How could anybody possibly live up here?" I was almost speechless at the fool's idiocy..."Where would they do their shopping?" I demanded. "How would they get supplies up here? What about toilets? What about the washing facilities? Use your head for God's sake, man." I decided there and then that the best thing for me to do was to get rid of Finch fairly quickly.

"Now, gather round men. This is the plan for this afternoon. I want you, Finch, to go down the way we came up. Take the hamper with you, pick-up the Range Rover in Clapham and drive it around to that pub in the valley down there! See it, man? It's marked on the map here, see? P!"

"That's the Post Office, sir, and you wouldn't get a drink there, even if it was open. The pub's actually marked 'inn' on your map. It's the Hill Inn at chapel-le-Dale."

"Right, right I know that. You drive round to the Hill Inn and meet us there. Partridge and I will be in the bar, probably having lunch there if they have a decent menu! Right, any questions?"

"Humph! Keys? Shall I take the keys?"

"Of course you take the keys, man. Give him the keys, Partridge, for God's sake."

"You've got 'em, sir. I gave 'em to you on the car-park, for safe-keeping, you said."

It took me two or three minutes to find the keys, by which time we were feeling decidedly chilled. I was annoyed with Partridge, not just because of the keys, but because if I don't look after things myself I strongly suspect things will get lost, or not get done. These are grown men and should be able to organise their lives without looking to me for guidance all the time.

"Right off you go, Finch. Cheerybye, good luck."

Clearing his nasal passages with more force than I would have thought possible without causing serious internal injuries he stepped out into the wind and was immediately buffeted away in the general direction of the descent. From the shelter we watched his hunched wind-blown figure stagger over the rim of the plateau, the hamper on his shoulders visible for several seconds after his body had disappeared from view.

"I say, Partridge, I've been meaning to ask you this all week. Is there something the matter with Finch? He seems to have difficulty breathing at times, snorts a lot, don't you think?"

"Can't say as I've noticed, Captain. He keeps very much to himself, he does."

"Well, I suppose one has to with an unfortunate condition like that. Come on Partridge, let's get moving. I think it's time we were sitting by the fire in the pub now, follow me."

I led the way across the summit heading roughly in the same direction as Finch but branching to the left as we reached the edge. We caught a brief glimpse of his stumbling, and presumably snorting, figure as he moved uncertainly down the track to our right. It will do him good I thought, develop his character a bit, I firmly believe that one's chaps should be allowed to use their initiative on occasions, providing they are well supervised, of course.

I enjoyed the descent to Chapel-le-dale. There was just one awkward moment when I suggested a short-cut across the moor rather than follow the duck-boards. I'd sent Partridge on ahead to scout out the ground when he suddenly let out a cry of distress and disappeared up to his thighs in quagmire. Fortunately he had the presence of mind to hold his equipment bag aloft, and it was possibly this extra weight which accelerated his downward movement. However, yours truly came to the rescue, as usual, and at the risk of getting my new brogues thoroughly soaked I hooked my walking stick under his arm and managed to drag him to safety. One does one's duty, for very little thanks, I might add. The rest of the trek to the hotel was uneventful. Partridge appeared to be lost in his own misery and seemed reluctant to respond to my attempts at jocularity. What made it worse, I suppose, was that being so soggy and muddy we could hardly allow him into the inn in that condition. He seemed quite comfortable on the bench outside whilst I enjoyed the warmth of the log fire and a rather reasonable meal of Yorkshire pudding served with beef and dumpling stew. I didn't forget Partridge though; I sent out a pint of the landlord's best bitter and a packet of beef-flavoured crisps. One of the maxims I picked up in the army and which I've always adhered to is, ' look after your men first.' If you want their trust and loyalty then you must consider their needs almost as much as your own.

I must have dozed off at some stage during the afternoon. Probably the heat of the fire, the exercise and the landlord's very palatable ale had induced this somnolence. Anyway, I was awakened by the landlord who wished to know if I required any more to drink as he was about to close the bar. Glancing outside, I noticed that the light was already failing so I declined his kind offer, feeling that it was time we made a move to get back to base. Pleasantly replete I forced my aching legs to the door, wished the landlord 'good day', and stepped outside.

The icy blast which hit me when I left the shelter of the building nearly tore the breath from my body. I looked around but there was no sign of Partridge at all; I wandered down to the car-park but that was completely deserted. There wasn't a soul in sight anywhere. I returned to the inn and tried the door, but it was locked. I banged loudly on it for some time, but no reply. All the lights were out, I made my way round the back of the building but there was no sign of life anywhere. It was very cold, it was rapidly getting dark, and it was beginning to snow; I had to do something quickly. I hunched up inside my waterproof and set off down the lane in the direction of the village, my intention being to telephone the cottage for assistance.

That evening was a long cold bitter experience. I could not get any one to answer the phone in the cottage and I spent a most miserable time sheltering in a telephone kiosk watching the snow piling up against the door. I was rescued, eventually, by the memsahib who had, unfortunately, on that particular day decided to stay over in Harrogate for the evening. She was not pleased to have to drive out in a snowstorm, I'll tell you.

I'm writing up this report in front of a blazing fire in the cottage, but I'm still chilled to the marrow even after a hot bath. I haven't seen either Partridge or Finch yet, apparently it's the staff's night off and they've all gone to the pub, but the Little Lady told me that Partridge had said that he thought I was staying the night at the inn and so he'd set off to walk down the valley. Fortunately, he told her, he'd managed to get a lift to Ingleton, and on being dropped-off there had come across Finch in the Range Rover who had got lost trying to find the way to the inn. A sorry story, and not one I found easy to follow, but a very disappointing end to the expedition; I shall have more to say to those two in the morning.

Wednesday

The ascent of Gordale Scar, North Yorkshire (GR 916641)

Feeling refreshed and relaxed after a good night's rest, and not being a person to hold a grudge for very long, I forgave Partridge and Finch for their stupid incompetence on the previous day. I informed them, however, that it would no longer be convenient for all the staff to be off duty on the same evening. I would draw up a duty roster and pin it on the daily information board in the morning. I ignored the snort from Finch, but it did remind me that we had a full team out today. It was, I understood, going to be an extended trek with rather a difficult climb to negotiate at one point. So besides The Snort, we had the jumped-up-Snipe, the encyclopaedic gardener, and the bovine Partridge, whose main attribute on these trips seemed to be his mule-like ability to carry heavy loads over rough ground for a minimum amount of fodder.

The early morning drive to Malham was delightful. As we neared the village I pointed out the grey limestone mass of Malham Cove, a perfect backdrop to the natural stage on which we were about to perform feats of courage and endurance. Well, it rolled off the tongue in almost Churchillian fashion, I thought.

For a short time we followed the rippling and youthful River Aire, fresh now in its embryonic state completely unaware of the pollution and exploitation waiting for it down the valley. Rather like life, I thought, the beauty of the morning inspiring the philosophical side of my nature. A fresh young child with beautiful innocent thoughts soon to be faced with the corrupting influence of so-called civilisation. Didn't Rousseau, or somebody, have something to say about that? I can vaguely remember Nanny Simpkins saying something like that just before I went up to College.

"This is part of the Pennine Way, chaps," I announced, catching sight of a nearby signpost.

"Did it last year," grunted Snipe.

I bit my lip, repressing my annoyance. One tries to tell these people, to educate them, to give them the benefit of one's experience, and all they do is brag about what they've done. It's quite impossible to tell them anything. We turned left and followed a smaller stream through the woods to Janet's Foss.

"Smell the scent? "I asked. "Wild garlic," I explained.

"Ramzans," retorted Finch.

"I beg your pardon, Finch?" I snapped quite annoyed at the lad. There's no need to be obscene. Any more outbursts like that I shall deal with you most severely." Couldn't help thinking that my grandfather would have horsewhipped the scoundrel for that, but staff are not that easy to come by nowadays, even though I try to reach the minimum wage. I forced myself to remain calm.

"That's the botanical name for it, sir. Ramzans for wild garlic."

I looked at him carefully but his expression appeared perfectly guileless so I let it pass this time. A bird darted along the surface of the stream and I quickly changed the subject.

"Look everybody. A kingfisher. Did you see it?"

"Dipper, sir," said Snipe emphatically.

"Dipper?" I queried.

"Definitely, sir. A dipper. They walk on the bottom of the stream."

I looked at his face. Does he think I'm as stupid as his mates? He returned my scornful look with such an innocent open expression that I had pity on his stupidity. Poor soul, I thought, he really believes these folksy fairy tales, I'm glad we didn't have him with us yesterday when we went up Trow Gill; he'd have been terrified.

We sat by the pool at Janet's Foss and had our morning coffee. I admired the formation over which the water was streaming.

"We could do with some of that limestone for our rockery," I said indicating the rock.

"That's tufa, is that," Snipe said sharply. "You can't have any of that; this is a National Park. You can't go round nicking stuff from here." His voice faltered when he realised to whom he was speaking.

"Er I'm sorry, sir." he added, realising that he'd spoken out of turn. "It's just that I'm a volunteer warden for the National Park Service, and er, it's my job to protect the countryside as much as I can."

Good God, I thought. Did we fight all the way through the last war to be told what we can and can't do by a bunch of little pompous parvenus in ill-fitting uniforms? I think not. However before I could marshall a devastating attack and put the little brat in his place, Partridge got to his feet and started clattering about with the table and chairs, and packing away the rugs and equipment.

"The next bit's the difficult bit, Captain. So you'd better lead the way now, I think," he said.

"Right," I said, somewhat mollified by the simple man's faith. "Follow me then, chaps."

I was not really prepared for the scene which met my eyes as we rounded the final bend in the narrow ravine. There was no way forward. The track was blocked by a waterfall. I'd been feeling ever more and more apprehensive as we'd moved between these intimidating overhanging rock walls. It seemed to get darker, danker and more eerie the further we penetrated. Now there was no way forward, we were faced with a waterfall flowing straight down the rocks in front of us. Still higher I could see the water pouring through a massive rocky aperture. No way was I climbing up there! Whilst I was studying the problem Snipe, in his yellow oilskins, pushed passed me, splashed across the pool of water in front of the rocks, and started clambering up through the waterfall.

"For God's sake, man!" I shouted, but my words were lost in the roar of the water.

Partridge then shouted in my ear, "Come on, Captain, it's nobbut a bit o' watter." He followed Snipe up the waterfall, the equipment bag balanced on top of his head, spraying the water out around him like a giant umbrella. I was fastening my Gore-Tex jacket up to the neck and wondering whether it would be more sensible to go back the way we'd come when Finch came up behind me and nudged me into the pool.

"Get yer feet on them ledges through there, sithee."

Peering through the streaming water I could faintly discern one ledge at least, but it was wet and slippery and not particularly inviting. Finch pushed past, a trifle impatiently I thought,

"Just follow me, sir, I'll show you."

He climbed up through the fall, the spray descending on me as I followed. It wasn't too bad once one got started, I realised, and there was a little cave part of the way up which provided some respite from the water for a time. Then nervously hand over hand, seeking rocky holds amidst the foaming torrent I clambered to the top. I must admit to a strong sense of relief, and a weakness in the legs when I rejoined the others.

"Wow!" I exclaimed, both relieved and exhilarated. "That was some climb."

"Well done, Captain," Partridge said.

Snipe and Finch, a little higher up the slope, were sharing some little private joke which had Snipe in convulsions and Finch, yet again, severely endangering his olfactory passages.

"Right-o chaps. Let's get moving again." I felt it best to bring some order to bear and get the group on the move.

I ordered a rest stop at the top of the steep incline as Partridge was obviously in need of a breather. He said it didn't matter but I thought it wise to exert my authority and overrule him for his own good.

Rested and re-organised we walked above the stream valley for a time before branching off towards a stile onto the road. A brisk walk up the road and across some common ground brought us within sight of Malham Tarn. Snipe was keen on tackling Great Close Scar, a grassy mound edged with limestone outcrops overlooking the Tarn, but I was having none of that and told him to unpack the luncheon gear here and now and settle on the grass. We could see the Tarn perfectly well from here without upsetting our appetite with any more life-threatening manoeuvres.

For lunch Cook had prepared a rather nice tuna salad and we had a very pleasant picnic. Afterwards I stretched out on the rug and closed my eyes, the better to appreciate the beauty and stillness of this idyllic spot. Minutes later, or so it appeared, I was rudely awakened from my nap by some fool tugging at the rug beneath me.

"What the...?" I muttered somewhat annoyed. It was Finch, of course.

"Sorry to disturb you, sir. But it's nearly two o'clock and time we were on the move again. It's a fair way back to the village from here."

"Right, Finch," I said, determined not to show my annoyance. "You get the gear together. I'll recce the route ahead."

Finch would have made a good lance-corporal in my old unit, but it is quite obvious that it takes a different class of person altogether to provide true leadership qualities. One could almost say that leaders are born into the role. For instance, in my position, the men respect me because they know they can rely on me to see them through, especially if the going gets tough.

I led on past the water sinks and down towards the dry valley leading towards Malham Cove. I drew the attention of the men to the way the stream disappeared underground at the sinks, and explained the properties of limestone and how caves were formed.

"The stream used to go down this valley," I indicated. "But now it sinks here and comes out under the Cove."

"No, it doesn't, sir," contradicted Snipe. "They put coloured dye in here and it didn't come out there."

"Well, where does it come out, then?"

"I can't remember exactly, sir. Aire Head Springs, I think, just below the village."

Ah. At last, something the little know-all wasn't quite sure about. "Well," I said, trying to control the superior tone in my voice. "I think you'll find, Snipe, that if you look at the configurations of this valley you'll realise that my hypothesis is the correct one."

"I'm not so sure, sir. I did a field study week up at the Centre here as part of my degree course and we did a lot of studies on the water table."

My turn to snort, and I must admit I quite enjoyed it. "Water table, Snipe? You need to get out in the countryside, man, to do any really serious geographic study."

I felt much better after that exchange and strode down the dry valley leaving Partridge and Finch to pick up the equipment, and Snipe to recover his composure. It was not until I was standing on the limestone pavement looking out over the Cove that we were all assembled again. I thought it wise to caution them about the drop.

"Keep well away from the edge, men. It's very very dangerous."

"I know, sir. I've climbed it." Snipe again.

I didn't even bother to look at him this time. They must live in a total dream world these people. I suppose it's the only way they think can get any respect by making outrageous claims like that. I made no comment but just edged away gingerly along the pavement, stepping carefully across the grykes until I reached the steps and followed them to the valley bottom. I carefully studied the stream which emerged from the base of the sheer rock wall, surreptitiously checking to see if there was any sign of dye. There wasn't! Looking up at the sheer rock face towering above me, I was certain that nobody could climb that, except perhaps Superman. And that, I decided, was probably where Snipe got his wild ideas.

I was brought back to the present by him addressing me from the side. "They've been in there," he grunted, nodding at the stream.

"Who have?" I asked, thinking what now? Bloody water sprites, or something.

"Cave divers," he answered. "They're trying to find a big chamber under there."

I snorted; it occurred quite involuntarily and took me completely by surprise. It was exactly the noise Finch was wont to make. I remember wondering at the time if it was some kind of infectious condition peculiar to the Yorkshire Dales.

The walk alongside the stream was pleasant and I stayed out in front not wishing to hear any more ridiculous and extravagant claims. I enjoyed a quiet pint of ale in the Lister's Arms whilst Snipe went off to fetch the Range Rover. Partridge and Finch sat outside on the bench enjoying the beer I sent out to them. Leaning on the bar passing the time of day with the landlady I reflected on yet another successful expedition. Not only were these outings valuable in allowing the men to gain a sense of achievement, I thought, but it also allowed them to see me in a more human role. One is all too often just a figure of respected authority rather that a human being who shares the same life, the same problems and the same joys. Adversity and challenge are great levellers, I concluded. I must remember that phrase the next time it's my turn to address the Lodge.

Thursday

Victoria Cave, North Yorkshire (GR 839650)

Settle is a picturesque, bustling, little market town. At one time, like its neighbours Skipton and Clapham, it was a traffic bottleneck and the scourge of through-travellers on the old A65. Since then bypasses have been constructed and these places have reverted to relative backwaters. Signs by the roadside now advertise their attractions and seek to induce the passing motorist to enjoy their rural charms.

We parked up on the big car-park and wandered through the market place. As soon as one leaves this square one begins to climb. First up a narrow cobbled street which leads to walled track and finally to a delightful green path onto the higher fells. It was hard walking but not unpleasant in the chill air of early morning. It had every promise of being a beautiful day and I was looking forward to another day of adventure. I was feeling very much fitter than at the beginning of the week and I felt sure that I had already lost sufficient weight to be a credit to the Little Lady at any poolside party. I called rest stops fairly frequently on the way up. I did not want to distress the men unduly at the start of the day and besides which, dramatic views were unveiled as we climbed steadily out of the valley.

I'd been inclined to leave Snipe behind on this trip, but as both Finch and Partridge had pleaded for his inclusion, I relented. It behoves one to show magnanimity on occasions. I felt, however, there was more than a little self-interest on their part; suspecting they were more interested in his load-carrying capacity than they were in his enjoyment.

We surmounted one rise and I was taking the obvious route down the valley with the limestone crags on my left sparkling in the sunshine. I felt a new spring in my step and invigorated by the fresh nip in the air I strode out briskly in the lead. I was halted by a call from the rear. I stopped, half-amused at the dependency these people already had on me. It was similar to waiting for one's child to catch up: I can remember what it was like when young Piers used to call out in the same way before he went on to boarding school.

"Hold on a minute, sir." It was Finch. He caught up, gasping rather stentoriously, I was pleased to note.

"The best route is up through that outcrop up there," he said, pointing almost vertically above his head.

"What?" I said, incredulously. "Are you mad, man? We'll never get Partridge and all the equipment up there."

"Oh, I'm all right, Captain," Partridge interjected. "No trouble to me, sir. And when we get up there it'll just be time for the coffee break, sir."

I was less than convinced. The route up through the limestone cliffs looked a bit severe to me, but not wishing to show any anxiety in front of the men I raised no objection. I've always believed that leading from the front was the hallmark of a true leader.

"Right, Finch, lead on. The sooner we get there the sooner we get the coffee break." It was as I had thought. It was not an easy route up. Admittedly there was a gap in the escarpment and a rough track up through the rocks but I was not all that comfortable with the steep drop behind me. However, once on top all was forgotten: the views in every direction were nothing less than dramatic. Ingleborough, Penyghent, Whernside each glinting in the sunlight and crowned with a dusting of snow; in the far distance the range of Lakeland peaks similarly coated. Closer at hand over the crags of Warrendale Knots was the massive ridge of Attermire Scar, with the black hole of Victoria Cave prominent in its face.

"Wonderful!" I exclaimed in delight. "The beauty of this vantage point, men, is that you can see the places we've visited during the week. There's the Celtic Wall over there." I pointed out. "And look, behind it is Ingleborough. You can see our actual route up to the summit." Needless to say the men did not appear to share my enthusiasm; they were more interested in the coffee and the chocolate biscuits.

"Here you are, Captain. Hot coffee and a plate of biscuits," Partridge said placing them on the low table.

I was entranced by the view and even whilst I enjoyed the break I felt obliged to try and instil a little more appreciation into my companions.

"Don't you ever get the feeling, chaps, that you'd like to get out there," I said, opening my arms expansively to take in the full vista, "and explore the whole area? Climb every mountain, follow every valley, see what's round the next bend?"

"I know what's round the next bend, sir. I've been round 'em all," retorted Snipe. "Done the Three Peaks Walk loads a' times, the Lyke Wake Walk, the Dalesway, the Pennine Way..." he tailed off as though too exhausted to list all his claimed achievements.

Course he would have done, I thought. The jumped-up jackanapes. He's been everywhere, done everything, probably got the bloody T-shirt as well. "I suppose you've got the T-shirt as well, Snipe?" I said in a light-hearted jocular manner. He stood up, slowly unbuttoned his jacket, opened it with a flourish to reveal the words, "SEEN IT, DONE IT, BOUGHT IT in large letters across his chest. Well, I was just speechless. Such blatant arrogance.

The next stage of our journey was through the Warrendale Knots, a series of limestone plugs stretching like the stumps of a particularly bad set of teeth across the intervening valley. We stood at the entrance to Victoria Cave and peered into the gloomy depths. I was relieved when I saw the warning notices advising people not to enter the cave because of recent rockfalls. I'd always felt somewhat nervous of confined spaces after Nanny Simpkins inadvertently locked me in the dog kennel during a game of hide and seek.

Snipe and Finch never fail to astound me with their gullibility, or indeed the way they sought to test mine. They maintained, and I leave you to judge how credible this may be, that the remains of elephants, hippos and rhinos have been found in this cave. Well, I ask you; does that sound likely? I tried not to sound too contemptuous but I fear some degree of scorn must have been apparent in my tone of voice.

"Skeletons of sheep," I suggested. "Chicken bones, pork chops," I added. "Picnickers sitting here in the cave mouth, throwing bones over their shoulders into the cave?"

"Exactly, " said Snipe. I must admit, momentarily, I was pleasantly surprised to have his agreement on something. But then he continued in his usual vein, "but not present-day picnickers; prehistoric picnickers."

I managed to get a quick snort in before he went on with his insane analysis.

"Prehistoric man dined on these extinct animals and left the bones and other rubbish in one corner of the cave. Over the years this pile of cast-off detritus accumulated and we now have a record of life in these parts stretching over thousands of years."

"Rubbish," I exclaimed. "You're trying to tell me that archaeologists base their studies on the fact that council binmen, or the equivalent in those days, failed to do their job properly?"

"Exactly," he said, in that clever way of his. "Why do you think binmen, even nowadays, always leave a bit behind in the street after every collection?"

My mind grappled with this statement for some time, so much so that I was hardly aware of the route we followed from the cave. I know we reached a narrow metalled road and after some fifty or so yards we stopped for lunch. A pleasant grassy bank in front of a small limestone outcrop afforded a comfortable picnic spot.

"Jubilee Cave," muttered Finch, nodded his head towards an arched entrance behind us. I grunted, without much interest I must admit, little knowing what was in store for me that afternoon. At present I was mulling over the fact that the Council Refuse Services were such an integral part of archaeological research.

The ham shank Cook had prepared for us was delicious, and with the pickled onions, mustard and rye bread we enjoyed yet another alfresco feast. I insisted Partridge repack the bones in the hamper, rather than dispose of them in the cave, so that future researchers should not be misled into the belief that pigs were kept in these caves during the twentieth century.

With a glass of mellow brandy in one hand and a King Edward in the other I gazed across the valley towards Ingleborough; such a peaceful tranquil scene. What more can a man want than this? Good food, a nice brandy, healthy adventurous exercise, good companions! Well, not exactly good companions, more like I was trying to work out a more precise definition to describe my companions when Snipe, who had been running on excitedly about the caves like some demented garden gnome called from behind me.

"Sir, come and look at this, sir?" His simple childlike request both touched and amused me.

"What is it, Snipe?" I said, with good-natured bonhomie.

"In here, sir. In this passage. It's all right, sir," he said noticing my hesitation. "There's plenty of room to walk about."

I do not know to this day what possessed me to enter the cave, I only know that I'll regret it for the rest of my life. I followed Snipe along the passage.

"I've been through, sir, you can get out at the other end. Come on sir, it's only a short way. It's like a show cave." With relief I heard Finch and Partridge coming up behind me.

"Aye, it's a little through system, sir. I've been through loads of times. Just keep going, and keep your head down. I'm right behind you." We turned to our right into pitch darkness. I stopped. "Hang on a minute." I shouted feeling along the wall for a light switch. "Isn't there a light anywhere?"

"Don't need one, sir. Can you see that light up front? That's where we get out. It's not far."

I peered ahead, yes there was a tiny speck of light, but it was minute. It could have been ten miles away for all I knew. I reached out for Snipe and grabbed the back of his jacket.

"Just bend down a bit here, sir and squeeze between these two slabs."

Oh, my God. I turned to go back the way we'd come, but in doing so cracked my head on the rock above. I cursed and sat down rapidly, cursing again as my seat splashed into muddy pool. It was then I noticed another shaft of light on the right of the cave. "There's another way out there, Finch. Why don't we go through there?"

"We're nearly there now, sir. Just follow Snipe. It's nearer to go on than to go back now, sir."

I seem to remember Macbeth saying something like that, but my mind was far too busy thinking about survival to recall the exact words. Anyway it didn't do much for him, did it?

Wriggling between the slabs was not easy for someone of my girth, and once through I found that the roof of the cave was very much lower on the other side. So much so I was forced to adopt a crab-like crawling movement to make any progress at all. The sticky mud on the floor of the cave did not facilitate forward movement in any way. Controlling my mounting panic I squelched towards the pinpoint of light which I knew was my only salvation. Then to my horror the light went out, in an instant my hopes were extinguished, surrounded by a clammy all-pervading blackness, lost in the depths of the earth, I cried out, "Help, the light's gone out!"

"It's all right sir, it's only Snipe going up through the hole. He's out now."

Indeed it was the figure of Snipe which had blocked out the daylight as, like a rat up a drainpipe, he'd shot to the surface. The guiding light shone once again and we, like the three Wise Men, headed towards it. A cold, and muddy coming we had of it, I thought, adapting Eliot to suit the occasion. Never did I think it possible that I would ever be glad to see Snipe's face, but I must admit that fact when his head appeared in the opening.

"Right sir, here we are. Just wriggle up through the hole and you're out."

Wriggle up through the hole? I'd got my head and shoulders into the narrow exit passage. After the dank underground it was sheer delight to be able to breathe the fresh moorland air and this helped allay the panic I'd felt earlier. I took stock of my situation; the panic returned almost immediately when I realised that my waist measurement exceeded the diameter of the opening by a good six inches.

"I'm stuck!" I shouted desperately.

"You're all right, sir. I can push you up from down here," Finch called up from somewhere between my legs. "Try and turn sideways a bit."

You can, perhaps, imagine the indignity of it all. The rough hands of Finch gripping my thighs and painfully forcing my lower extremities upwards, Yours Truly jammed solidly in the middle sweating profusely from a combination of pain and panic, and the diminutive figure of Snipe tugging ineffectually on my arms. To add to my embarrassment I became aware I was the centre of attention of a party of schoolgirls who had gathered behind Snipe and were staring at the spectacle with unashamed enjoyment.

"Take some of his clothes off! That's the only way you'll get him out!"

The voice was harsh and impersonal with a ring of authority to it. For a moment it reminded me of matron in my prep school and I was back there shivering in the queue waiting for the medical inspections to start.

Snipe suddenly appeared to be lifted out of the way and a huge female figure appeared above me. Without a word she tugged at the sleeves of my jacket and pulled it over my head, my pullover followed. She then seized my arms in an iron grip and yanked me upwards. I might at that point have gained my release but, unfortunately, the back of my braces snagged on a projecting rock, expanded to their limit and then sprang me back down the hole with such force that it catapulted my would-be rescuer down on top of me. Amid the confusion and the embarrassment of being closely entangled in such a compromising situation with a member of the opposite breed, I distinctly heard a roar of laughter from the girls. The Senior Mistress, as from her bearing I assumed she must be, was completely unfazed by the setback and again took command of the situation.

"They'll have to come off," she declared flatly.

I could sense rather than see the girls edge nearer the cavity. She pulled my braces over my shoulders and then tugged off my shirt. I was now down to my thermal vest and determined to retain that last remnant of modesty at all costs. The faces of the girls peering from behind their teacher were a picture of rapt attention and studious concentration.

"I'm going to unfasten your trousers a little bit, sir." The voice of Finch echoed up from the chamber below.

"No!" I screamed. "Finch, for God's sake, no!" but when have the fools ever listened to me? I kicked out wildly with my legs but it was to no avail. I felt my belt being unfastened, my zip released and the chill on my legs as my trousers slid down to my ankles. I groaned in despair.

"We're nearly there now, sir. But I might just have to ease your underpants down a bit, sir."

"No!" I yelled in desperation. "Stop it, Finch! You'll do no such thing, Finch, do you hear? Get off my legs this minute. Where's Partridge? I want to speak to Partridge. Partridge?"

"Here I am, Captain. What do you want me to do?" The voice seemed to come from above me. I found this confusing, was it an echo?

"Partridge?" I questioned, looking down.

"Up here, sir."

I jerked my head up in amazement. There was Partridge peering over the angular shoulder of the Senior Mistress.

"What the bloody hell, Partridge? What the hell are you doing up there, man?"

There was a horrified gasp from the senior mistress at my outburst and she turned to her charges," Stand well back, gels! This is no place for young ladies." There was a murmur of disappointment from the class, but I noticed there was only a token movement of withdrawal.

"I couldn't get through down there, Captain. The way out was blocked, so I came out the way we went in. I've come up here to help."

I fumed silently, adequate words again failing to come to mind when I needed them. I took a deep breath, "Look Partridge, for a start stop these people tearing my clothes off and then get me out of here."

"Right you are, Captain."

Partridge stooped down and wrapped his arms round my chest, then placing his boots on the rocks on either side, he leaned back and exerted his bull-like strength. The veins knotted on his forehead, his face turned red, then blue as his effort increased; there was a tearing noise about my midriff, underpants or stomach I neither knew nor cared, and then a scarcely perceptible upward movement, like the first movements of a cork coming out of a wine bottle. The speed of release increased and I let out a shout of sheer joy as I felt my body being yanked out of these rocky jaws. Partridge, taken by surprise at my release and still pulling with all his might, catapulted backwards down the hillside. Loyal to the end, he still retained a tight grip round my upper body and we tumbled over and over down the grassy bank straight into the group of schoolgirls. They scattered shrieking with what appeared to be more delight than horror. The Senior Mistress, with remarkable agility, leapt down the slope after us but her determined attempt to cover my embarrassment with her woolly hat only added to my indignity.

It was sometime before I had recovered sufficient equanimity of mind to be able to even think about the events of that day. Was it Dr Johnson who said that there was more to be endured than enjoyed in the human condition? I was inclined to agree. Needless to say the return walk over Attermire Scar was conducted in a silence which would have done justice to one of those ancient funeral corteges which carried the deceased from one village to another along the old corpse roads. Even Finch's snorts were muted and I was only aware of them as a dull background noise to my inner thoughts. The indignity, and the shame: I blush with embarrassment as I write. It was a weary and dispirited leader which led the way down the valley to the car-park.

No mention was ever made of that day's farrago in my presence. Indeed the long-term effects are still with me to this day. I still refuse to travel on the London Underground, and I never visit any gentlemen's toilet which is situated below ground level.

Friday

The Norber Erratics, North Yorkshire (GR 77269)

The 'Norber Eccentrics' might be a more appropriate name for our group, I thought, when Partridge informed me of our destination that morning as he came in with my breakfast tray. He laid out my walking apparel on the bedroom chair and I was pleased to note that it had been washed and pressed, and that my boots were dry and freshly polished. I think he, at least, was sensitive of my desire never to be reminded of the previous day's fiasco.

We started today's expedition in the car park in the attractive village of Horton-in-Ribblesdale. Dominating the valley on the opposite side was the classic profile of Penyghent, a lion with outstretched paws dozing in the morning sunshine. Today, however, our route lay in the other direction and we crossed the infant River Ribble by a footbridge and headed towards the railway station. I led across the railway line and followed the footpath over the Beecroft Estate, making for Sulber Nick, a cleft in the limestone outcrop which I knew from my map was yet another route to the summit of Ingleborough. I pointed this out to the men, feeling duty bound to keep them informed.

"Three Peaks' route," grunted Finch.

"We must try that next year," I said, not to be put off by his tone of voice.

"Are you coming up for a fortnight, then, sir?" Snipe asked.

"No," I answered, and was about to explain further when Finch was convulsed by an unfortunate paroxysm of spluttering. Wiping the tears from his eyes he apologised for holding us up and we pushed on up the fell-side and across the broken limestone pavement. Sulber Nick is a delightful little valley and the sheltered grassy location made the ideal spot for a coffee break so we settled down on the rugs. There, with the curlews calling and the lapwings wheeling around, one can really appreciate the bucolic charms denied to most city dwellers.

"We must be near their nest," Finch remarked, nodding up at a pair of lapwings, which were now becoming rather a nuisance with their insistent squawking. "If you get too near the nest one 'em will pretend to have a broken wing, or something, to lead you away."

I looked at him to see if he was serious; one can never tell with people like that. He seemed it, and to be fair to him, he probably thought it was true; country lore being difficult to eradicate in isolated communities.

"I think," I said, choosing my words carefully, so as not to offend the man. "You'll find that the lower orders of life are not really able to rationalise situations to that extent. Sophisticated thought processes like that need a far greater intellectual ability than are possessed by the bird population." There was a silence whilst they absorbed that information so I continued. "I know one can teach parrots to talk but they are only mimicking the human voice; they are not processing thoughts at the cognitive level."

"Well, how does the turnstone turn stones, then? And the oystercatcher catch oysters?" Finch rejoined some seconds later, obviously not convinced by my argument.

I was about to respond but Snipe piped up, "Oystercatchers don't catch oysters."

"Exactly," I remarked, glad of support at last from Snipe. "They haven't the brain power to open the shells".

"They don't use their brains, sir, they use their beaks. Anyway they eat mussels and limpets in this country". He said this with an air of finality and got to his feet and started packing away the gear.

The men were loaded up and all prepared to move away when out of the corner of my eye I saw a lapwing scuttling away on the ground dragging an open wing. I pointed across the fells in the other direction, "We need to take a left turn very soon and head across in that direction. Move out, chaps!"

The walk across the moor in the direction of Thieves Moss was very pleasant. We had mound of Simon Fell to our rear, Ingleborough's high table on our right and the leonine profile of Penyghent to our left. We walked in silence for some time with me in the lead and Partridge at the rear, coping magnificently, as always, with the loaded hamper. I was having some difficulty in identifying a prominent mountain on the horizon immediately in front of us. Surely it couldn't be Whernside? I stopped and unfolded my map from its case. Finch caught up with me. Noticing the direction of my gaze he said tersely, "Pendle Hill".

"Pendle Hill?" I repeated after a few seconds, not being able to find it on my map.

"Won't be on there, sir. It's in Lancashire. Where the witches come out on Hallowe'en, or so they say."

"Oh, yes, Finch." I retorted coldly. "Thank you very much," I did not intend to be drawn into any more primitive folklore.

I found Thieves Moss an interesting spot. Standing on the edge of the escarpment and looking down into the massive natural amphitheatre one is immediately reminded of the outdoor theatre at Epidaurus, where it is said that a pin dropped on centre stage can be heard from any point in the auditorium. I was never able to test this acoustic claim due to the many other people on the tour whispering Shakespearean snippets to friends and relations dotted about the arena.

A grassy track led invitingly over the moor and one could easily imagine travellers being waylaid in this isolated place by some debonair desperado on horseback. "Stand and deliver!" The dreaded call would echo in the night and some poor soul would be relieved of his wallet by a masked brigand who would then probably share his spoils with the villagers in the valley. I ventured to share this idea with Snipe when he came up. A decision I now regret as he immediately repeated it to Finch and they both doubled up in what appeared to be some kind of hysterical competitive snorting competition. Leaving them to recover in their own time I strode on, determined in future not to waste my observations on minds insufficiently developed to appreciate them. I think possibly some of the lapwing family exhibit signs of being higher up the evolutionary ladder than my companions.

Rounding one particular rise the whole valley of Crummackdale opened out before us. Instead of descending to our left however we made for the crest of the ridge directly to our front. When we attained this commanding height and were seated on a grassy terrace above the limestone scar I ordered luncheon to be served. As we enjoyed the first course, Cook's home made vegetable soup, I studied my map and the surrounding countryside. In the middle distance below us lay the village of Austwick, the houses huddled together for warmth like a herd of grey-slated armadilloes. It was a simile of which I was particularly proud, but on repeating it to my companions, found, as usual, it was completely wasted on them.

"Them's the Norber erratics," Finch gestured towards some dark rocks on the hillside. I'd not noticed them before, my gaze naturally taking in the wider horizons. Which in many ways is what someone from my background tends to do, leaving the smaller less significant items for those people for whom wide-ranging expansive thought is well outside the boundaries of their awareness.

On closer study the Norber Erratics were unusual. Standing around self-consciously, I thought, like strangers in a country pub on a Friday night; wishing they'd gone somewhere else. Some stones had obviously been placed there as some kind of memorial, shaped by some unknown sculptor and delicately balanced on pedestals overlooking the valley, possibly to commemorate the love of a rural swain for his lass. When I proffered this as a likely explanation Snipe and Finch snorted in unison. I was beginning to wonder if this was one of their Christmas party tricks; the special one, the showstopper, the one they felt obliged to rehearse at every opportunity.

"They were brought down from up the valley," Snipe informed us with his usual air of superiority. They were carried down here thousands of years ago by the glacier and dumped here when the ice melted." I caught a fleeting glimpse of that smirk of his when he added, "Actually they're from Northumberland."

"Oh, yes?" I scoffed. "With a prehistoric geordie fork-lift truck, I suppose." My scathing tone silenced the young upstart, or the Whipper Sniper I mentally nicknamed him, a rather clever play on words I thought. I had no regrets; I can only listen to his self-opinionated views for so long and then I feel it my duty to shut him up and remind him of his place.

After an extended lunch break, Cook's chocolate gateau is far too delicious to be rushed, we descended the hillside. We moved through a field of erratics as though paying our respects to rows of monolithic memorials in some Victorian cemetery. I think the reverence we felt was due in no small part to our awareness of the awesome forces of nature which had moulded this land in the past, and was still, in spite of our puny presence, actively carrying on the process.

The route to the lovely little hamlet of Wharfe was not as direct as one would have imagined from our position overlooking it, but by several contrived deviations and a series of ladder styles we attained a delightful walled track which led us directly into the heart of the tiny community.

The next part of our route lay along the road towards Helwith Bridge. I led the single file and insisted, in accordance with the infantry manual, on the requisite distance of seven paces between men. About half a mile on we were able to leave the road and follow a footpath on the left which led diagonally across the hillside to one of the lower ridges. What an astonishing sight then met our eyes. One minute one had been walking in rural tranquillity, the next minute one was gazing down on a scene from Dante's Inferno. Below us in a giant excavation lay the grey mephistophelian workings of the slate quarry. Well out of the public gaze, steadily and inexorably, like some giant slate-devouring monster chewing the heart out of the countryside. Grotesque dumper trucks throwing up clouds of dust in their to-ing and fro-ing about the grim landscape; massive wagons coming and going with clockwork regularity and the intensity of some urgent life-or-death mission. Glancing across the valley at the classic outline of Pen-y-ghent on the horizon, one was struck with the thought that man is considerably less successful at sculpting the landscape than nature.

A heron lumbered into the air on grey outstretched wings from the marshy ground as we descended, although it could just have well have been a white egret, for all I knew, which had adopted the natural colouring of the area. Local wild life could include grey swans, grey foxes and grey deer I suppose.

We edged round the quarry spoil heaps to Foredale where high above us under the limestone escarpment stood an incongruous row of stone terrace houses looking exactly like a rural Coronation Street. Instinctively one scanned the doors for a curlers-festooned head and listened for the raucous cry of 'hey, ower Jack!' echoing over the cobbles. On this occasion, the wind being from the wrong quarter, we were disappointed.

Somewhat dismayed at man's intrusive encroachment into the landscape we sought refuge in the hostelry at Helwith Bridge for a most delightful respite. I remembered my old pater's ex-army dictum; 'always feed the horses first, the men second and yourself last.' Horses not being in evidence on this expedition I immediately sent out a glass of bitter and a packet of crisps for each man whilst I ordered the steak and ale pie cooked, I was informed, on the premises that very morning. It was a delicious repast and together with a varied selection of ales it promoted in me a feeling of peaceful co-existence with the world and fully appreciative of nature's bounty. I raised my glass in a friendly salute to the men outside on the bench, but although they appeared to be looking in my direction, they may not have seen my gesture through the window.

The final part of the route was much more enjoyable; level walking along the left bank of the Ribble back to Horton. Dippers bobbed and curtsied on river rocks and then sped skimming along the surface of the water at our approach. I must admit, however, to some degree of relief as we neared the village. I was beginning to feel rather fatigued after the six, or more hours of strenuous mountain walking and an hour of eating and drinking at Helwith Bridge.

It had been a varied and interesting day. We had, I thought, when I was seated in the welcoming bar of The Golden Lion in Horton, seen the best, and possibly the worst aspects of rural life. A glance out of the window told me that the men had cleaned most of the mud off the boots and stowed away the gear and were now impatiently hanging about on the car park ready to depart. I waved my acknowledgement, ordered another pint of the excellent ale and settled down to jot down some notes in my pocketbook whilst the memories were fresh in my mind.

After some minutes I became aware of a face pressed to the window pane; it was young Snipe, the blasted whipper-snapper again. Angry at the intrusion and the invasion of my privacy I waved him away angrily. He mouthed through the glass, holding his fist to his ear "Telephone, sir. Her Ladyship for you."

There's always something, I thought. One cannot settle down for a minute without somebody bothering you about something. The one snag of being indispensable. I drank up quickly, apologised to the landlady for my hasty departure and crossed to the Range Rover. The Little Lady was calling to remind me that we had a dinner engagement at the Cranley-Johnstones on Tuesday week. She thought it best to remind me in good time. I was furious, not that I let my feelings betray me on the telephone. I glanced at the men for sympathy but they had that look of stupid impassivity on their faces, such a characteristic feature of people at their level, that I knew little fellow-feeling would be forthcoming from their direction.

On the drive back to the cottage I came to the conclusion that no matter how much one shares hardship and adversity with one's men there is always a social barrier over which it is impossible to cross; and the barrier is much higher on their side than it is on ours.

Saturday

The Worth Valley, West Yorkshire

Well worth a visit, Finch had said, in a despairing attempt at humour. The other men agreed; apparently they had all been born in the area and educated, to use the term loosely, in the town of Keighley. I'd never even considered them as having a past of sufficient importance to necessitate a return trip. However, since it was our final full day's walking I gave my assent. Noblesse oblige, I thought. One's rank is often proved in the way one allows one's subordinates a chance to express themselves.

The drive down the Aire valley was pleasant enough, but I was not impressed with the rather grim industrial prospect the place offered at first sight. The Downmarket Dale suggested itself to me as an appropriate name as I looked around but I kept the idea to myself so as not to offend the men on their day out. I consulted my map and informed my companions that the Worth was a tributary of the River Aire. I noted with excitement that one branch of it also flowed through the literary village of Haworth, and said as much to the men.

"Branwell were the only decent one of 'em," grunted Finch. He always expressed himself as though any contradiction would be unthinkable. I couldn't let it pass.

"How can you say that, Finch? His sisters produced some of the classic literature in the English language; all Branwell did was sit in the pub and drink himself into a stupor."

"Aye, that's what I mean, sir. He were the only normal one; he went in the Black Bull for a night out with his mates, while them women just sat at home writing boring old books."

What can you say in the face of such utter mindless philistinism, I ask you? I mean, is this all we've achieved after over a century of free education for the masses? I was speechless with despair for the future of mankind. I resolved that if I was the only one to carry the banner for a more enlightened approach to art and literature then I would carry it with pride and not be intimidated by ignorant clods from the lower classes.

"Do you mean to tell me," I said slowly, enunciating my words with great care, so that the importance of what I was about to say could not be misheard. "That literary masterpieces, such as 'Wuthering Heights' and 'Jane Eyre', have anything to do with having a night out with one's mates?" I added as much contempt as I could into that final phrase, sat back in my seat and silently dared him to respond.

"Well," he said. "When me and me mates on the OU Literature course have a night out in the pub we always seem to end up discussing literature in terms of the sociological background of the writers. Me and me mates decided that their books were just a psychological manifestation of repressed women in a male-dominated society."

I scarcely noticed the rest of the journey as I pondered on this last remark. I was just about to demolish his theory when we drew up outside the railway station in Keighley.

"Here we are, Captain," said Partridge. "This is where the Keighley and Worth Valley Line begins. There's five miles of single track right up the valley to Oxenhope, and they've got some really old steamers on the line."

What was the fool on about? Steamers? Surely the River Worth wasn't navigable at this point? I refrained from any reply, I think sometimes in their ingenuous way these simple souls tried to provoke me.

The early part of our route wandered along various twisting back alleys, or snickets, as Finch called them. It was interesting but decidedly squalid. Sometimes we caught glimpses of the beck other times the railway line, sometimes just accumulated rubbish. We gained a little height and a series of tower blocks hove into view on our left which did absolutely nothing for the aesthetic qualities of my nature.

"Nobody should have to live in the likes of those," I opined. "They're just an expedient way of accommodating large numbers of people inexpensively. I'll bet neither the architects nor the town planners live in them!" I added, to give weight to my point.

"I used to live in there, sir," Snipe said quietly. "On the ninth floor."

"Oh, I am sorry, Snipe." I said quickly, with some embarrassment. "I didn't realise."

"It's all right, sir. I didn't choose it myself. My mum and dad just happened to live there when I was born."

We followed a marvellously well-preserved cobbled road up a very steep hill and things began to look decidedly better. Looking back over the Worth valley one could pick out various settlements on the opposite side. Modern housing estates in serried ranks, older scattered farm communities and the railway line in the valley bottom. As one's eye swept down the valley one could see where it joined the main valley of the River Aire. On the far horizon was the bare expanse of Ilkley Moor with the twin aerials at Keighley Gate standing like rugby posts awaiting a conversion kick from the giant Rombald, apparently another local folk tale character, into whose details I didn't feel I had the time or the inclination to delve.

We had coffee in the charming village of Hainworth. What an idyllic collection of beautifully tended cottages, a credit to the farm labourers who lived there and worked the surrounding pastures. I said as much to my companions as we sat around the picnic table in the neat village square.

"I used to live here when I were a lad," Finch informed us.

"Did you really, Finch?" I remarked, in some amazement. "How delightful."

"It were bloody awful, excuse the expression, sir. There were no warm water, toilets were outside round the back, tipplers. We were frozen to death half the time, and if you wanted to go anywhere you had to walk there and back."

"But to live in cottages like these, Finch, surely?"

"Naw, they wasn't like this then, sir. It were only when the 'off cumdens' came in that they got done up. Most of the folk who live here now work in Bradford and Leeds; they only come back at night. After we left we went to live over the other side of the valley on the Guardhouse estate. Us kids thought it were great; hot water, bathrooms, gardens, other kids to play with: we had a real time."

This was the longest speech I'd ever heard from Finch and for the first time I felt I was getting some insight into the man. He was talking like a real person, a person with feelings and, I must admit, I found this vaguely disturbing.

The next part of our expedition took us along an elevated route which contoured the valley side. To the front, on the spur of another hill, we could see the village of Haworth, terraces of grey stoned houses clinging to the slope. We followed the lane through the village of Cross Roads, just a few cottages snuggled into the hillside, and crossed the main Keighley - Halifax road at the bottom. Following a track on the opposite side we made for a cleft in the hillside; a small lake in the pastures to our right complemented the view as we climbed the rough path. The moor opened up before us as we levelled off at the top but what demanded our attention was not the vast expanse of moorland ahead but an enormous wind turbine perched on the brow of the hill. The massive white propeller was spinning slowly on its mast as though warming-up prior to take-off. The sun glinted on the blades at each rotation and the effect was one of total unreality, I stood transfixed and stared at it. I think it was the shock of seeing something so completely out-of-place that temporarily stunned me. I can only compare it to the feeling I had when I walked from the Tuilerie Gardens in Paris and was confronted by the triangular greenhouse some fool had erected in front of the Louvre.

I was the first to speak, "I suppose one has to be environmentally conscious nowadays and look for ways of providing energy without polluting the atmosphere." Not being at all sure of the way my companions would regard this feature I felt this was a rather clever non-committal way of opening the debate. I was surprised at the reaction, especially as it came from the normally impassive Partridge.

"You what?" It sounded almost like a snarl, and I instinctively stepped back a pace.

"Begging your pardon, Captain. But that thing there is a monstrosity. That pollutes the whole neighbourhood by just being there. One insensitive, selfish person ruins a whole valley so he can get cheap power for his generator. Sir, my mother has lived in Haworth all her life. She lives there because she was born there and she enjoys the views from her window. Then one day someone comes along and builds a bloody great ugly wind turbine right in front of her window. And the Council allowed it! I'll bet they thought it were going to be like a little Dutch windmill, sir. It's the same for all the people in Haworth, and the thousands of visitors, we don't deserve beautiful places if we let 'em get away with this. How would you feel, sir?"

"Er, I agree with you Partridge," shaken by this impassioned outburst. "I think it is an eyesore and totally unsuitable in a position like this." Fortunately my instant agreement seemed to have a calming effect on Partridge and the rather fiery shade of crimson which had suffused his face faded to a more equable tint.

"There are some more over there on top of that hill," Finch said as we trudged across the moor. "About two dozen of them."

I followed his directions and there sticking up on the horizon was a skyline full of whirling wind turbines. Now fully aware of my companions' feelings on the matter I was able to mount one of my favourite hobby horses.

"Why is it," I said, "That mankind always seems to get it wrong? They destroy old buildings in the towns and replace them with glass and concrete monstrosities, they build houses likes rows of boxes in the green belt and they stick up things like these in open countryside. Why do they do it?"

"I'll tell you, sir," Finch said in a confidential tone. "Firstly, because we let 'em get away with it. Then there's the corruption, you know back-handers and such like. I don't always mean bundles of fivers in brown envelopes, but you know, discreet contributions here and there, support for this or that project. And then, of course, friends in the right places are always very useful, and if you've got a bit of money it's not all that difficult to make friends anywhere."

This was all beginning to sound very revolutionary and I was beginning to regret my earlier comment. After all many of my friends had money, as well as influence, and that didn't necessarily make them corrupt. And the fact that I'd just happened to go to the same school as Palmer-Dykes didn't help me to obtain that last big dockland contract. I distinctly remember his wife saying as much when they stayed with us in our villa in Portugal.

Our route now lay down the hillside towards the village of Oxenhope. We had been entertained by the sight and sound of a steam engine chugging its way up the valley below us. A nostalgic picture of white clouds of steam billowing against the green of the valley, the rhythmic rattle of wheels over sleepers, the piercing whistle as it passed through level crossings: I did enjoy "The Railway Children", such a time of innocence and goodwill.

We stopped for lunch in Oxenhope. The Bay Horse was a friendly hostelry and it was warm enough to dine at an outside table. I think Cook had made a special effort today as it was one of my favourites; fresh salmon sandwiches, home-made pies, mushroom pâté things, and a side salad; for desert we had apple pie and custard, and all washed down with a pint of the landlord's full-bodied ale.

Whilst the men were re-packing the hamper I popped into the bar to express my thanks to mine host for his good services and sample a drop of the Napoleon I'd spotted above the bar. In the mellow mood I was in I was soon persuaded by the men that it would be a far nicer experience to travel back to Keighley by train than to slog through the muddy pastures they assured me lay before us on the river bank.

Requesting one first class and three third class tickets at the tiny prehistoric booking office I was informed, by a most pleasant young lady in a peaked cap, that first class travel was not generally available. Even in the far outposts of the North West Frontier it was possible to travel first class, I informed her, but she was quite adamant that such a facility was no longer possible in Yorkshire. Although, she did offer me the chance to book a seat in the Pullman car on its special Easter service; however, the thought of waiting three weeks for it to arrive rather lessened its appeal.

In the event we waited some twenty minutes or so before we were made aware, both audibly and visibly, of the train's imminent arrival. I'd previously assumed that the tableau of figures crouching in statuesque immobility at the end of the platform, pencils poised eternally over open notebooks, was a sculpture of the Bronte Sisters. However, the call of the whistle acted like some life-awakening injection on the group. I watched in amazement as they rose, stretched aching limbs as if emerging from some long hibernation, adjusted anoraks, picked up their flasks with a robot-like precision and moved awkwardly to the edge of the platform. In their eyes one could see the tiny flickering spark of excitement, a pilot light to ignite the senses and rekindle the dormant flames of passion.

Whilst considering these literary allusions it occurred to me that it would be remiss of us not to visit the important literary shrine on our route. Never one to shirk a decision, however onerous the consequences, I instructed Snipe to travel to Keighley on the train with all the expedition impedimenta whilst Finch, Partridge and myself would detrain at Haworth, visit the Bronte Museum and be picked up later by Snipe in the Range Rover.

The Black Bull, at Finch' suggestion, seemed an eminently suitable place to rendezvous. I found the stroll up the cobbled Main Street quite fascinating, the quaint tea shops redolent with Victorian atmosphere. The souvenir shops and antique shops displaying their wares much as they would have done during the time of the Famous Sisters. Finch, of course, feigned a complete lack of interest, dismissing the whole experience as 'a tourist charade.' I didn't rise to the comment on this occasion, as I was enjoying a particularly tasty Branwell burger at the time. It didn't, however, stop me thinking that some people are so lacking in refinement that they are quite unable to appreciate the value of their own heritage.

At the top of the street both Finch and Bartlett expressed a wish not to visit the Bronte Museum as they both, so they said, had suffered many such trips in the past whilst still at school. Needless to say I did not attempt to dissuade them, as unbelievers can ruin the atmosphere on any devout spiritual occasion. One would not wish to make a pilgrimage to Mecca, for example, in the company of the BNP Holiday Club.

I found the Museum experience most rewarding, and not a little emotional. It moved me greatly to see the clothes worn by the sisters, and to observe the petite delicate shoes worn by Emily Bronte herself brought a lump to my throat; and noting the size probably more than one lump to her feet. The original rooms in which they studied, played, wrote their masterpieces took me back in time to a world in which there was time to think, to express oneself, to enrich the lives of others with lofty thoughts. And such tragedy! Early deaths, constant bereavements, disappointments and unrecognised genius. Whoever it was wrote, 'full many a flower is born to blush unseen' knew very well what she was talking about.

I left the parsonage in a deeply reflective mood. Temporarily overcome with emotion I expressed a wish, almost a prayer in fact, that somehow, wherever they were, the Sisters would feel that a sympathetic, appreciative soul had crossed their threshold today and humbly paid his respects.

I'd left Finch and Partridge on the car park but they were now nowhere to be seen so I wandered into the adjacent churchyard. The quiet tranquillity of the setting blended perfectly with my present mood and induced inspirational thoughts of a profundity which I had not felt all week. If three young girls, from their background and times, could write novels with such depth of feeling, then what might someone with my advantages of birth, intellect and sensitivity achieve? At this point, I regret to say, my musings were violently interrupted by a piercing shriek from a group of schoolgirls who were gathered round a nearby memorial stone. I looked at them sharply with a disapproving frown and was horrified to see in their eyes the glimmer of recognition. Then, as I stared at them, the awful realisation dawned on me; they knew me! These were the same girls who had been present at my most ignominious moment when, unclothed and helpless, I'd been trapped in that cave mouth! My deductions were further confirmed when the familiar head and angular shoulders of the Senior Mistress rose above the group. I involuntarily backed away and attempted to avoid eye contact but, unfortunately, as I did so I stumbled over some decorative funerary urn and sprawled backwards onto a gravestone slab. Like a Mother Superior protecting her novitiates from the attentions of some notorious flasher the Senior Mistress swept her charges to safety, casting just one disdainful glance over her shoulder towards me, presumably to check that I was not preparing to strip off and roll in their direction.

I slunk out of the churchyard in a subdued and thoughtful frame of mind, still feeling the warm blush of embarrassment on my cheeks. To have one's sublime moments of spiritual inspiration dashed to the ground in such a devastating fashion had left me totally demoralised. It did not take me long to decide, like Branwell I suppose, that a couple of brandies might be the best thing to calm an agitated soul. As soon as I reached the main street I was hailed from the doorway of the Black Bull. It was Finch. "In here, sir. We're in here. Come and see where Branwell used to drink."

I needed no second invitation and joined them in the bar. Their remarkably good humour, I decided, owed itself more to the ale they'd been drinking than any natural conviviality on their part. We spent the next hour in literary discourse, and with all due modesty, I feel I really improved the occasion and influenced the thoughts of my companions. The lively exchange of ideas, particularly with Finch, who I learned during the course of the afternoon was in the process of writing some thesis or other on the Brontes, was particularly edifying. My spirits rose, possibly inversely related in some way to the descent of the brandy, I later thought; but good fellowship, good ale and good conversation resulted in a memorable afternoon...as far as I can recall.

"There is nothing which has yet been contrived by man, by which so much happiness is produced as by a good tavern." I felt it felicitous to remark, finding once again one of the Dr J's bon mots entirely apposite. We all drank to that observation with hearty approval, and then to Branwell and each of his sisters, and their father, then if I remember, to Heathcliff and the two Cathys, then all the Lintons we could remember. Some time later we were joined by the genial host who bought a round and introduced his comely wife, who bought another. After which we thought it only proper to pay our respects to the landlord of the White Lion across the street, where the hospitality was equally welcoming and so the afternoon past in what I can only describe as a pleasant atmospheric haze.

The cobbles in the Main Street seemed to have a life of their own and our descent thereof was more like surfing than walking. The Old Hall at the bottom appeared to be most likely place to establish our equilibrium but I can remember little apart from the efficient service from behind the bar. One glass had hardly been emptied when another miraculously appeared.

The latter stages of this particular expedition are even less clear in my mind. I seem to remember that Snipe appeared some time in the evening; here my recollection is not perfect, but I seemed at one stage to be supporting both Finch and Partridge at the same time.

The atmosphere then inexplicably and suddenly changed, we were in a place which I can only describe as having a decidedly Indian flavour. I vaguely remember standing up and reciting a few lines from Kipling which I thought fitted the occasion; this was then followed by some altercation or other, incongruously involving a group of wild-eyed Pathans. I believe we sat outside on the restaurant steps for a while after that. Anyway, details of the incident are so indistinct in my mind that I cannot really vouch for their accuracy.

Sunday

Kingsdale, North Yorkshire (GR 700780)

Our last day; in many ways I shall be sad to leave. One can get used to a more basic lifestyle, especially if one makes the effort to get out into the countryside and experience the hardship at first hand. Or should one say, first 'foot'? It is easy to maintain one's good humour in an area so richly endowed with spectacular scenic beauty. It lifts the spirit and forces one to consider one's own unique position in the natural world. To return to a warm welcoming cottage in the evening after a hard day on the fells, relax in the jacuzzi, and then sample yet another of Cook's culinary masterpieces in front of a blazing log fire must surely be one of the best of life's simple pleasures. One sometimes envies the simple Yorkshire lifestyle: not for them the stress and worry of financial manipulation, the bustle of city life or the responsibility of executive management.

It took a little while for my head to clear that morning and I was also troubled with an unpleasant burning feeling in the back of my throat. When I peered into the bathroom mirror it misted over rapidly as if exposed to a blast from some fiery dragon's breath. I had decided to give the staff a special treat today in recognition of the hard work they had put in during the week. The Little Lady was to join us this morning so nothing strenuous was planned; a short walk, lunch in a country pub, and a drive in the Dales would suffice.

Our first call was to take Cook into Skipton to catch the National Express bus back to town; with any luck she would be back home in time to prepare breakfast for us on the following day. With Partridge at the wheel, me alongside navigating, the memsahib in the back seat and Snipe and Finch in the boot we took the A65 up to Thornton-in-Lonsdale. After stopping briefly to book Sunday lunch at the Marton Arms, we drove up the country lane and parked at the top of the hill overlooking Kingsdale.

What a picture. I spent some time pointing out the various landmarks to the memsahib whilst she was painting her nails and getting ready for the walk. The air was crisp rather than cold and, apart from the Little Lady, we moved fairly quickly as a team up the hillside. We were heading for the Turbary Road, an old drovers' track which follows a level route along a high shelf on the north side of the valley. When we reached the track the Little Lady was nowhere in sight so I ordered Finch to go back and assist her whilst Partridge organised the coffee break. Some time later Finch appeared with the memsahib; she seemed to be having some difficulty walking over the uneven ground. I had informed her before we started that knee length fashion boots might be fine for extended shopping expeditions but the high heels might be a problem on the softer ground of the fells. She informed me that she wouldn't be seen dead in the sort of clod-hopping boots I favoured, so I left it at that.

As we strolled along the track Snipe began to annoy me again. He seemed very keen to point out any pothole we came across. He'd go into great detail about its depth, its severity, the number of pitches and so on. Having tried for the last few days to completely blot out of my mind my own cataclysmic caving experience I was not well pleased at being constantly reminded.

"Snipe?" I said at last. "Will you just shut up about caving? We're here to enjoy the countryside. Nobody is the least bit interested in what it's like under the ground." That silenced him and with an air of resentment he fell back and walked alongside Partridge. I could hear him muttering under his breath from time to time but never loud enough for me to hear or to disturb my enjoyment.

A shout from Finch caused me to stop and turn round. He was miles away and he and the Little Lady appeared to have stopped. He was waving his arm and pointing back in the direction of the Range Rover. Partridge came up to me at that point and said. "Her ladyship's going back to the car, Captain. She's had enough!" As he spoke I could see that she and Finch were already moving away from us.

"Right," I said decisively, consulting my watch. "We'll make our way back to the inn for lunch."

We stayed in the Arms rather longer than we expected. I think the men enjoyed their meal in the tap-room, at least they didn't complain as far as I know. I was just glad to get away from their company for a time. I felt that, during the week, they had on occasions been inclined to take liberties. It would do them good to be on their own for a while. Unfortunately, the Little Lady was not in the best of moods; she was complaining bitterly, first about the state of her boots and then about the condition of her skin. She kept scrutinising her face in her compact mirror and then rushing into the ladies room with tubes of moisturising cream, or some such emollients. To be honest I was more interested in the superb home-cooked lunch which, washed down with two or three pints of real ale, induced in me that feeling of relaxation and well-being which is such an antidote to minor domestic worries.

With some reluctance we left the warmth of the inn, collected the men and continued our journey. Our tour took in the village of Dent, where we stopped briefly whilst the Little Lady visited the ladies room in the inn, I popped in for a brandy whilst the men waited in the car. Next we drove over to Ribblehead as I was eager to show the memsahib the impressive Batty Moss viaduct on the Settle-Carlisle railway. We didn't get out of the Range Rover but we were able to drive right under the arches and see at close range what an impressive structure it was, and when I briefly opened the windows we experienced at first hand the conditions the labour force had had to face in this bleak northern outpost. One could only but admire their resilience and fortitude, and one felt that the viaduct remains a very fitting monument to their labours.

I didn't wish to renew any unpleasant memories of Chapel-le-dale so we chose the other road which went to Horton-in-Ribblesdale by way of Selside. Snipe, who had not spoken to me since the exchange on the Turbary Road, piped up from the boot at this point.

"There's a famous pothole just up there, sir. Alum ..."

"Shut up, Snipe!" I said sharply, not giving him chance to finish. "Nobody is interested. Let's just enjoy the drive, shall we?"

This was the way we usually toured the Dales. Apart from the fact that we hadn't brought the Sunday newspapers with us, it was just like one of our Sunday runs. Two or three valleys, stop for coffee, read the papers in a lay-by, a nice pub lunch, a couple of pints and back to the cottage to watch television; days to remember!

And so it was on our final day on our springtime break. I'd learned a great deal, both about myself and about other people. I think I can say, with great humility, that the shared experiences enriched all their lives, and I truly feel that I also gained something from the experience. As Dr Johnson once said, "a man always makes himself greater by increasing his knowledge." I could only concur with the great man, and possibly add, with all due humility, that a man who increases other men's knowledge is even greater still.

Next morning we said our farewells to Finch and Snipe who would act as caretakers-cum-gardeners for the summer months. I was touched to receive a parting gift from Snipe just as we were leaving. In spite of our vastly different backgrounds and intellectual capacities I think I finally gained his respect, possibly my common touch and innate sense of fairness had won him over.

The gift? Well it was not that important after all. Just a few photographs of the week's expeditions, not worth keeping really. I didn't even know he had a camera with him on the caving expedition. I just wish the Little Lady hadn't caught sight of that undignified shot of my semi-naked shape sprawling down the hillside into a crowd of giggling schoolgirls. The scribbled note on the back, "He who bares his bum to the world reveals his inadequacies," didn't make the explanation any easier.

The Power Broker

Kenneth Allbright was a dull person. Everybody knew that, his parents knew it, his friends knew it and his teachers knew it. He'd been a dull baby, a dull infant and a dull youth. His parents, Mr and Mrs Allbright, were disappointed, naturally, but over the years they had become accustomed to his quiet unassuming existence. Even as a baby, he'd never been demanding and had always seemed content with his own company. He never shouted or cried, or indeed expressed his feelings in any way.

When he was five years old Kenneth had been given a pocket calculator for his birthday. This had been the start of a lifetime's interest in the manipulation of figures. Even the instruction manual with its list of improbable uses held a fascination for the young Allbright and he'd soon committed them all to memory. "He'll grow up to be a top accountant, mother." Mr Allbright remarked to his wife one evening during a game of snap. "Just you wait and see."

His wife was too engrossed in the game to reply there and then, but the following evening, before they started playing she murmured, "An accountant, dear? Do you really think so?"

To mark the occasion of Kenneth's eighth birthday his parents bought him a copy of Bradshaw's Guide.The effect was immediate; he disappeared into his room in April and none of the family could remember seeing him again until December. He astounded the assembled uncles and aunts on Christmas Day however by his ability to recount, from memory, the times of trains to any given town in the United Kingdom. And if anyone wanted the Bank Holiday variations or Sunday specials, he could supply those too.

On his tenth birthday the young Allbright was presented with a personal computer. Kenneth's complete absorption in it worried his mother, to such an extent that one evening she twice interrupted a game of pelmanism to comment on the fact.

"Have you spoken to our Kenneth at all this month, dear?" She enquired timidly, as her husband was thinking deeply about the position of the Queen of Hearts. There was no immediate reply so half an hour later she repeated the question.

"Er, what's that?" said her husband sharply. "Don't you think our Kenneth's becoming a little er withdrawn? Socially, I mean."

Mr Allbright considered the question for some time before replying and then looking directly into his wife's eyes he said, "How do you mean, dear?"

"Well," she said, glad of the opportunity for a prolonged discussion. "He seems to spend an awful lot of time on his computer, he never talks to anybody and he hardly ever goes out, does he?"

"That's because he's got everything he needs here, isn't it, my love. He can always discuss things with us if he wants to, and if he feels like an evening of fun he can join in with us, can't he? No, our Kevin's all right, he's one of the new generation. He's at the fore-front of the dawn of technology."

"Kenneth, dear," she corrected. "Well, if you think it's all right I suppose it is," she concluded, and they settled down to finish the game in earnest.

Kenneth's school career had been significant by its total lack of significance. At the primary school the teachers never knew he was there until he'd left, and then only because he'd left his cap behind in the cloakroom. A frantic search through the class registers confirmed, to the headteacher's horror, that Kenneth had achieved a one hundred percent attendance record for the previous five years.

After that first, less-than-distinguished, dip into the pool of knowledge Kenneth disappeared into the maelstrom of the local comprehensive school. He emerged in another five years, considerably shaken by the experience but in no way academically stirred. His mother, however, was pleased to note considerable improvements in his social life. Kenneth had become a member of two school societies; the Computer Club which met in the school library once a month, and the Train Spotters Society. The latter arranged trips, a few times a year, to locations such as platform 9 at Leeds City station. Kenneth was an enthusiastic flask-carrying member. Many Sunday mornings saw him wrapped up in anorak, muffler and cap; notepad and Bradshaw's Guide in mittened hands, shivering in anticipation as he waited for the six-thirty from Doncaster to come up the line.

Looking back affectionately on these formative years Kenneth often thought that this is where his horizons were extended and his lively imagination given sustenance.

Kenneth's first job after leaving school was as a temporary clerk in the offices of the Inland Revenue. His aptitude and enthusiasm for the work routine impressed his superiors to such an extent that within a month he was offered a full-time superannuable post. His future looked secure and his mother and father were delighted with their son's achievement. To further his knowledge of the subject Kenneth enrolled on an evening course in accountancy and tax management at Bulford College of Further Education, soon to be known as the University of Greater Bulford.

One evening over their hot cocoa and biscuits Mr Allbright confided to his wife, "You know, dear. I'm really proud of the way our Kevin's got on in the world. It's what I always hoped to become myself but I just never got the chance."

His wife sighed and murmured "Kenneth, dear," under her breath. She looked at him sadly, "Never mind, dearest. You might qualify for early retirement in a couple of years and then you can get out of teaching for good."

Needless to say Kenneth's grasp of Information Technology and his complete lack of interest in any of the usual distractions to which youths of his age are subjected, ensured exemplary comments from his tutors, and outstanding marks in his final examinations. He graduated from the College with the plaudits of the tutorial staff ringing in his ears.

The following week he took another step up the career ladder in the Tax Office. A Grade 7 Clerical officer may not seem important to the uninitiated but to Kenneth it was the start of a path to power or, as he modestly confided to his parents that evening, "The first step up the staircase to the stars."

One very useful contact he made on his college course was a young man called Shokat who had shared the same table as Kenneth in the very first lecture they had both attended. Impressed by Kenneth's dedication to the subject and his encyclopaedic knowledge of the tax system, Shokat, and many others, it should be said, used Kenneth as a walking source of reference. Indeed it was in no small part due to Kenneth's guidance and help in the coursework that Mohamed won the James Duckham Award for the highest marks in a final assessment. Shokat scored 99% and Kenneth, who finished second with 98.8%, was the first to congratulate him.

Shokat was not slow to show his gratitude and he helped Kenneth to land a part-time evening job auditing the books for the family shop, run by various uncles. Kenneth enjoyed the challenge of preparing VAT returns and unravelling the complexities of what appeared to be a very rudimentary bookkeeping system. His unparalleled skill in tax avoidance measures and corporate financial management soon endeared him to the brothers Fazal and he rapidly became a key figure in their organisation.

Apparently there were seven brothers in the business, but Kenneth never met them altogether and, as people, they remained only shadowy figures in the background. Not so their business figures however, in Kenneth's mind these were always crystal clear; and because each brother had a different surname, a common factor in such households Kenneth was told, and a different bank account, it helped Kenneth maximise the fiscal advantages for the organisation. What did surprise Kenneth in the early stages, however, was the huge annual turnover for a corner shop in a place like Bulford. He supposed it was connected with the C. & H. Import Agency run by one of the brothers in the room upstairs.

Kenneth, it should be said, was not in the least bit concerned about money as such, and the bin-liners full of five, ten and twenty pound notes held little interest for him. It was the allocation of figures to the various columns which absorbed his attention and which gave him the most creative joy when he managed to effect a balance.

At the end of the financial year the brothers Fazal expressed their gratitude to Kenneth by providing him with a company car, not a new one, but it was the thought that mattered, as Kenneth's mother said. Kenneth was more than delighted with his X registered Corolla. He proudly parked it behind the line of Mercedes whenever he called at the shop. Even when he was pulled in by the police for having neither valid tax nor MOT certificates it did in no way detract from his appreciation of the brothers' kindness.

After a couple of years the Fazals' business, due in no small part to Kenneth's expertise, had expanded from a small corner shop with doubtful appendages into a burgeoning business empire. The brothers now owned the newsagents next door, the curry house next to that, the post office on the corner, the private hire firm across the road and most of the houses in the street. This row of terraced houses had been sub-divided into units and were a great help to the Department of Social Security whenever temporary accommodation was needed.

The filing cabinets in Kenneth's bedroom were overflowing with information on all these transactions, plus the back-up discs of all his accountancy work. His room, with its battery of technological hardware, including computers, scanner, fax machine, and a photo-copier, more nearly resembled the nerve centre of a major financial corporation than a one-man accountancy business in a suburban semi. Each day Kenneth meticulously pinned the market pages from the Financial Times on the wall over the bed, keeping the edges in line under the printed maxims he'd made when he first started college. He set great store by these two profound tenets and, although the paper was now yellowing with age, they were a constant reminder to him of his importance in the business world. He felt a surge of enthusiasm course through his body whenever he read the bold black capitals.

BEHIND EVERY SUCCESSFUL BUSINESS THERE IS

A DEDICATED ACCOUNTANT

THE HAND THAT BALANCES THE BOOKS

SHALL RULE THE WORLD

At Kenneth's instigation the Fazal Brothers discreetly filtered certain funds into the local party political system. Not directly, of course, but there were certain organisations which were a front for this kind of practice. Political laundrettes, in fact, which ensured that none of the dirty linen appeared on the public washing line. Kenneth maintained that these donations should be regarded as long term investments. The fruits of which may not be immediately obvious but which may include, at a much later date, easing of certain regulations in the granting of planning permission, preferential treatment in council property purchase, perhaps even some municipal honour for one of the brothers, or a candidature nomination for the council or the local bench. One never knew where the seeds might fall, and how big they might grow in the fulness of time.

It was about this time that Kenneth left the Fazal Brothers' employment, partly because they were now fully operational but mainly to concentrate on his advanced studies at the university.

It would be kinder to the reader to skip the next five years of Kenneth's progress. Suffice it to say that his extra mural studies earned him a first class honours degree in economic management which then allowed him an opportunity for further study, and eventual recognition as a full-blown chartered accountant. Kenneth now occupied a very senior clerical position in the Inland Revenue and was generally recognised, more as a name than as a person, one must admit, as one of the leading authorities on business taxation.

Whilst he had been studying he had also worked for a short spell in the evenings doing the books for a family of builders. Charlie Rooke was the eldest of three brothers and they'd just been awarded an enterprise grant to kick-start, or pump-prime, their business. Recommended to Kenneth by the man at the newsagents they sought his advice on the financial side. Whilst their ability to hammer in nails, and mix concrete was unquestioned, their ability to understand the Council's application forms and guidance leaflets was very limited. Before they enlisted Kenneth's assistance their policy had been to drive around the neighbourhood in a battered Transit low-loader calling at houses and offering to lay tarmac on garden paths or drives. On these work-seeking sorties the brothers sat in a row in the cab, each brother distinguished by the colour of his woollen hat. Charlie wore a green one, Jeff the red and Len the blue one. According to the books their only assets, apart from the woollen hats, were the Transit, a wheelbarrow, a pick and three shovels.

With Ken's advice, and the support of his name, the Rookes managed to raise money from selected financial institutions and entered the property development business. They purchased derelict property, barns, disused chapels, churches and village schools. Indeed any building which possessed some character, and could be sympathetically and economically restored, was frequently demolished and the stone used elsewhere and the site developed in a more financially rewarding fashion.

Over the next few months contacts were made, both within the trade and also in the various regulatory bodies. Kenneth's assistance during the negotiating periods was, as always, indispensable. He was able to offer sound financial advice, sometimes even at a personal level, to all the interested parties in the transaction. Kenneth dealt with all clerical matters whilst the Brothers Rooke continued to swing the pick and organise the labour force. Working very much in accordance with the 'on the lump' method of employment, they knew just which public house to call in, and at what time, to obtain the services of whichever artisan was needed; be it brickie, plumber, joiner, plasterer, or general labourer.

It was one contract above all others, however, which made the Rooke Brothers the household name they are today. Once again Kenneth's contacts in the corridors of power were of inestimable value. Tenders were invited for the cable-laying component of a multi-million pound project for a Government-approved communications network. By one of those remarkable strokes of luck one often gets in the business world, the Rookes' tender was the nearest to the figure the Council had in mind; it was accepted, and from then on the brothers never looked back; over their shoulders occasionally, but not directly backwards.

Kenneth's business acumen guided the family Rooke into the purchase of former quarries and defunct mining systems. Often these were obtained for knock-down prices as many of the owners, Council or private, were unable to maintain their upkeep, especially with regard to public safety. Indeed on one occasion the owners of an old quarry were in the process of being sued by a hiker who had inadvertently fallen down one of their shafts. Apparently the owners had failed to maintain the warning signs and the security fence and a Mr. Martin Rooke-Hughes (no relation) from Liverpool had had the misfortune to tumble in. He had, unfortunately, suffered severe psychological stress which was highly likely to keep him off work for the rest of his life. Naturally he was suing for present and future loss of earnings as well as compensation for injuries received. The Rooke Brothers however came to the rescue and the quarry changed hands. Charlie Rooke himself generously recompensed Mr Rooke-Hughes for the accident and indeed, it was rumoured, later gave the injured walker a light job in the stone-breaking section of one of his quarries.

Never slow to acknowledge their appreciation for favours received the brothers, at their own cost, built Kenneth a bedroom extension over the existing garage. This allowed him to expand his office and update his records by the installation of the latest microfiche system.

In a matter of months, as is well documented in the local press, the Rookes' became well-known local philanthropists and many worthwhile causes had occasion to be grateful for their generous donations.

Kenneth left their organisation shortly after Charlie Rooke became chairman of Bulford Rugby League club. He obviously enjoyed this fairly undemanding role because one day Kenneth overheard him speaking to one of his fellow directors, "I can buy 'em and I can sell 'em," he was saying, "...like carcases of meat in a slaughter house." Kenneth had often heard the fans refer to the team as the 'steam pigs' but had never known why before.

Some time afterwards Kenneth heard, through his contacts, that the Rookes had successfully tendered for the widening and resurfacing of the whole of the British motorway system. So the three shovels, the pick and the wheelbarrow would come in useful again, he thought...as well as the old quarries in the Yorkshire Dales! Local village industries were revitalised, once-peaceful country lanes throbbed to the sound of heavy goods vehicles, double-glazing salesmen prospered and quiet backwaters of bucolic charm joined the mainstream of economic progress.

The following year Kenneth opened up as a fully registered chartered accountant and within weeks was approached by the Sayed Brothers, joint principals of an Middle-Eastern business cartel. They wanted him to become their full-time financial adviser in the United Kingdom. The offer could not have come at a better time for Kenneth. His present post in the Tax Office was becoming increasingly more administrative and he longed to get back to the real love of his life, the manipulation of raw figures. The Inland Revenue were sorry to lose someone of Kenneth's ability and dedication and, as a touching reminder of the happy hours he'd spent with them, he was presented with an automatic tea maker, a year's subscription to Computer Weekly and a pair of warm woollen mittens.

The Sayed Brothers were interested in investment properties, business take-over situations and indeed any venture which might produce maximum profits from a minimum outlay. Naturally the Sayed Bros did not want to be seen to be the prime movers in these arrangements, nor for that matter did Kenneth. The one strong and enduring characteristic throughout his life had been his anonymity as a person; indeed this was the one feature by which he was recognised by many of his colleagues.

"Haven't seen much of Kenneth Allbright this month," one would remark.

"That's all right then, he must be O.K." was the standard response.

Kenneth suggested to the Sayeds that a number of holding companies be established, each one ever so slightly obscuring the affairs of the next. The simple juxtaposition of the letters and words in the title of the A & B Import and Export Co. for example, often provided sufficient obfuscation to deter many unwelcome investigations.

By now Kenneth was as sensitive to the fluctuations of the FT Index, the Dow Jones, the Nikkei and the Hang Seng as he was to the variations in his own heartbeat and temperature. These financial agencies had almost become a part of his metabolism and whatever time of the night or day he would sense significant movements of change, sometimes even before they actually happened. A hot flush in the early hours of the morning, for instance, would often wake him from his light sleep; a quick check on his laptop would, perhaps, confirm the need for immediate action in the face of a falling index in Tokyo. Needless to say the Sayed Brothers benefited enormously from this facility and many an ailing company found itself in the control of strange hands even before it knew the reason why.

One particular productive source of acquisition was with companies in receivership, often the result of cash flow problems, perhaps even induced by the B. & A. Export & Import Co. itself. Kenneth was able to arrange take-overs through one of the associated companies, settle-up accounts with the more persistent creditors, and either redevelop the company with a sudden in-put of cash or simply sell off the assets and keep the company name for future use. These were profitable exercises and, as with his previous principals, Kenneth recommended that some money should be discreetly diverted into the funds of certain political parties, and less surreptitiously, a smaller amount into well-publicised charities. Investments of this nature, he pointed out once again, often proved to be invaluable in the long term, and they were easily offset in the books against depreciation, or some other nebulous item.

This type of accounting held a tremendous appeal for Kenneth, because not only was he dealing with complicated accounts but he was also able to develop a system which concealed both the source of the donation as well as the recipient. The Sayed Brothers were delighted with this system because, as they explained to Kenneth, often in their export programme it was better that competitors were not aware of where the goods were coming from, or indeed going to. End-user certificates were all right in themselves, they reasoned, as long as they didn't reveal too much factual information.

The Sayeds prospered under Kenneth's guiding hand and it was not long before most of the larger department stores in Bulford, and many of the prestigious hotels in the county, were under their control. Not obvious control, of course, but if the outer layers of the onion could be peeled away, in the very centre you would find the Sayed Brothers, tears welling up in their eyes as they banked the proceeds. And behind them, as inscrutable as a professional poker player risking home, car and marriage on a pair of twos, you just might, on a very clear day, discern the blurred image of Kenneth Allbright seated at his computer. Kenneth was not, as you can guess, a person to indulge in idle thoughts. His brain, like his computer, was programmed to deal with figures, not conjecture or philosophical concepts.

It even surprised him one day when, in a rare moment of reflection, he considered how fate had decreed that he should be central to the development of business empires. How ironic, he thought, that the great imperialists, this proud nation of shopkeepers, should itself be colonised by shopkeepers from its former conquests.

It was not long before other people, some of them in quite important positions in government circles, began to be aware of Kenneth's abilities and influence. Unknown to Kenneth, and, incidentally, to everyone in the Cabinet, security investigations into his background were carried out over a period of months. His telephone was tapped, he was followed to and from the supermarket, his mail was opened prior to delivery and close surveillance was kept on his bedroom window through high-powered binoculars from the roof of the off-licence across the street.

Reports were sent directly to the Chairman of the Party. It was felt that a man of Kenneth's stature, who could discreetly direct hundreds of thousands of pounds into deserving causes, needed to be cultivated...once his credentials had been checked, of course. Kenneth would have been delighted with the results when they landed on the Chairman's desk; just one page of A4 with double-spaced lineage contained all his life history. No mention of any doubtful liaisons with women, or men! No apparent vices, doesn't drink, smoke or take drugs, lives with parents, never goes anywhere, has never been anywhere, frugal lifestyle, only indulgences an X registered Corolla and an extensive filing system. Strongly recommended by Councillor Ghulam Fazal JP. Chairman of the Finance and General Purposes Committee, Bulford, and spoken very highly of by Sir Ben al-Sayed, recently knighted for his services to British industry. An excellent reference from C. Rooke, Managing Director of The Rooke Development Industries plc. and President of the Society for the Preservation of Rural England. The Chairman re-read the notes, a smile fleetingly crossed his patrician countenance as he stamped it with his official seal, initialled it and briefly added, "Follow up ASAP"

We come now to a dramatic stage in Kenneth's life. Dramatic perhaps is not quite the right word, because the effect was cataclysmic in the extreme. Kenneth met a woman! And what a woman she was. Kenneth had spent his entire lifetime in social isolation, content to manipulate inanimate figures on a computer screen. The female figure had not come within the compass of his awareness and none of his previous experience had prepared him for anything, or anybody, quite like this.

They'd bumped into each other, well to be more exact, she'd bumped into him, or rather into the back of his Corolla whilst he was parked outside the supermarket waiting for the rain to abate. The young lady, a strikingly attractive blonde, had been most upset at the accident and apologised profusely, even though there was hardly a mark on her white Audi TT. She had felt unsteady on her feet, she told Kenneth, probably the shock she explained, as she grabbed his arm to steady herself. Kenneth, always the gentleman, suggested he assist her into the supermarket restaurant where she could sit down and recover her composure over a cup of coffee. She readily agreed and supported by Kenneth's protective arm they made their way into the coffee bar. After the initial embarrassment of having a young lady on his arm, and the fear that he might meet someone he knew, unlikely though that might be, he quite enjoyed the experience. If he'd thought about it he had more chance of being struck by lightning on a sunny day than meeting someone he knew, but Kenneth was past rational thought; his mind had been taken over by strange and apparently uncontrollable forces. Her perfume lingered about him as he went for the coffee and he couldn't resist the temptation to smell the shoulder of his jacket where her head had rested during the walk from the car park.

They exchanged names and addresses and Kenneth found Victoria a fascinating companion. He discovered during the course of the next half hour that she, like him, was enthralled by computers and hi-tech equipment, and that her job as personal assistant to Sir Miles Longe MP, a well-known and long-serving back-bencher, involved a fair amount of bookkeeping and accountancy. Kenneth's heart skipped a couple of beats when he heard this; how wonderful life was, half-an-hour ago he was alone! And now a beautiful creature, from a species he'd never realised existed, was looking into his eyes and telling him how much she admired him.

Naturally their friendship developed rapidly after this initial contact. Kenneth could hardly disregard the good fortune that benign fate had placed in his path, could he? Victoria was fascinated by his expertise in financial management and it was not long before he was helping her with her personal accounts as well as those of the Honourable Member. In spite of the fact that Victoria was based in Sir Miles's office in Westminster she was still able to see Kenneth quite frequently as Sir Miles's constituency, and many of his directorships and consultancies, were in the North of England.

Kenneth and Victoria's mutual passion for figures reached its ultimate joy of expression in Kenneth's bedroom-cum-office, seated in front of his visual display unit. Kenneth's fingers fluttered over the keyboard with a lightness he'd never before experienced, and with Victoria's head resting gently on his shoulder he was intoxicated by the perfume of her presence. Their minds met, their thoughts coalesced and the joint product, fruit of their labours, came to life on the screen in front of them. Kenneth had never in all his life felt such an intense degree of satisfaction, not even when the Fazal Brothers presented him with the Toyota Corolla or when the Rookes built an extension to his bedroom, or the Brothers Sayed gave him a box of dates one Christmas.

Weeks passed in a haze of newly discovered feelings and sentiments. Blissful hours in the evening were shared in the glow of the computer screen as side by side Kenneth explained the mysteries of the financial universe to the second great love of his life. Victoria was a willing student and Kenneth was extremely proud of the diligent way she approached the subject and the searching intelligent questions she asked.

Kenneth was happy to advise Sir Miles on his financial investments and, after one particularly successful venture in the Middle East, Kenneth was introduced to the Party Chairman. A gentleman, like many other successful politicians, who was able to defy all known physiological principles and speak for long periods of time without actually breathing.

The upshot of the meeting was that some weeks later Kenneth was offered a senior position in the Chancellor's advisory unit at Party Headquarters. The starting salary was extremely generous, but it was only when Victoria said, when he spoke to her on the telephone, that it would give them more time together that Kenneth was convinced that it was the right move for him. Kenneth was glad about this because he had not seen much of Victoria since January when she went on a fact-finding tour of the West Indies with Sir Miles. Apparently it was to undertake a comparative study of the motorway system, or something equally important, she'd said. Anyway when he called her the following evening at the Rooke-al-Sayed Hotel complex in Kingston, Jamaica, to tell her the good news the answer-phone said she was not available at the moment and would the caller ring back in three weeks' time.

Kenneth had a nasty shock two weeks later when there was a mysterious fire-bomb attack on his office bedroom in Bulford. A number of empty petrol cans were found at the scene, from which the local police deduced that there was probably some degree of malicious intent. However their extensive enquiries over the next couple of days failed to discover the person, or persons, responsible. The inspector assured Kenneth that the file would remain open until the culprit, or culprits, were apprehended. The insurance company meanwhile, in keeping with the small print on the back of the policy, withheld reimbursement until the investigation was satisfactorily concluded.

There was a great deal of damage to Kenneth's office, the Fire Damage Assessment officer later reported that major structural failings in the original building and its materials had largely contributed to the extent of the damage. Kenneth's prized filing cabinets and computer systems were completely destroyed. Most of the original documents, such as the Fazal Bros. Import files, the Sayed Bros. arms shipments file and the Rooke Bros. property transactions were lost in the inferno. Fortunately Kenneth had recently updated all his copy discs and had already moved them into the secure unit at his new office in London so he was not unduly worried. However, when he telephoned his former associates, he was quite surprised at their annoyance. It seemed excessive for such an unimportant matter, especially when he'd been at pains to assure them that their precious records were still perfectly safe.

Kenneth, now settled in his new job, was able to co-ordinate all the extraneous activities of Party Members and advise them on appropriate declaration procedures to prohibit unnecessary scrutiny. Kenneth's expertise was also invaluable in the privatisation of former public organisations. His intimate knowledge of the financial market enabled the government to choose exactly the right time to float the issues to maximise speculators' profits. Members also found his suggestions useful regarding the early disposal of shares in companies which might be adversely affected by such an eventuality.

The Party was extremely happy with Kenneth's advice. Members of Parliament, it was felt, had slept easier in their seats since Kenneth had re-organised their finances. It had always been a source of some embarrassment to have to declare vested interests; it seemed to smack vaguely of distrust, some MPs thought, quite out of keeping with their status in the country. People who have been chosen to rule, and given the authority to make decisions for other people, should be allowed to get on with it without constant interference, was the prevailing thought, Kenneth found.

Kenneth often wondered what had happened to Victoria over these last few months; perhaps it was a very extensive motorway system. Kenneth was kept extremely busy and he was in such demand by Members of Parliament that he really had little time to think about her.

Kenneth was not usually given to malicious thoughts, but it did occur to him that the information he held on most elected members in the party could be very damaging to the government, as well as to the individuals concerned, if it got into the wrong hands. He therefore devised a computer-controlled safety system to protect his records and kept the entry code a closely guarded secret.

Before the year was out Kenneth had become what was loosely termed one of the 'wise men'. These were the key advisers to the Government on economic matters, and it would have been difficult to make a better choice than Kenneth. To develop the analogy still further Kenneth thought of himself as the man in charge of the gold. He guessed the chaps responsible for the frankincense and myrrh were there to conceal any possible whiff of corruption which might arise from some of the policies.

Kenneth had just about reached the zenith of his ambitions now and he was, when he had time to dwell on it, extremely proud of what he had achieved from such a humble start. He was the faceless controller at the centre of a powerful government, and the trusted confidante of most MPs and Ministers. However, he did have certain advantages over them. Whilst their actions were constantly monitored by the increasingly intrusive media and whingeing constituents, he could make decisions without the annoying trammels of democratic control, or the nuisance of public accountability. Kenneth was the complete antithesis to those media-created personalities, those of little ability who are puffed up like inflatable dolls by the publicity hype, and then, when no longer needed, are left to deflate in some ignominious corner.

Kenneth's incredible technical ability was allied to clinical efficiency and single-minded dedication, and these attributes were condensed and centred on the task under consideration. Kenneth's dedication often reached such intensity that his actual persona became completely absorbed into his work. At such times it was difficult to separate man and project; for a time he became synonymous with the project. Kenneth's personality, therefore, was something which could not be equated with the usual personal characteristics but more with the technical and emotional qualities of a robot.

Mr & Mrs Allbright had not heard from their son for some months. This was not unusual because they knew that he was so caught up in his work that he would forget about them from one year to the next. They were, however, surprised to receive a postcard from him in August of the following year. There was a picture of Copacabana Beach on the front...very nice and sandy, Mrs. Allbright thought, but far too many young ladies wearing too little clothing to be healthy, she informed her husband. The printed message on the back read:

Dear Mr & Mrs. Allbright,

Having a nice time, weather good, wish you were here. Moving on tomorrow, urgent business in Nicaragua. Love Kenneth. The postmark was dated 21.07.95 and the stamp franked 'MI5 Paid Brazil'.

"What's this Nicaragua?" Kenneth's mum asked. "It doesn't sound too respectable, if you ask me. Do you think Kenneth'll be all right out there?"

"Of course he'll be all right, dear," her husband retorted. He's a fully qualified chartered accountant, isn't he? Important people need men like Kevin to look after their business interests...so they have to take care of them, don't they?"

In November of that year Mr and Mrs Allbright went up to London on a day trip to visit the Board Games Trade Fair at Earl's Court. They called at Party Headquarters to enquire if their Kenneth would be coming home for Christmas. A very nice gentleman in a bow tie and dinner jacket, who was standing on the step hailing a cab at the time, told them that Kenneth was on such important, and top secret government work, that it was unlikely they would ever get to see him again. They thanked the Minister for his time and apologised for interrupting his work and made their way home.

"Usual club, guv?" they heard the driver say to the Minister, as they made their way to the bus stop.

That evening after a game of ludo, when Kenneth's parents were winding down with their cocoa and biscuits Mr Allbright said to his wife, "I told you our Kevin would get somewhere someday, didn't I, dear?"

"Kenneth, dear," she murmured automatically. "Yes, you certainly did...er...where is he then, exactly?"

"He's in Central America, Mother. He'll be up to his neck in accounts, buried in his books if I know anything about our Kevin. Anyway, we know he'll be all right, didn't the Prime Minister tell us the Government would take care of him?"

A look of pride crossed Mrs Allbright's face and she smiled gently as she laid out the cards for the last game of patience of the evening. Kenneth's colleagues, however, had a much more realistic approach to the possibilities and the following day a quiet ceremony was held in the office.

The Party Chairman concluded his moving and emotional address with the words, " and so it is with pride, as well as sadness, that I dedicate this new filing cabinet to the memory of our dear departed colleague er..er," at this point, momentarily overcome with emotion he raised his handkerchief to his face, he paused briefly and glanced at his notes before he was able to carry on with his valediction. "Er..our esteemed colleague, Kevin Allbright, whose mysterious disappearance in Central America may never be fully explained. This engraved plaque on the top drawer," he indicated the small brass plate with his left hand, "will, I hope, serve as a reminder to all those who use the system, that their services, whilst often unsung, are still of vital national importance. As Kevin himself might have said - behind every successful government there is an efficient filing system. To lay down one's files for one's country is surely the ultimate sacrifice. I now call upon Sir Miles Longe MP, a close and very dear friend of Kevin's, to read the very moving epitaph engraved thereon.... Sir Miles!"

Sir Miles, in a charcoal grey suit and black tie, cleared his throat and stepped forward. He solemnly read the inscription, "The Kevin Allbright Memorial Filing Cabinet, 1959 – 1997. He filed for freedom and the right to remember."

Both men were clearly moved by the occasion, Sir Miles brushed a tear from his eye and the Chairman blew his nose. The latter then graciously thanked the staff for attending and ushered them out of the office and closed the door.

"Fancy a snifter before you go, old boy?" he said to Miles as he slid open the top drawer of the filing cabinet and pulled out a bottle of whisky and two glasses. "It's been a trying day; I think we've earned this." Sir Miles nodded his agreement and the Chairman poured out two generous helpings. The men raised their glasses in a silent toast and downed the contents, proving once again that sentiment is not entirely lacking in the higher echelons of power.

Reflections In A Ginger Pot

One

Skipton in the Aire valley in North Yorkshire is a small market town with a population of about 14,000. It likes to be known as the gateway to the Dales, but this tends to overlook the fact that Airedale actually starts much further south.

Arthur and Carrie Duxbury have lived in the town in the same suburban semi-detached for the past twenty years. Their house was identical to the other fifty houses on the same estate, and their domestic routine probably much the same as their neighbours.

It was early morning and Arthur had just come into the kitchen where Carrie, in her white fluffy dressing gown, was already seated at the table going through the morning's mail.

"Anything in the post this morning, love?"

"Just the usual, a few bills, some leaflets, oh," she added as an afterthought," and a letter from me mum."

"What again? That's the second this week. Is she running a correspondence course in home management, or something?"

"Hey! Don't you go knocking my mum. She's been very good to you, in fact, better than you deserve. She's very concerned about us. You working every day of the week and me stuck here at home slowly going round the twist."

"Oh no! Carrie, don't start that again please, not at this time in the morning. You know I've got to be at the shop seven days a week or we'll never manage."

"You could have a day off sometimes. All work and no play makes Arthur a right pain in the bum."

"Well, why don't you come in and do a day or two in the shop? It'd widen your horizons, you know; broaden your outlook a bit."

"You must be joking! All that dusty, musty junk - it's like being in a bloody mausoleum. Full of ancient out-of-date crap, the previous generation's cast-offs."

"Nay, love, come on. You sound like your mum when you talk like that. You think because something's modern it must be good. You forget, the old stuff was designed to last by craftsmen. They're really well made and, " he hesitated as if unsure how to put his feelings into words, "and, if you want to know, some of the shapes are really lovely."

"Bloody hell, here we go again. Hark at 'im. I know exactly what you see in a piece of furniture, Arthur Duxbury, bloody profit. You're like all the rest, you are. You want to buy at the lowest price and sell at the highest: the furniture itself has nowt to do with it. You know, I think, if I had Queen Anne legs you might take a bit more notice of me. Then again, you might just sell me on to the trade."

"Nay, lass, you're being ridiculous again." He glanced up at the clock on the wall. "God, look at the time, I must be off. You know I like to open on time at 9.30. Don't like to see a queue waiting." He added jocularly. "See you tonight about seven, love."

Arthur picked up his car keys from the hall table and after a quick glance in the wall mirror let himself out of the front door.

Carrie watched his car drive away, took out a cigarette and lit it and sat down at the table again. "Another day, another drag," she muttered as she picked up her coffee cup. She shuffled through the pile of mail, commenting on each as she did so. "Can do without that, and that. That's useful, soap coupons. Now what's mum got to say?"

She opened the envelope and was surprised to find another one inside, "What the hell is this?" she exclaimed. She read aloud the address on the second envelope, "Miss Caroline Anne Wadsworth, God. It's twenty five years since I was called that."

She opened the letter and read quietly, obviously very absorbed in the contents. Her face registered a mixture of disbelief and bemused surprise. She put the letter down slowly and stared out of the window. After a few minutes she shook herself out of the dream-state and muttered. "I don't believe this. What the bloody hell is going on? Where's it come from?"

She hurried into the hallway, the letter flapping in her hand, picked up the telephone and dialled impatiently. "Oh come on, mother! For God's sake, pick up!" Her fingers tapped nervously on the hall table as she waited. "Hello, mum? It's Carrie. Yes, fine thanks, and you? Yes, he's gone, just gone. Yes. yes, lovely day. Look mum, about this letter you sent on, the one you got yesterday addressed to Miss Caroline Wadsworth. Yes, I know that's me, well it was me once. It just came through the post? Well it was just a surprise, that's all. No, it's from a friend I've not heard from for a long time. No, I'm going to get on with the cleaning and then I'll go down to the supermarket. No, the big one in the new precinct. Right I'll see you at the weekend as usual. 'Bye mum. See you later. 'Bye".

She replaced the handset, sighed and went back into the kitchen. She settled down at the kitchen table again and slowly and carefully re-read the letter aloud.

24 Water Street,

Skipton, tel.3021

Dear Caroline, I am very fond of you and would like to take you out one evening if you can manage it? You will know me because I work in the next office to you and we have spoken to each other in the canteen occasionally. Perhaps you would like to go to a dance, or the pictures, or even a walk on the canal bank. Please ring me, I think we will get on well together.

Yours, James Preston

"Caroline?" she repeated, "I haven't been called that for years. And that phone number's not right, but it does look familiar".

Carrie sat for a while staring out of the window, then thinking aloud, "That address seems familiar too. Water Street, Skipton. God, it can't be him, can it? What the bloody hell is he playing at?"

Carrie gradually became aware that her door bell was ringing and by the sound of the impatient jabs on the button the person had been waiting for some time. She hurried to the door; It was her close friend, Jane.

"Oh, hi Jane come in."

"Hey, what's going on? I thought you had a fella in there."

Carrie gave a hollow laugh, "That'll be the day, won't it? Come in, Jane, coffee? Sorry I haven't quite got going this morning."

"I called to see if you wanted a lift to the supermarket. We can do a bit of shopping and then have one of those delicious cream cakes in the cafe."

"Sounds good, I'll just get dressed and put me face on. Won't be a minute, help yourself to the coffee. Oh, and by the way, just have a read at this letter I got this morning."

When Carrie returned some ten minutes later, Jane looked her up and down and gave a little cry of admiration.

"Wow, very chic! Here, what's all this about?" She said indicating the letter. "Is he your fancy man?"

"Don't be bloody daft, what would I do with a fancy man? All right, don't answer that," she added, when she saw the look on Jane's face. "I don't know what the hell it's about, came right out of the blue, addressed to my maiden name at my old address, my mum's house."

"So much for the new, improved postal service, eh?" Jane said cuttingly.

"No, just look at the date on the envelope. Posted in Skipton two days ago."

"Well, who is this guy, do you know him?"

"I can vaguely remember him. At least, I think I know which one he was. He worked in the outer office at Wilkinson's when I was secretary there... but that was twenty five years ago. I never went out with him... though I always knew he fancied me. From what I remember he was a very shy, reserved sort of lad, not bad looking, mind. I remember now, he used to look at me through the partition window, but it's all such a long time ago, another world, different people."

"Well give him a ring then, he might be really interesting now, or better still... rich!"

"He might be a bloody nutcase, more likely," Carrie said sharply.

Jane persisted, "Look Carrie, what have you got to lose? I think it's really intriguing. Ring him up, tell him you're married, but you wouldn't mind having a chat about the old times."

"But why should he write now after all these years, and as though we were still working at Wilkinson's? Anyway Wilkinson's closed down...about twelve years ago, I think."

"There's only one way to find out, lass, and that's to speak to him."

"Do you really think so? It's funny, you know, but it doesn't make me feel like laughing. It disturbs me, like a voice from the past speaking to me. I don't understand it...and that's what frightens me."

Jane moved around the table and placed a comforting arm across Carrie's shoulder. "Look, you're taking it too seriously, Carrie, that's your trouble! There'll be a simple explanation, it's probably just a joke, somebody's winding you up."

Carrie shrugged her shoulders, "Yeah, I suppose you're right. Anyway, I can't ring him now, it's too early."

"What about your Arthur? Are you going to tell him about it?"

Carrie gave it some thought for a while before answering and then in a rather doubtful tone, "I suppose so, though whether he'll listen is quite another thing. He gets home at seven, has his dinner, reads the paper, watches telly a bit, falls asleep, wakens up and goes to bed! Gets up next morning - repeat performance! If anything disturbs the routine he goes berserk, he just can't cope with things that aren't planned ages before or, if truth were known, owt at all out-of-the-ordinary."

"Sounds bloody marvellous. Come to think of it though, Jack does more or less the same. Hey, do you want me to ring this guy for you?" Jane said brightly, stressing the 'me'.

"No, it's all right, thanks." Carrie replied quickly. "I'll give it some more thought first" then rapidly changing the subject. "Come on, we'd better get going, we don't want to miss out on the sticky buns, do we?"

"I must say, Carrie, you look very grand for a shopping trip. Is that the new outfit you bought the other week? Perhaps we'll meet this mysterious James Preston, eh?"

They laughed their way out into the street, but there is more genuine mirth in Jane's high spirits. Underlying Carrie's laughter there is the excitement of the new, the strange and it has to be said, the romantic, but the whole package is tinged with a fair amount of apprehension.

Two

That evening Carrie had just served the evening meal and she and Arthur were sitting facing each other across the dining table in the kitchen. They didn't usually have much to say to each other and the early part of their conversation followed the familiar desultory fashion. In fact, these early exchanges could have been pre-recorded and played back each evening thus saving valuable eating time.

"Had a good day today, Arthur?"

"Nar, nothing much doing - trade's really bad at this time of the year." Trade was always bad, whatever season of the year, "Aye up, though, nearly sold that duchesse dresser I was telling you about, but the bloody know-all said it were the wrong top for it, tried to beat me down on price."

"Well was it?"

"Was it what?" queried Arthur, his eyes and mind fixed far away on a pristine piece of furniture.

Carrie sighed, "Was it the wrong bloody top?"

"'Course it was, but he couldn't tell from where he was standing. Big 'ead!.. I've never known a trade with so many big 'eads in it. You know, they're experts after a fortnight and bloody authorities after a month, you can't tell 'em owt! To hear them talk they've either just spent ten grand, or have ten grand to spend for some big foreign buyer, that no one ever sees, mind. Dreamers they are - walking, talking, bullshitting dreamers, that's all." Arthur yawns loudly, "Cor, I'm tired out today. Think I'll just have five minutes read of the paper on the settee." He pushed back the chair and made as if to leave the table.

"Did you enjoy your meal, by any chance?" asked Carrie pointedly.

"Oh, yes, thanks love, it was lovely." He moved into the lounge, switched on the television, picked up a newspaper and flopped down on the settee with an exaggerated sigh of contentment.

Carrie remained in the kitchen clearing the table and stacking the washing-up on the draining board. She felt this was probably the best time to broach the difficult subject of the letter. With a damp dish-cloth in her hand she stood in the lounge doorway. "Arthur," she said hesitantly. "I got a really unusual letter this morning, did I tell you about it? It's from a lad I used to know years ago when I worked at Wilkinson's."

"Oh, aye?" Arthur replied vaguely, obviously completely absorbed in the newspaper. "I see here City have signed a new striker. They must be bloody barmy. Just listen to this, love. He's thirty-five years old, hasn't played in the first team this season, and is recovering from a serious knee injury. He'll fit in bloody well with our team though, he'll look like superman compared to that lot! You know what I always say, if you buy right you can always sell right."

Carrie yelled, "Oh, for God's sake, Arthur! I'll scream if you say that again. You bloody well drive me mad with your sayings." She paused, in the belief that she'd established a connection with her husband's brain, calmer and more controlled she went on. "As I was saying, I got this letter from a lad I've not seen for twenty-five years."

"No, it says here he's thirty-five!" Arthur interrupted, his mind still totally focussed on the important things in life, "thirty-bloody-five," he went on. "He's that slow the groundsman painted him the other day in mistake for a corner flag." Arthur chuckled at his own joke and rapidly warmed to the theme, completely unaware of the effect it was having on his wife who was still standing by the door, fuming to herself and looking at her husband with utter contempt. "You know, I reckon if he warms up before t' match he'll be too knackered to play. Hee, bloody hell, anyway, everybody knows the Board of Directors are damned sight faster than the players. You ought to see 'em move when they bank the takings on a Monday morning."

Arthur stifled another yawn, "God, I really am tired tonight." He rested the newspaper on his lap, closed his eyes and settled back on the settee.

Carrie watched him for a few seconds, "Pathetic" she murmured, a look of disgust on her face. She took the letter out of her apron pocket, went into the hall and quietly closed the door behind her. She checked the letter in her hand, picked up the telephone and carefully dialled the number. She cleared her throat and waited nervously. A man's voice answered, deep and quite well spoken.

"Hello, is that James Preston?" Carrie asked tremulously, annoyed with herself for the breathiness in her voice.

"Yes, James Preston speaking. Who is that?"

"It's Carrie, er, Caroline," correcting herself. "Caroline Wadsworth. I got a letter from you."

"Caroline, is it really you?" The excitement in his voice was obvious. "Hey, I'm delighted you've rung, I've been trying to pluck up courage for ages to get in touch with you. Do you fancy going to the pictures one night this week? Say Friday or ..."

"Hold on, James, just a minute; slow down, will you? You don't seem to understand. I'm married now, have been for a long time."

There was significant pause at the other end of the line before a shocked, exclamation "What? I don't get it. I've never seen a ring on your finger. You're kidding me aren't you? Look, let's just meet and talk properly. I hate to have important conversations on the telephone, you never get true reactions. It'd be much better if we met, don't you think so? I've always wanted to take you out but never dared ask till now."

Carrie was completely baffled by his reaction but her curiosity and inherent romanticism proved a more powerful combination than mere protocol. "But why now, James? After all this time?"

"Don't know really. I've been thinking about you for a long time. Like I said, never dare give it a try, and there was my mother to think about. Sadly she passed away a couple of months ago, God rest her soul."

"Oh, I am sorry to hear that. I don't really keep up with the local Skipton news; I don't live in the town now."

"Don't you?" queried James, the surprise evident in his voice. "I thought you walked to work every morning. I've seen you coming up the drive in all weathers, even in your wellies at times."

"Look, James," said Carrie patiently. "Let's get this straight. I haven't worked at Wilkinson's for years, you must be mistaking me for someone else."

"No, of course I'm not. I could never do that, you're the only one for me. Do you remember that staff photograph we had taken on that trip to Blackpool? You're sitting on the grass at the front eating an ice-cream. I'm right behind you, remember?"

"Yes, I do actually," Carrie said thoughtfully, "freezing cold day it was too, if I remember. As a matter of fact I still have that photograph somewhere, though I haven't seen it for ages."

"Well, what do you say, then? Let's just meet and have a chat, Caroline. I'd love to see you again, OK?"

The urgent tone of pleading in his voice rather deterred Carrie from committing herself to an early meeting, excited though she was by the whole romantic scenario.

"Er, I'm sorry I can't manage it at the moment, James, but I will think it over and ring you again sometime."

"Yea, all right, Caroline, but try not to leave it too long, please?" A note of resignation in his voice quite apparent. "It's been really great talking to you."

"Yes, it's been nice talking to you. 'Bye, I'll speak to you later." She gently replaced the handset. "Nice, but bloody weird," she murmured as she returned to the lounge.

Arthur was still sprawled on the settee fast asleep, his mouth wide open and sheets of newspaper scattered all over the floor. Some 1960s pop music was blaring out from the television. Carrie just shook her head in disgust, "Jesus, love's young dream", she muttered and went through into the kitchen to finish the washing-up. She had just got to the kitchen sink when the sound of the telephone ringing made her start with apprehension, "Oh, my God!" she exclaimed, her first thought being that James was ringing back and that Arthur might answer the phone. Still wiping her hands on a tea towel she hurried through the lounge to the hall. Arthur, thank God, was still on the settee, grunting incoherently at the subconscious interruption. Carrie picked up the phone and nervously answered. With overwhelming relief Carrie recognised her daughter's voice. "Oh, Helen, it's you, love."

"Well, who did you think it was? It didn't sound like you at all when you answered the phone. Are you all right, mum?"

"Yes, 'course I am. Er, just a bit of a sore throat that's all."

"I rang you earlier but you were engaged."

"Oh yes, I was chatting to a work friend I've not seen for a long time."

"Is Dad there? I want him to get a piece of furniture for me if he can."

"He's fast asleep in front of the telly at the moment. Tell me what you want and I'll pass the message on."

"It's for Jim, my new boyfriend, you'll like him, Mum, he's really great. Very polite, in a sort of old-fashioned way, if you know what I mean, anyway you'll meet him soon. He's furnishing his flat in Victorian style and he wants a small mahogany chest of drawers. I wondered if Dad could get him one."

"OK love, I'll ask him and get him to give you a ring later. How's Sarah?"

"She's fine; she's out at the moment with her boyfriend, so I'm tidying the flat up. It's my turn today. Tell Dad I'll probably call in at the shop to see him during the week."

"Right, love. I'll see you later then, 'bye." Carrie passed through the lounge on her way back to the kitchen and noticed that Arthur's eyes were open though he was still half-lying in the same position on the settee.

"Good God, it's moving," she remarked sarcastically with a disdainful glance. "That was your daughter on the phone. She wants to know if you can get her a small chest. Her boyfriend wants one."

"Well, if he's going out with our Helen that's all he will get."

"There's no need to be vulgar, Arthur. A small mahogany chest. He wants it for his flat so she's coming in to see you this week, she says."

"Aye, righto, I'll fix him up: small chest for the boyfriend, right." He yawned and stretched extravagantly then settled down again and closed his eyes. "Thought I might go for a run tonight."

"You haven't been for a run for twenty odd years," Carrie scoffed. " It takes you all your time to get out of the bloody chair."

"Didn't say I would. Just said I'd think about it," he muttered, his head drooping onto his chest as he dozed off again.

God, he's off again, she thought. It's like living with a zombie; the only time I see him he's semi-comatose, either first thing in the morning or last thing at night. He's only actually alive when he's somewhere else.

Carrie finished off in the kitchen, checked the back door, put out the light and moved quietly through the lounge taking care not to disturb the snoring mound on the settee. Once in the bedroom Carrie rooted through the wardrobe drawer. The one that is hardly ever used except as a storage place for things that might never be needed. Carrie found the cardboard box she was looking for and took it over to the bed, put on her reading glasses and then sifted through the stack of old photographs. With an exclamation of satisfaction she selected one particular photograph and held it up to the light to see it more clearly. It was the old photograph of Wilkinson's works trip to Blackpool. Carrie picked up the magnifying glass from the dressing table and focused first on her own face and then more closely on the face of James Preston standing immediately behind her. Carrie smiled to herself, she'd never even realised he was so close to her until he'd mentioned it earlier that evening.

The noise of Arthur stumbling and cursing his way up the staircase rudely interrupted her reverie and with a guilty start Carrie hurriedly replaced the photograph in the box and stuffed it back into the drawer and then sat at the dressing table busily brushing her hair.

Arthur burst into the bedroom, "By, bloody hell, lass. I'm exhausted! Big German buyer coming in tomorrow." He put his arms around Carrie's shoulder and bent his head to kiss her neck.

Carrie shook him off violently and snapped, "Just get off, will you? You've not had a word for me all night and you just think you can bloody well grab me when it suits you. Well it's not on, so you can think again. I'm not here to just pander to your desires whenever you feel the urge."

Whilst Carrie ranted on Arthur had already moved away and started undressing; he quickly got into his pyjamas, yawned a couple of times and slipped into bed.

This didn't affect Carrie's flow in the slightest, "I thought we were meant to share things in a marriage. It's all one bloody way with you. Expect everything when you want it and yet not prepared to do a bloody thing, unless it's convenient for you - so good night!"

But Arthur was fast asleep. Probably dreaming of the enormous profit he was going to make out of the big German buyer on the morrow. Carrie got into bed, glanced once at the recumbent form of her husband, settled herself down and then viciously pulled the duvet over on to her side of the bed.

Three

Memory Lane was the name of Arthur's antique-come-second-hand shop in Cavendish Street. It was a simple one-roomed shop with an area to the rear in which Arthur did his restoration work. The stock consisted mainly of assorted second-hand furniture, very occasionally a couple of quality pieces and always a few shiny repro items to fill up the empty spaces. Arthur was busily and noisily hammering a plywood back on to a small chest of drawers in his workshop area when the bell on the shop door rang. This indicated one of various possibilities. Could be a customer, possibly a seller, usually a time waster, often a pensioner seeking warmth on a cold afternoon, or generally always, one of his many trade acquaintances seeking anything they could get for as little expenditure as possible.

Arthur hurriedly hid the hammer and the nails and wiped over the top of the chest with a dirty rag. He looked up, his dealer's welcoming you-can-trust-me-smile automatically on his face, but it quickly changed to the genuine article when he saw his daughter standing in the doorway. She was an attractive pleasant girl, who had inherited many of Carrie's facial characteristics, particularly her blonde hair, exactly the same shade as her mother's. Helen had, however, a high degree of self confidence and was much more assured and outgoing than her mother, not exactly an unusual difference between the generations.

She greeted her Dad cheerfully, "Hello, Dad, did Mum tell you I'd be calling? I'm looking for some drawers for a friend."

"Hello, love. Yes, she did say something about it. Mahogany chest wasn't it?"

"Mm, a small one," she confirmed, looking around the shop. "Any dark wood, it's for a bedroom."

"Aye, well I've nothing in at the moment, lass. But this chap's calling today and he might well have one. How much does your friend want to pay?"

"I think about thirty quid, or thereabouts. Well not much more than that."

"You'll not get much for that, I'll tell you. You might get one at the auctions, but there'll be plenty to do on it. Anyway, I'll see what I can do for you."

"Thanks, Dad. The shop looks nice. Jim, that's my boyfriend, is right into antiques. His Dad had a houseful at one time."

Helen noticed for the first time the chest at the back of the shop that Arthur has been working on, "What about this one, Dad? This looks all right, won't this do?"

"I haven't quite finished that one yet, it still needs a bit of fine restoration work on it. 'Course, I don't have to tell you what it is, do I?"

"Don't you? I like it though, is it Georgian?"

"Well, I would say that's highly likely. Late Georgian at a guess. I've a chap coming in today who specialises in Georgian furniture and he'll be able to date it for me." Guys like Arthur always had some back-up in the trade who, for past favours received or debts forgotten, would confirm or reject the provenance of anything from a Tintoretto to a tin can.

"I don't suppose thirty quid'll buy something like this, will it?" Helen asked, looking in her purse.

The antique dealers spiel, internalised to the extent that it was impossible to stop even when family was involved, sparked into life immediately. "Well not usually, that's for sure. I've got about fifty in it already, what with the work I've done on it. I'll tell you what I'll do, since it's for a friend, I'll let him have it at trade price - fifty quid. Cash, that is. I'll just straighten it up a bit. I could have it ready for the weekend, if you like."

"All right, Dad. I'll have a word with Jim today. Will you save it for me if I put a tenner deposit on it?"

Arthur nodded his head and swiftly trousered the tenner, "OK lass, no problem."

The brass bell on the door sounded again as a middle-aged couple came into the shop.

"Is it all right if we just have a look around?" the man enquired deferentially as though entering a museum of fine art.

"Of course, come in," Arthur said in his breezy shopkeeper's tone, only just managing to stop himself rubbing his hands together in anticipation. "Just browse around and if there's anything special you want to know just ask."

Helen took the opportunity to slip out at this stage, promising to call and see her Mum over the weekend.

Arthur went and stood by the counter near the door. He could hear quite plainly the whispered conversation between the couple. The woman was speaking, "Here, look at that, Harold. Your mother had one of them. Look!" At this point there was even more of a dramatic stage whisper. "It's forty-five pounds. Whatever did she do with it? Eeeh, some of the stuff she had, if she'd saved what she had she'd be worth a fortune now. Remember that roll top desk she had in the kitchen; used to keep her bread in it, where did that go?"

"Nay, I don't know, probably got thrown out when she got that formica table from your Alice."

Arthur had heard this sort of conversation many times before, in fact just about every day, if truth were told. Though the latter concept was not by any means an everyday occurrence in the trade.

The woman came across to Arthur, "Excuse me, we was looking for a cabinet for the telly and video, weren't we, Harold." Harold nodded his agreement as though he had been programmed to do so over a long period of time.

"Aye, smallish one though, where we can get 'em both in, and out of the way, like."

"What about that one, Harold?" She pointed in the direction of the chest of drawers on which Helen has just left a deposit. "You could take the top two drawers out and put some doors on it, couldn't you? Video'd go in't bottom drawer, it'd be ideal would that, I think."Having organised the next few weeks of Harold's life in a matter of seconds she turned to Arthur. "How much is that? That one there."

"Now, let's see, 'onest little chest is that, very desirable piece, late Georgian I'd say, or early Victorian possibly. Can't get 'em anywhere nowadays. Unfortunately I've got someone very interested in it already, but, if you definitely wanted it, and came up with the cash, it'd be yours. Mind you it's a quality chest, is that. Now, best I could do on price, bearing in mind all the work that's gone into it, would be, er, let's say eighty five - they're fetching well over a hundred in t'centre of town."

"Well, what do you think, Harold? I think it'd look lovely in t'lounge, don't you think?"

After many years of practice Harold always thought what he was told to think so there was no real difficulty there. He pondered a while and took out his tape measure and fiddled with pencil and paper but Arthur knew a done deal when he smelled one and he stepped in with his killer blow.

"Look I'll tell you what I'll do." He studied his wrist watch carefully. "Now let's see, this other couple said they'd be in to let me know definitely by two o'clock, it's nearly five past now, so if you want it I'll let you have it for seventy-five, and that's a real rock-bottom bargain price, that is."

"Right,' said the woman. "We'll have it. Pay the man, Harold. And let's get it home."

Four

Carrie and Jane were having lunch in the supermarket restaurant. Jane was desperate to find out what happened to her friend with regard to the mystery man who fancied her.

"Well, what happened then?"

"How do you mean? What are you talking about?" Carrie answered, knowing full well what her friend meant. But she wanted to give the impression that it wasn't important, that it had almost slipped her memory.

"You know damn well what I'm talking about, Carrie," Jane retorted in mock anger. "The mystery man. The letter. Did you go and see him?" she persisted.

"I did not!" Carrie said emphatically. "It's quite ridiculous, it's obviously some kind of joke, " she paused before adding mischievously. "I did ring the number though."

"And?" snapped Jane impatiently. "Go on! Oh, you are irritating, Carrie. What happened, for God's sake?"

"Oh, nothing much," she replied in a matter-of-fact tone. "He sounded very nice, very polite, a bit strange and not quite with it, if you know what I mean."

Jane persisted with her questions and Carrie told her the general gist of the conversation she'd had with James.

Finally Jane retorted, "And you mean to say you didn't fix anything up? Well I'd have arranged to see him. Bloody hell, Carrie, the fella's been thinking about you for twenty-five years, he must be really red-hot by this time. Don't dither about, girl. This might be your last chance for romance."

"Jane, I'm surprised at you. You wouldn't really see him, would you? What about your Jack?"

"Look, I'll tell you something about our Jack, Carrie He thinks more about his bloody maggots than he does about me. He's off fishing at every opportunity. Up at five on a Sunday morning, comes back for his tea about six in the evening, bolts it down, watches telly for an hour and then down to the pub to talk to his stupid mates about flaming fishing again."

There was real contempt in Jane's voice and it prompted Carrie to ask in a concerned voice, "Oh, I am sorry, Jane. Aren't you two getting on right well, at the moment?"

"Oh, don't worry about us. We get on just fine," she said brightly. "Providing we don't have to be alone in each other's company for any length of time."

Carrie grinned ruefully, "I suppose it's the same with us, really. The most important things in Arthur's life are his antiques. Oh, and bloody football!" she remembered painfully. "When sodding football's on the telly his brain seems to leave an empty body behind; sometimes you can almost see a thought bubble over his head, a picture of himself in his knee-length shorts running on to the field and the commentator saying, 'and this is what the fans have been waiting for, Arthur Duxbury, idol of the northern crowds. Listen to the roar as the League's top scorer comes on to the Wembley turf. Bloody hell!" she snorted in disgust. "He played about three times for the Church Youth Club when he was a kid, since when, of course, he's been the leading authority in Europe on team selection and tactics."

The women had a good laugh at this and the many other failings of their menfolk in the kind of purgative session which allowed them to put up with their dissatisfaction of married life. It led Jane to reflect rather philosophically on the past. "You wonder, don't you?" she went on. "If this is all there is to life. It seems great when you're eighteen to get your independence and have a man of your own, and your own place, and all your mates are as jealous as hell, but twenty years on you realise you actually gave up your freedom for someone you hardly knew and," she added as a ruminant afterthought, "what's more, if you'd met him now you wouldn't be the least bit interested."

Carrie couldn't help but agree, it summed up her relationship with Arthur both accurately and painfully.

Jane continued to push Carrie into some positive action. "Give it try," she urged. "Add a bit of excitement to your life. You've nothing to lose, have you? Opportunities like this don't come very often, you know, and we're bloody fools if we don't recognise them, and even more stupid if we ignore them."

Carrie nodded her head in agreement. Jane was right. She would give the guy another call, but she had to admit she did feel a certain amount of apprehension about the whole thing. "Yes, I think you're right, Jane. I'll give him another ring. I must admit the idea excites me but it still frightens me a bit, it's weird, really. He's got me thinking of a time when life was full of hope and interest, and adventure and, I suppose, what I might have been if I'd taken the other path."

"What other bloody path was that, then?" Jane retorted.

"Oh, there were lots of different paths in the woods in those days, Jane," Carrie murmured vaguely. "But I...I took the one more travelled by...and that," she continued thoughtfully, "has made all the difference."

"Oh, bloody hell", Carrie complained. "Here we go again, get the violin out, you're a deep one, you know, Carrie."

On the other side of the restaurant, so far unnoticed by Carrie and Jane. Carrie's daughter and her new boyfriend, Jim, were having lunch. Helen was sitting with her back to the wall facing out into the restaurant. Jim was telling her how glad he was that she had agreed to come out with him and how he'd been trying to get up enough courage to ask her for ages.

"Well, I'm glad you did ask," she said in her usual forthright manner. "I was going to give you until the weekend then I was going to ask you out."

Jim's face registered surprise and also delight at this remark and his voice immediately had more self confident tone about it, "Were you really, Helen? I'm surprised you even thought about it."

"Don't be silly, you're a very attractive man; a bit unusual, mind you, but I like a man to be a bit different."

Jim smiled at this, obviously please at the compliment, "Different? How do you mean, different?"

"Well, you're not always on about drinking lager, football and fast cars, sex, hi-tech gadgets and all the rest of that laddish bullshit."

Jim nodded thoughtfully, and answered slowly, "Oh, I see."

Rather worried that she might have offended him Helen felt obliged to expand on the theme, "Well, for instance, you're interested in antique furniture, and you've a certain old-fashioned way about you, almost as though you've been born twenty years too late. You don't seem to fit in with the modern life-style somehow."

"Oh, thanks very much; that's made my day," he replied with an amused expression. "You make me sound like some species of fossil."

'I mean it all kindly, you dummy," laughed Helen. "I find your approach most attractive, and I love the consideration you show to other people, 'specially me," she added and reached over and touched his hand affectionately.

A group of people moved from an intervening table and Carrie noticed Helen across the room. She waved and attracted her attention, getting a smile and wave of recognition in return. "There's our Helen over there, Jane, " she informed her friend, "with her new boyfriend, I guess."

Jane swivelled around in her seat, "She's a lovely girl, Carrie. She's the spitten image of you when you were that age."

"Aye, fortunately she does take after me, in looks, as well as brains," Carrie remarked cockily.

"And modesty too, I'll bet", countered Jane. "This coffee's good, isn't it?" she said changing the subject, "and the cakes aren't bad. I like this place; they do some good food in here."

Carrie agreed, "Yes, and there's plenty of choice on the menu, and a bit of life about the place. You know plenty to look at whilst you're eating."

'You mean like that old guy over there." Jane inclined her head towards a table on the left and added. "The one who fancies you?'

"Don't be ridiculous! Jane," Carrie expostulated, but was still interested enough to enquire which old guy. "Where? I'll bet he can't even see this far."

'He's always here leering in your direction, anyway. Just you take notice."

"Get on with you," Carrie remonstrated You make stuff up just to get my reaction. I know you."

Helen and Jim finished their lunch at the far side of the cafe and headed towards the exit. On the way they stopped at the table where her mother and Jane were seated. As she approached their table, Helen began by, way of introduction, "Mother, this is Jim, a friend of mine."

Carrie turned round with a smile of greeting, straight into the face of James Preston as she remembered him twenty-five years ago. Her smile froze into rigidity, her jaw dropped open, acute shock registered on her blanched face and she spluttered and choked on the food in her mouth. With tears and bewilderment in her eyes she gasped for breath looking ever more like a floundering fish on fishmonger's slab.

There was total confusion around the table, Helen was slapping Carrie on the back to relieve the choking, Jane was reaching over to control Carrie's shaking hands, people were turning around to look at the scene, crockery smashed on the floor which then drew the attention of a member of staff who came over to help. All the time Jim stood well back from the table, appearing to be quite detached from the whole incident. Jane forced Carrie's head between her knees and the assistant rushed off in search of the First Aid Officer.

Seconds later the background music faded and the tannoy crackled into life, "Would the First Aid Officer report to the restaurant immediately, please? Mrs Middleton to the restaurant now, please."

Carrie, meanwhile, had recovered from the choking fit but her eyes were still staring wide and her face and body were tense with shock. Helen had her hand on her mother's forehead and pleaded with her to concentrate and look at her. "Mother, look at me. You're all right."

There was a minor commotion near the door of the restaurant as a large officious woman barged her way through the crowd of onlookers. "Excuse me, please! Excuse me, sir, would you make way, please? Step back, if you would please," she reached the table and took immediate control. "Now then, what seems to be the trouble, madam?" She said breezily as she seized Carrie's wrist and studied the fob watch on her lapel. "Mmm, state of shock." she concluded. "Let's get her to the First Aid room," she said to Helen and Jane. She put her arms under Carrie's shoulder and heaved her bodily out of the seat, "Come on, madam, on your feet please." She issued various other orders to anybody who was near, "Bring this!" Pick up that!" Get hold here!" and Carrie was half-carried, half-dragged out of the restaurant by Matron, Helen and Jane, across the foyer and into a small First Aid room under the stairs. Jim followed the party but took no part in the proceedings; he simply watched from a discreet distance and after a few minutes slipped quietly out of the supermarket.

Five

Arthur Duxbury and his friend, Bill, spent most lunch-times in the bar at the Brown Cow and this particular day saw no change in the pattern; they had been on their favourite bar-stools since midday. There were four other men in the bar, two youths of the shaved head and tattoo variety, and two elderly men, one of whom talked incessantly at the other one whose face registered complete impassivity. Snatches of the overheard conversations covered the talker's opinion on a wide range of subjects including women priests, Saddam Hussain, the Al Qaida threat, the French farmers, water pollution, and footballers' wages. The elderly listener maintained his inscrutable mien, just occasionally making minor adjustments to his hearing aid.

The youths on the other side of the bar were re-living some fracas in the town centre at the previous weekend. Their conversation seemed to be entirely about the justification for some violent and aggressive action against another party who had the temerity to look at them in the pub. The account was liberally sprinkled with many a "do yer know wharra mean," and nodding donkey-like confirmations from the other one.

"Owt much doing, Arthur?" Bill asked, after a contemptuous glance at the youths.

"Oh, aye, one or two deals going through, Bill." Arthur answered brightly. Business was always thriving in conversations like this. "By the way I sold that chest I got from you yesterday."

"What, not that bodged-up piece of crap? I got that off that rag-tatter that comes round; the rogue wanted a fiver for it. I said, nay bloody hell lad, it's nobbut firewood, is that."

Arthur was disinclined to agree, "Ah, it were a lot better than you thought, Bill. I think it might have been Georgian."

"Georgian, my arse", Bill snapped. "Only Georgian piece I've seen with a plywood back and a chipboard top."

"Nay, steady on, Bill," Arthur remonstrated, in an attempt to justify his claim. "It weren't as bad as that, it did have a bit of a Georgian look to it. Anyway," he went on not at all reluctant to change the subject. "Here, while I remember, that big German buyer's around again. He gave me a cheque for thirty grand last year to fill a container with bureaus and desks. He doesn't mess about, so keep your eyes open. I'm not telling anybody else. We'll just keep this to usselves. I want two hundred of 'em; doesn't matter if the legs are broken, 'cos we're taking 'em off anyway to pack 'em in."

Bill nodded his head, "Right, I can get hold of a few. When's the container going?"

"End o' next month probably, so there's no rush yet. But keep it to yoursen, them villains'll up the asking if they know I'm after some."

"Trust me, Arthur. By the way I sold a couple of roll- tops yesterday. A grand each I got for 'em; they'll be going to the States. This guy, who's an agent for this American buyer, always comes to me. I did him a favour once. I might have told you about it before, we'd been in a bar in Leeds doing a deal when these two toerags tried to mug him outside. Lucky I came out just behind him. I'd done a bit of unarmed combat in the commandos, know what I mean? Well I soon sorted them out and since then he's always come to me for owt special."

Not to be outdone by his mate Arthur was quickly in with his reciprocal self-elevation. "Aye, I've a customer like that. Japanese he is...or Chinese. I forget which. Spends thousands with me every year; he's going to finance me on a trip to Tokyo... or is it Peking?" he said thoughtfully. "Somewhere like that, anyway," he added, as if the ultimate destination was of little importance, " it'll be next year sometime to see what sort of stuff they want out there. I'm gunna learn Japanese next month. I'm starting one of them courses you see in the papers. Do you know the ones I mean? Learn Japanese in three weeks. That'll do for me! You just put them in your cassette player and you learn to speak the language in less than a month. I might learn Spanish the month after that, and then Italian before Christmas, depends where the markets are." A sudden thought occurred to him, "Here, Bill, what do the Israelis talk?"

Bill retorted promptly, "Money. That's what they talk, money. But from my experience not very much of it."

There was a lull in their conversation whilst Bill went to the bar to recharge their glasses. Arthur settled for just a half pint this time as he maintained that he had a customer coming to the shop at three o'clock to look at an empire cabinet.

"What is your best on that cabinet, Arthur? That Manchester shipper I know might just be interested in it."

"Well, let's see" Arthur said slowly, naturally reluctant to be the first to name a price, an anathema to any self-respecting dealer. After some thought and mental computation he finally said. "Well, I've got about two hundred in it so it'll have to be about two forty if you want it. That's cash, mind you," he added quickly. "No more bloody cheques", he said vehemently. "I took a cheque from a punter the other day, only for thirty quid, mind you, a little repro ginger pot, it was. Bloody cheque only bounced this morning, didn't it? I got his address and card number though, Preston, his name was, so watch out for him."

"Right, thanks for the tip-off. Cheers", acknowledged Bill. "Bloody good price for a repro pot that, Arthur, wasn't it?" he queried.

"Well, you know what I always say, Bill. If you buy right you can always sell right, but, if you buy wrong you can never sell right. To tell the truth Bill, I didn't like the look of him as soon as he came in. He looked as though he'd come straight from the Oxfam shop, do you know what I mean? Sort of flared trousers and big-lapel sixties jacket. Said he wanted a present for his new girlfriend. I thought, if you can afford a girlfriend at your age, pal, you can afford to pay me a bit extra for the present."

Bill nodded, "Right, but I'm still surprised at you taking a cheque."

"Well, he was public, like," Arthur said in justification. "I never take 'em from t'trade. That lot try to get stuff by cheque, mark it up and sell it on for cash, keep the profit and get the cash in the bank before the bugger bounces. Anyway, "he added as a conclusive determinant, "cheques mess the books up; too many people can see what you're doing."

Bill eagerly agreed and quickly took the opportunity to air one of his periodic moans about the system, "Aye, and that can be bloody dangerous! The more they see, the more they want; there's accountants, bank managers, tax inspectors, VAT men. I often wonder why the hell I bother; supporting that bloody lot, I mean! You know there's a massive pyramid of non-productive bureaucratic layabouts sitting on my shoulders, and they've just about knackered me, I'll tell you."

They'd now dealt with most of their own and everyone else's problems and Arthur was about to get his coat and return to the shop when the telephone rang on the bar. The barman answered it, had a short conversation, put his hand over the mouthpiece and called Arthur over to take the call.

"Bloody hell, business is bucking up," he muttered as he moved over to answer it.

His jolly tone changed after a few seconds, however, and his face expressed concern at what he was hearing. He hung up and turned to Bill, "It's the wife, she's had a funny turn at the supermarket, some kind of shock our Helen says, I'd better get over there right away." With a quick word of goodbye to Bill he grabbed his coat and hurried out into the street.

Six

Carrie was sitting in the first aid room in the supermarket. Mrs Middleton was standing over her taking her pulse and checking her matron's watch on her lapel. Jane and Helen sat on each side of Carrie their faces still retaining worried expressions. Carrie was trying, obviously unsuccessfully, to reassure them about her condition. Her face was flushed and she was totally embarrassed about the whole situation.

"I feel much better now, Mrs Middleton, honestly. Thank you very much for all you've done. I feel really silly for all the trouble I've caused. I don't know what came over me, I don't really", she lied. She knew damn well what had caused it but she could hardly go into details with Matron standing over her, and with her daughter there too. What Carrie needed right now was time on her own to think things over. "It must have been the heat and the rushing about," she added lamely.

"Dad's on his way, Mum." It was Helen back from telephoning her father. "He was in the pub with Bill."

"Bill Matthews?" queried Jane.

Carrie answered before Helen could reply. "No, I don't think you know this Bill, Jane, and take my word for it, you don't want to. According to him he lives in a Norman manor house, paved courtyard, mullioned windows, the lot."

"Really? Sounds interesting," Jane said, obviously impressed and eager to know more.

"Oh, it is. Apparently it's the only one there is on that particular council estate," Carrie said dryly. "The house is called Five Acres, five belly-achers more like when all the family are in."

Jane glanced up at Carrie, realised she was joking and they both laughed. "Right. You're feeling a lot better now, aren't you?"

Mrs Middleton and Helen thought so too, because the former excused herself and bustled off to her duties and shortly afterwards Helen left for work. She urged her mother to take it easy and promised to telephone her that evening. Jane and Carrie were now left alone in the small first aid room.

"He'll not be too pleased about being dragged out of The Brown Cow before closing time, I'll bet," Carrie said, referring to her husband.

Jane leaned over towards Carrie and in a confidential tone said, "Look, Carrie, before Arthur arrives, what exactly was it that shocked you so much. It frightened the life out of me, I'll tell you. It was just when your Helen introduced her boyfriend, it was as if you'd seen a ghost."

"That's just it, Jane. It was!" she exclaimed.

"Was what?" queried Jane sharply.

"A bloody ghost", Carrie replied despairingly. "That boy Helen was with was James Preston."

"Oh, come on now, Carrie," Jane scoffed. "What are you on about? You can't be serious?"

Carrie was adamant. "I'm telling you, Jane, that was James Preston. No bloody doubt about it."

"Don't be daft, Carrie. That lad was only about twenty-five or six, about Helen's age."

"I know, I know," Carrie agreed desperately, "but that's what he looked like when I knew him. Definitely him. Good God, I've been thinking about him enough just recently to know. There he was, out of nowhere, standing right in front of me, and with my own daughter. I couldn't cope with it, that's why I freaked out, and that's the honest truth."

Jane thought for a moment before speaking, "Well, if you think about it, Carrie, it couldn't be James, could it? He's far too young. He must have reminded you of him and, because he's been on your mind, you were shocked by the likeness."

Carrie was rapidly tiring of all this analysis, "Perhaps you're right, Jane. I'm stupid, aren't I? Getting worked up like this. What am I going to do now? I've upset your plans, embarrassed Helen and her boyfriend, and on top o' that Arthur'll play bloody hell about his routine being disturbed."

Voices could be heard in the corridor. "Don't worry, Carrie. I'll sort Arthur out and I can take you home. I think he's here now."

The door opened and the Assistant Manager ushered Arthur into the room. He seemed very concerned and moved quickly over to Carrie and took hold of her hands, "Are you all right, love? What happened? I came as quick as I could."

Jane took over the responsibility. "She's all right, Arthur. Just got a bit overcome with the heat in the shop, that's all. She's fine now, aren't you, Carrie?"

Carrie nodded in confirmation and managed a weak smile," Yes, I'm all right, Arthur, really. It's good of you to come. I think our Helen must have panicked a bit to ring you. Jane says she'll take me home in a minute."

Arthur shifted about uneasily for a minute or two and then decided he was totally superfluous to requirements, muttered something about a big American shipper coming in that afternoon and made his departure. His relief at his escape would have been obvious to the least observant passer-by.

When he was out of the door Jane and Carrie exchanged glances as if to say now we can really talk. Jane was first in, "so, what are you going to do about Mr. Preston now, girl? You're obviously very affected by him. What's the next step?"

"Oh, I don't know, I'm all confused, I think I'll just forget about it." She paused for a second to consider it further. "Or I might ring him up and ask him if he was at the supermarket." She looked at Jane for approval but got a resounding rejection instead, one she half expected it must be admitted.

"That is bloody ridiculous, and you know it, Jane," she snapped. "Just phone the guy up and arrange to have a coffee with him. I'll come with you, one afternoon, if you like. That'll answer all the questions and set your mind at rest, what do you say to that?"

Carrie agreed, involuntarily yawning as she did so: she suddenly felt very tired, too tired to argue that was for sure. She said as much to Jane who solicitously gathered all their shopping up and then linking arms like a couple of pensioners heading for a night out at the bingo hall they left the supermarket.

Seven

That same evening Helen and Jim were seated in the lounge bar of the White Lion discussing the supermarket incident. Helen was desperately apologetic, feeling that Jim might somehow have taken offence, she'd been worrying about it all afternoon in the office

"I'm sorry about this afternoon, Jim. My mother is all right now; but it was a bit of a worry at the time, I can tell you. I thought she'd had a heart attack."

"No need to apologise. I'm just glad she's OK; not a very good introduction to the family, was it?" he said wryly. "What exactly was the matter with her?"

Helen related what the nurse had said about her mother being in a state of shock.

"She just looked up at me, went deathly pale and seemed to sort of collapse. I didn't know what to do so when you went into the medical room I thought it best to keep out of the way."

"You did right," Helen agreed. "She seemed very confused for a while, but after a cup of tea she was back to normal. She didn't seem to know what caused it. Stress, I think." Helen paused for a moment before continuing. "She's not getting on too well with Dad; he's at work all the time... Or it might just be her age, I don't know. I rang her before I came out tonight and she sounded fine. Dad wasn't there, of course, he'll be working over again, down at the Brown Cow with one of his big foreign buyers.'"

Jim missed the sarcasm and asked if her dad did much export business.

"Well, to hear him talk you'd think so. Mind you, they're all alike that lot!" she said contemptuously, "Either, they've just completed a big deal, or about to fix one up. It's all part of the traders hype, bullshit it's called in les refined circles."

Jim laughed at her bluntness, "You don't think that highly of the business, then?"

"No, don't get me wrong, Jim. I don't object, really. I just don't accept everything they say. For instance they can always go one better than you, whatever it is. Their deal is always just that bit better than yours. For example if you've got back ache they'll have had a spinal transplant, or if you'd had a triple bypass operation they'd have been totally reincarnated, or something stupid like that. They fantasise about the deals, as well, each tries to impress the other, and what's more, each goes along with the other's exaggerations." Well into her stride about the failings of the antique dealers, Helen continued. "Another thing I've noticed is that whenever you do a deal with them, whatever it is, you've always got the feeling that you're losing out in some way. Quite honestly I think 'suspicion' is the main characteristic of the trade, for a start they all suspect each other, and then they all suspect there's something wrong with the stuff they've been offered."

"It sounds a funny carry-on to me," Jim remarked thoughtfully. "I told you my Dad was interested in antiques, didn't I? I haven't seen him for over ten years but he did leave a little Chinese pot behind when he left. The top's a bit chipped but it's quite attractive and I'm very fond of it."

"Where's your Dad now?" Helen asked.

"No idea, really. When they split up we didn't see much of him. I thought he'd gone down to London, but I don't really know. My mum never spoke about him after he left."

"That's very sad," murmured Helen sympathetically. "I'm sorry, perhaps you might try to make contact again sometime."

"Yes, I have thought about it. I ought to. It's funny really, isn't it? We can't choose our parents, we sort of inherit them in reverse, so I suppose we ought to do our best to try to understand them."

"I wonder how many of our relatives we'd choose as friends if we had the chance?" Helen suggested, "and yet because we're so close to them for so long we always feel such a strong obligation towards them, don't we? Then as an afterthought she asked, "Were you fairly close to your father, Jim?"

"I was for a time; I looked very like him when he was a boy. Some photographs I saw of him, when I was a kid, I thought were photographs of me. Weird, really, I felt as though I'd had some kind of previous existence, and there I was looking out of some old-fashioned yellowing photograph at myself. I'd like to see him now, if only to see what I'll look like in twenty-five years time. It's frightening, isn't it?" he concluded. "I mean, to think there's a pattern already made for you, you just follow it and you can see how it'll turn out from the picture on the front, like a knitted sweater."

"God, that is a totally depressing thought," Helen retorted. "When I look at Mum I'm determined not to have her narrow-minded outlook. Hey," she exclaimed looking at Jim for support," you don't think I'm going to look like her when I'm her age, do you?"

"Your Mum is a very attractive mature woman, and you are a very attractive young one," he answered diplomatically and added, "so you can't lose."

"And you are just a young smoothie," she scoffed smiling, pleased with the reply. "You'll get on very well with my mother I'm sure. I'll have to watch it."

Eight

That evening Carrie was sitting by the kitchen table reading the newspaper; the evening meal was already in the oven and she was waiting for Arthur to come home. The telephone rang and Carrie went into the hall to answer it. It was her husband; he would be late home, delayed at the shop. Carrie replaced the receiver and went back into the kitchen muttering to herself, "Japanese buyer. Big bloody deal. Must have a juke box in the shop now, the rat! Stuff his bloody dinner, honestly he must think I'm as thick as the rest of his dozy mates".

Carrie's irritation was obvious as she slammed the kitchen door. Then an idea occurred to her and she took James Preston's letter from her handbag, marched back into the hall and dialled his number. She straightened her hair in the mirror and cleared her throat with a little nervous cough. A man's voice answered.

"Hello," Carrie said. "Is that James Preston?"

There was an immediate note of excitement in the man's voice, "Caroline, is that you?"

They exchanged a few inconsequential pleasantries then Carrie broached the subject that had been on her mind all evening. "You didn't by any chance go to the supermarket this afternoon, did you James?"

"Supermarket?" He repeated, obviously puzzled by the question. "How do you mean? No, 'fraid not, I've been working all day. Sometimes I go in the evening, but not today, why do you ask?"

Carrie dismissed the question as unimportant, muttering that she thought she'd caught a glimpse of him when she was shopping. James again denied that he'd been there, adding that he didn't get out much during the day to go shopping. Carrie changed the subject realising that this line of inquiry wasn't getting her very far.

"Where do you work now, by the way?"

"I'm still at Wilkinson's," he answered. "Have been for years. Time I moved on I think. Well, you know where I am," he added as if the question was unnecessary.

"But Wilkinson's closed down years ago," Carrie persisted.

"Well, they went bust, didn't they? Some years ago, that was, but they were taken over by Martin's then, we always call it Wilkinson's mill though, same job, same place, same faces, same wages," he added wryly.

"Oh, I see," said Carrie, relieved to get what seemed to her to be the first reasonable explanation for the situation. "Do you still work in the office there?"

"Yes I do. I'm in charge of that section now, the Customer Accounts Department."

"Ooh, that sounds a bit grand does that, James. What about your family life, if you don't mind me asking?" She wished she'd never asked because James's answer took them back into the weird world of times past.

"Not at all, Caroline." he went on blithely. "I've always been fond of you and thought about you a great deal. I think we're very right for each other."

" Wait a minute, James", interrupted Carrie forcefully determined to get the situation sorted. "Let's get this straight, I'm married and I've got a grown-up daughter. Remember we haven't met for twenty-five years. So it's highly unlikely we'll have anything in common now," she paused for breath. "Are you married? Have you a family? Where do you live? I don't know anything about you at all."

James's voice was surprisingly calm in spite of this barrage of questions. "That's precisely why we should meet, Caroline. We've wasted enough time already. I was married, once, but I haven't seen her for years. I have a son as well, but he went with her when we separated. I think she married again shortly afterwards. I haven't seen either them since. I live over on Water Street, got a nice little terrace house there. It's small, but it's clean, and it's paid for. You're welcome to come over and look round, if you like."

Carrie felt a bit chastened by this apparent openness, "Look, James, I'm sorry if I seem to be prying into your private life. We're only talking for old time's sake. I've too many commitments here at the moment."

"That's all right by me, Caroline," James said quietly. "I quite understand. Whatever you want. I've kept silent about you for so long, another week or two won't bother me. I'm just glad we're actually talking to each other at last. Look, ring me whenever you want to, I don't often go out and I'll always be delighted to talk to you."

Carrie, now quite weary, agreed to call him later. The leaps between the real and the unreal were beginning to tell both on her nerves and her general composure and she was glad to get out of the conversation and back to her own thoughts in the kitchen.

Nine

Carrie was dozing on the settee in the lounge that evening when Arthur finally returned home. In spite of his efforts at a stealthy entry Carrie awoke. The almost inaudible click of the latch sufficient to alert her security conscious instinct

"Ooer, what time is it?" she grumbled.

"It's about eleven. Sorry I'm late, love."

"Big German buyer, was it?" Carrie muttered sarcastically.

Arthur didn't react to the sarcasm, he was too wise for that; he knew from experience when he was on shaky ground, and how quickly the tremors could reach seismic proportions.

He answered very mildly and politely, "No, love, a Japanese customer actually, he buys a lot of stuff off me. Mainly cabinets, apparently they sell right well over there. They're short of space, you see, and they can fill 'em up with all sorts of stuff."

"What? Like the kids, you mean. One on each shelf and they can still see what they're up to," she snapped, not in the least bit mollified. "Anyway, your dinner's in the oven. It should just about be done now, it's been in since seven. I'm off to bed." Carrie stalked out of the room and switched off the TV set on her way out.

"Oh, thanks, love," said Arthur. "I'll be up in a minute," as if that was of any interest to his wife. He breathed a sigh of relief and went into the kitchen for his dinner. He'd handled that rather well he thought to himself.

Next morning Carrie was tidying up after breakfast after Arthur had left for the shop when there was tap at the door and her daughter came into the kitchen. "Hello Mum", she said brightly. "I've just popped in to see how you are today. See if you've got over yesterday."

Carrie assured her that she was quite all right now and it was just a bit of a turn. "but why aren't you at work?" she queried.

"I'm on flexi-time now, Mum." She explained. "I can start at anytime up to ten o'clock. I'll make it up tonight as I'm not seeing Jim until later on."

Since Helen had broached the subject, Carrie felt she could ask a few pertinent questions of her own. "What do you know about this Jim, Helen? Is he local?"

"Oh, yes," said Helen more than happy to talk about him. "He's got a flat down Water Street." A cold shiver went down Carrie's back at this information and she gave an involuntary start, fortunately unnoticed by her daughter, who carried on, "and he works in the office at Marsdens, in the Estimating Department, quite a good job, I think."

"And what about his family?" Carrie persisted, eager to find out as much as possible whilst the opportunity was there. "Do they live round here?"

"I think his mother lives locally but his dad moved down south some years ago, but he hasn't seen him for a long time. Jim tells me he was very interested in antiques, which is a bit of a coincidence, isn't it?" She broke off as she'd obviously remembered something important. "That reminds me, Mum. Jim wanted Dad to value this for him." She reached into her carrier bag and placed a small ginger pot on the kitchen table. "It's a keepsake from his dad."

Carrie looked at it closely without picking it up, "Well" she said slowly, "your dad sells stuff like this, he gets them from Manchester or Preston, or somewhere like that."

"Oh, I don't think so, Mum." Helen scoffed. "Jim thinks the world of that, says it's been in his family for years."

Carrie was still doubtful but she didn't say anything to her daughter who dashed off to work shortly afterwards leaving Carrie to finish tidying the kitchen.

A few minutes later the front door banged. Carrie looked up from the kitchen floor dust-pan in hand, "For God's sake, who now?" she muttered. "Helen?" she called.

Her husband answered, "No, it's only me, love. Forgotten me bloody invoices, was going to do me books today. You know I got all the way into town before I remembered, a right bloody nuisance." He burst into the kitchen. "Hey up! What's this?" he exclaimed, great surprise evident in his voice, as he noticed the ginger pot on the table. "What the hell is that doing here?"

"What?" said Carrie, looking up, not sure what he was on about, then following his gaze. "Oh, this pot? Our Helen just brought it in. Her boyfriend wanted you to value it for him."

"The hell he did!" Arthur retorted angrily. "The cheeky bastard. Well it's worth thirty quid and I'm having it back right now."

"What are you talking about?" Carrie said indignantly? "It's been in his family for years, it's an heirloom!"

"Is it buggery!" shouted Arthur. "It's a bloody repro, is that. I ought to bloody-well know, I ship 'em in from Taiwan every three months, don't I?" He picked the ginger pot up to examine it more closely. "Look, it's chipped as well. There's a bloody great Harry Ramsden on the lid," he pointed to the chip on the lid. "I'll tell you something now, love. This pot has been in his family for about four bloody days. I know because I sold it to him and what's more, the bastard still owes me for it!"

"Oh, surely not, Arthur. There must be some mistake. Helen's boyfriend gave it to her to show it to you. She just left it here before you came back."

"Her so-called bloody friend, Mr Cheque-bouncing Preston, passed me a cheque for a bank account that had been bloody well closed for twelve years."

Carrie gasped, her knees went suddenly very weak and she sat down quickly. The mention of the name Preston and the twelve year time gap had produced the same shock effect as seeing Helen's boyfriend in the supermarket.

"Hey up, what's up, lass?" Arthur reached over to his wife and put his hand on her forehead. "Are you sure you're all right, love?"

Carrie shook her head in dismay, "Oh, I don't know what's going on." She admitted. "It's beyond me, is all this."

In an unaccustomed flash of consideration Arthur offered to make his wife a cup of tea. "I'll sort this Mr. Preston out; it's nowt for you to worry about," he said, misconstruing completely the reason for her state of shock.

Carrie, however, needed more information, and she needed it now. "What does this Mr Preston look like, Arthur?'

"Look like?" Arthur repeated and he gazed up at the ceiling as if forming an identikit picture in his mind. "Bloody queer old bird, if you ask me," he said at last. Looks as though all his clothes have come from t'Charity Shop. Good quality, mind, but sort of musty and years out-of-date."

"Well, how old would he be, do you think?" Carrie asked trying to get a more exact picture from her husband.

"Why? Do you know him or summat?" queried her husband looking at her face inquiringly.

"No," Carrie demurred. "It's just that Helen's boyfriend is called Jim Preston."

"Well, I'll be damned," exploded Arthur. "Is he really? It couldn't be him, though. This chap must be at least my age, and he looks a lot older and worse for wear. Our Helen wouldn't have owt to do with an old dodderer like that, that's for sure."

"No, you're right. Anyway, Jim's a smart young fella, very good-looking, and polite. He wouldn't have anything to do with bad cheques."

Arthur wasn't convinced, "You can never tell, love." he said. "After all, he did bring yon pot in, didn't he?" With the promise that he would sort things out with Helen and her boyfriend Arthur picked up the ginger pot, for safe keeping he said, collected his accounts folder from his desk and went back to work. Carrie remained seated at the table, her chin on her hands and gazed thoughtfully out of the window for a long time.

Ten

In the Duxbury kitchen that evening Arthur was sitting on the settee reading the newspaper. Carrie told him that they had been invited to Jane's for drinks on the following evening, Arthur grunted his approval, "Aye, it'll be nice to have a drink and a chat with Jack again. Oh, by the way," he went on," I spoke to our Helen on the phone about that bloody ginger pot. I told her it were mine anyway and it were worth thirty quid to me. She didn't believe me, but I know I'm right. Anyway, it doesn't matter now because I sold it for cash this afternoon."

"You did what?" exclaimed Carrie angrily.

"I sold it on, I told you; to a right polite young chap who came in. He looked around a bit and then bought it; actually paid for it in old pound notes, bank'll change 'em all right. Said he'd saved 'em up in an old tin box to buy a present for his dad. So that's one problem solved."

Carrie had become increasingly irritated as she listened to her husband's confident dismissal of the problem. "Is it hell as like," she asserted. "I don't care if he paid thirty pounds, thirty gold sovereigns or thirty pieces of bloody silver. What about Jim Preston's pot that Helen brought in? What's she going to say to him, for God's sake?"

"Well, what about it?" countered Arthur. "It wasn't his, was it? Wait till I see him. I'll bet he doesn't come here asking for it! I wish he would, I'd tell him a thing or two about his dad, or whoever he is."

"You're going to cause a lot of trouble for our Helen if you go on like that, you are."

"Well, if he is bloody crooked it's better she knows now than when it's too late," Arthur asserted.

Carrie was very doubtful about her husband's direct approach. "I think you've been a bit too hasty, Arthur. I do really. Shylock's bloody antique shop, pay up or it'll cost you an arm and a leg, literally"

"Hey, I'll have you know, lass, a good antique shop civilises a neighbourhood," Arthur said light-heartedly.

"You what?" Carrie queried, caught off-balance by his change of mood. "Who said that? What the hell are you talking about?"

"I'm talking about Mr Bloody-smoothtalking-cheque-bouncing Preston, that's what I'm talking about. He said to me, 'a good antique shop civilises a neighbourhood, my good man.' Believe you me - two minutes later he did me with a dud cheque. Can you credit it?"

"Can I see it?" Carrie asked. Arthur's face expressed his usual puzzled expression as he tried to grasp her meaning. "The cheque, you dummy. Can I have a look at it?"

"What the bloody hell for?" queried her husband.

"I'm interested, that's all," Carrie explained as non-commitally as possible. "I once knew a chap called Preston. I told you about him the other day but you never bloody-well listen."

"No, I can't say I remember, love. The cheque should be in my briefcase, front section, with the accounts, but I've left it at the shop. I'll bring it home tomorrow."

"Talking of tomorrow, we'll be going over to Jane's about eight o'clock so don't be arranging to work over. And don't forget your briefcase."

Next morning as Arthur was going out to work Carrie again reminded him about the two important things in his life: home by seven to smarten himself up for the party and the briefcase. When Arthur had left in his usual hectic and disorganised rush. Carrie sat down for a few minutes peaceful recovery, a cup of coffee, and a glance at the morning chat show on television. A regular antidote to the frenzy of the previous half hour.

A sharp blast on the doorbell and the sound of someone coming into the hallway in a rush caused her to stand up quickly in doubtful anticipation. It was Helen, obviously very distraught. Her face was red and tearful and her mother immediately crossed the room to comfort her. Helen clung to her mother and sobbed out the problem. "Oh, Mum. It's this letter I got from Jim this morning. He's gone away. I don't understand it at all. We had such a lovely time last night, then, this morning I got this letter," her sobs subsided and apart from a the occasional sniffle she was composed enough to tell her mother the rest of the story. "The funny thing about it, Mum, is that it was posted yesterday afternoon, look at the stamp. Anyway, he says he's going away and won't be seeing me for sometime." At that she broke down again and it was some minutes before her mother could calm her down by suggesting that perhaps he'd been called away on urgent family business or a relative's sudden illness.

Helen was far from convinced, and handed the note to her mother. Carrie's face stiffened as soon as she saw the handwriting, her hand trembled and she turned away so that Helen wouldn't see her reaction. She swallowed hard and tried to steady her voice; the handwriting was exactly the same as in the letter she'd received from James Preston.

"Mmm, doesn't say much, does he?" Carrie managed to mutter. "Going to find his father, that's about all."

"I know, but he told me he hasn't seen his dad for years, why now all of a sudden?"

Carrie looked at her daughter and said thoughtfully, "You don't think it had anything to do with your dad, and that bloody ginger pot, do you, love?" She knew just how indiscreet her husband could be and what a fuss he could create.

Helen however dismissed that as a possibility, "Oh no," she explained. "Dad was stupid about that, but me and Jim talked about it last night and he just laughed it off. He wasn't bothered about it at all. I told you, we had a great evening, a few drinks and then went for a curry, there was nothing wrong at all."

"Well, I don't know," said her mother not entirely convinced. "But I reckon he'll get in touch soon," she added, in an attempt to lift Helen's spirits. "He'll probably ring you tonight and explain." She paused for a moment, going over the circumstances in her mind. "It is peculiar though, the posting, I mean, before he saw you last night."

Looking into her daughter's tear-stained face Carrie realised guiltily that she had been thinking more about the effect upon herself than on her daughter. Her voice had a forced cheerful ring to it when she spoke. "Look, wipe your face, love. They're not worth crying about, believe me; it'll all sort itself out in time. You can spend too much of your time worrying about what other people are doing. You've got to get on with your own life." Having expressed her bit of home-spun philosophy Carrie realised that she had a great deal to do that afternoon and hoped that that would conclude the matter but Helen was still mumbling amid the sniffles.

"I thought he was such a nice man, Mum; always so polite and considerate, not at all like the loud-mouthed posers you get nowadays." It looked for a moment as though Helen might break down again so Carrie tried to jolly her up and get her out of the heartbreak mould.

"Yes, I know, love," she said briskly. "Come on now, there'll be a simple explanation, wipe your face, it's nearly ten o'clock," this latter piece of information immediately wrenched Helen out of her despair and into time's reality.

"Oh God, it isn't is it?" she exclaimed getting to her feet. "I've still some time to make up from yesterday. I'll just pop upstairs and smarten myself up, won't be a minute, Mum."

Carrie called after her as she left the room, "You can give me a lift into town if you will, love. I've a lot to do today."

While she waited Carrie put on her coat, checked her appearance in the hall mirror, and patted her hair into place. Her daughter returned a few minutes later looking freshly scrubbed but slightly red about the eyes. The two women left the house arm in arm, their clinging presence a comfort to them both.

Eleven

Jane's house was a large suburban semi on a middle-class estate. It had the statutory three square metres of garden to the front, a tarmac drive to the side leading to the garage and the obligatory conservatory extension to the rear. French windows from there led to a small paved patio with green plastic garden furniture tastefully arranged in a half circle.

When Carrie and Arthur arrived the conservatory area was quite full; a dozen or so people were milling around. However, Jane spotted them immediately and greeted them effusively. "Carrie, Arthur. Great to see you both. It's ages since we've all had a drink together. Come in, help yourselves from the drinks table in the lounge, Arthur. Supper's supposed to be ready about nine. Jack's in the conservatory, Arthur, if you want him. I want a quick word with Carrie."

Arthur was only too pleased to get away and head for the bar as the two women started discussing the new curtains in the conservatory. As soon as he was out of the way Carrie whispered urgently to her friend, "I've loads to tell you, Jane," Carrie's voice was full of repressed excitement. "I don't understand half of it; it's like one of them surrealist paintings, do you know what I mean? A lot of it seems quite real but there are parts which are, " she paused to get the right words, "are just sort of, impossible, like. You know, they couldn't possibly exist."

Jane was now visibly excited too, "Go on, tell me more. I find it really fascinating; it's more of the mysterious Mister Preston story, isn't it?"

Carrie smiled at her friend's enthusiasm, "How did you guess? Well, as a matter of fact, it is; and, it might well be fascinating to you, perhaps, but it's a bit frightening and totally confusing to me."

They are momentarily interrupted by Arthur's return with the drinks, but Jane soon packed him off to find Jack in the lounge with the forceful instruction to tell Jack to get off his bum and mix with their guests. "Honestly," she remarked to Carrie when Arthur had left. "Jack's totally useless; he leaves everything to me, if he thought he could get away with it you wouldn't see him again tonight."

Carrie nodded her agreement. And was about to divulge the interesting information she had acquired in the last few days when the large imposing figure of Sylvia, one of their neighbours, bore down on them. She wanted to discuss the new curtains in the kitchen, the price, the quality, the shade, every last detail in fact. Carrie caught Jane's eye and with a slight grimace moved away, mouthing, "speak to you later' as she went. Jane managed to extricate herself from Sylvia after some minutes and went after her husband. She found him seated on the settee in the lounge, glass of beer in hand and his mates around him. "Jack! Jack, dear!" she called in the refined voice she kept for social occasions. "Can you spare a moment, please?"

Jack reluctantly disengaged himself from his group of cronies and edged towards the door. Jane, still retaining her social smile hissed through her teeth, "Get the hell in here and do something, will you?" Almost simultaneously switching her voice to her refined version, "would you see to the drinks, dear?" Then back again to the hissing witch, "Just you get in here and look after people. It's not just a booze-up for your bloody mates, you know."

Jack attempted to take the heat out of the situation. "We were just discussing what would be the best way to make our wives really happy," he said ingratiatingly.

Jane was having none of it, "You're bloody joking," she snapped. Then added hopefully, "Tell me, you're all going on a six months fishing trip, is that it?"

Jack muttered something about being unfairly accused and drifted away to see to the guests.

Carrie came over for a few words, "God, that woman, Jane. She wanted to know where you got everything, how much you paid for it, and who fixed it up for you."

"Probably one of Jack's creditors, taking stock for when he goes bust, " Jane remarked sourly.

"He's not in trouble with the business, is he?" Carrie asked anxiously.

"Well, if he isn't, it'll be the first time that I know of. No, I'm only joking," she added with half a smile. "I think."

"We're not going to get chance to have a chat here, are we, Jane? How are you fixed for coffee tomorrow?"

"Fine, all right by me" Jane said. "Is it about you-know-who?"

"Well, more like about I-don't-know-who. Of course, it bloody is. What else? I've just about cracked the case now; well, I think I know what's going on. Can you manage about ten o'clock, do you think?"

"I should think so. I'll just tell Jack I'm going to Preston for the day."

Carrie groaned at her friend's feeble attempt at humour, "You'll do no such thing. You'll keep as quiet as the grave about this little lot. Right, tomorrow then...and now back to the merrymaking," she said with mock enthusiasm.

The evening dragged on in a familiar pattern, the men had too much to drink whilst the women sorted out life's essentials. Partners drifted together, argued briefly, moved apart and flirted elsewhere.

Most of the guests had already left and Carrie and Arthur were at the door. "You've had too much to drink again," Carrie complained. "Now I'll have to drive home. Why is it whenever there's any free food or drink you've got to eat and drink as much as you can?"

"You're only young once, that's what I say." Arthur responded not coping too clearly with his esses. "We're here to enjoy ourselves, 'ere give us a kiss, love."

Carrie angrily shrugged him off just as Jane came up to the door to see them out.

"By, you're looking lovely tonight, Jane, " Arthur said unperturbed by his wife's rebuff. "Is it time I were getting my arms round you for the last waltz?"

Jane stifled a pretend yawn, "God, he must have had over his two pints tonight; well past his sensible level." She turned to Carrie and asked, "Why is it when men get drunk they start thinking about sex? When they're sober they're crashing bores always on about fishing, football or golf, and when they're pissed they're just as boring about sex."

"Amazing, isn't it? It numbs their brains, reduces their performance, and yet they're so stupid they think it does the exact opposite." She glanced into the lounge where a few of Jack's friends were still drinking. "Slobbering drunks are quite revolting, aren't they?" she said reflectively. "Trouble is: I've got to take this one home with me."

"Well, I'm quite glad about that," retorted Jane. "I couldn't do with two of 'em about the place."

"Where is Jack, by the way? I haven't seen him for a while. We want to say goodnight and get off."

"Oh, he's around somewhere," Jane answered without much interest. "He was trying to chat up one of our neighbours half an hour ago. He's ignored her for the past three years but he's suddenly noticed she's got a bosom and it seems to have blown his mind. I think he was telling her about the one that got away last Sunday, if not, it was the biggest bloody exaggeration I've ever heard of, believe me."

"Well, we'll get off anyway, Jane. Thanks for a lovely party. Must remember what it's like whenever I'm tempted to feel sociable." She grabbed her husband by the arm, "Come on, you. We're going now. And for God's sake straighten yourself up. To Jane in the doorway, "He's like a bloody rag doll, boneless as well as legless. Goodnight everybody! This is my prize for the night," she shouted as she guided her husband's faltering footsteps down the garden path.

Twelve

The next morning Carrie and Jane were seated in a quiet corner of a coffee bar in town. "I'll bring you right up-to-date, Jane. Thank God we can talk without constant interruption. I told you about that so-called Chinese ginger pot, didn't I?"

"The one Arthur sold? And then swore it was the same one Helen brought home."

"Right, and the cheque signed by James Preston bounced, so when Arthur saw the pot again he took it back right sharp, and sold it again within twenty four hours, for cash, or so he said."

"Oh, did he? You didn't tell me that."

"Well, he did," Carrie went on quickly. "But that's by the way. Let me tell you what I found out after that. Our Helen got a letter from Jim, you know the new boyfriend?"

Jane nodded, 'Yes, yes, I saw him in the restaurant."

"She got this letter yesterday and brought it round; very upset she was about it." Carrie spoke very slowly to emphasise the importance of the next piece of information. "The handwriting on that letter was exactly the same as on the letter I'd got from James Preston and, " Carrie paused for even further emphasis," what's more, the same as on the dud cheque that Arthur took."

'What?" queried Jane incredulously. "Are you sure?"

"I'm bloody positive," Carrie declared emphatically. "I've spent enough time studying it, haven't I?"

"Bloody hell!" Was all Jane could manage. They held each other's gaze for some time without actually seeing anything as they tried to work out what that actually meant.

After a few seconds had passed Jane asked what was in Helen's letter.

"He said he was going away for a while, to find his father, he said. Helen was terribly upset about it; you see they'd been out the night before, and yet somehow the letter had been posted that afternoon."

"God, that's queer, isn't it?" muttered Jane.

"Oh, it gets a damn sight queerer than that, Jane," retorted Carrie. "Listen to this. I telephoned that number again yesterday, the one James Preston gave me, and I couldn't get through, got the unobtainable tone. Checked with the operator, she said the same thing, so I got on to the supervisor. Now, get this, she said, that that line had not been in use for over ten years! I said to her, I said I'd spoken to someone on it only this week. She said I must have been mistaken, had mis-dialled or something. Her records showed that the number had never been re-allocated since the last subscriber had it disconnected. She wouldn't give me the name."

"But you spoke to him twice on that number, didn't you?" Jane shivered, " Oh, I don't like this, Carrie, it's spooky; it's making me feel funny. Is it a joke, do you think?"

"No, I don't," Carrie replied. "It's crazy, and unreal, and it doesn't add up but there are connecting links which do. When I get them all together I'll understand."

"What are you going to do now, then?"

"Hang on, I haven't finished telling you the tale yet," Carrie protested. "There's more. I had a bit of spare time yesterday so I thought I'd check on the address where the Prestons were supposed to live, 24 Water Street. I went down there and looked around, there was no one in at 24. Actually, it looked really dirty and unlived in."

"You just didn't go up and knock on the door, did you?" Jane said in amazement. "What if he'd come to the door?"

"Look, Jane," Carrie explained. "I was past caring. I had to find out somehow; it was driving me round the bloody twist. Anyway, no reply. So I went next door, and here I had a bit of luck. An elderly couple lived there. I told them I was trying to trace an old friend and that the family, the Prestons, had lived next door at one time. The couple invited me in and made me a cup of tea, grand couple they were. It took them absolutely ages to get round to telling me anything I wanted to know. We went through every neighbour who'd ever lived there, and remember, they'd been there for fifty odd years. Well, eventually, they did get around to agreeing that they remembered the Prestons, but they thought that Mr Preston had died about ten years ago." Carrie imitated the old couple's reminiscences, 'Let's see, our Sandra, that's our granddaughter, lovely bairn she is etc. well she's 21 next year and she was nobbut nine or ten at the time. Was it our Sandra, Hettie, or was it young Shane? - our Jill's lad.'" Carrie laughed, "You know how they go on, well, I had that nearly all afternoon. I know more about the history of their family than I do of my own."

"Anyway, you found out some useful stuff, didn't you? Which Mr Preston was it that died, then?"

"Ah well," Carrie continued. "After that I went round to the Gazette's office then to check on that."

"By hell, Caroline," Jane said in admiration. "You did some hard graft yesterday."

"I went through the files of past copies of the paper about that time. Thank God it's a weekly and not a daily. It took me ages but I found it." Carrie took a slip of paper out of her handbag. "Listen to this." She read aloud from the paper. "October 4th 1969 James Preston, aged 25 years, beloved son of Frederick and Hilda Preston of Skipton and husband of the late Mollie. Service at St. Columba's Church 10.30 am. on 10th October followed by cremation at Overcrag Cemetery."

"My God, Carrie," Jane exclaimed. "25 years old. That's the lad you knew, isn't it? I don't get this at all. Who wrote to you then? Who did you speak to on the 'phone? Who bought the bloody pot?"

"You tell me, Jane, you tell me," Carrie said desperately. "You know as much as I do now. I've just one more thing to do now," she went on with more determination in her voice, "and I daren't do it on my own."

"Oh no! Bloody hell, no!" exclaimed Jane, quick to realise the implication. "You want me to go to the sodding cemetery with you, don't you?"

Carrie nodded her head.

"Oh, Carrie, do I have to?" Jane pleaded. "It gives me the creeps just thinking about it."

"Well, how do you think I feel?" Carrie retorted. "Remember, I spoke to the guy on the telephone only the other day."

The two women stared at each other in silence as they struggled with the complexity of their own thoughts. Jane was the first to break the silence. "Right! We don't have to worry about a thing; we're just going to visit the cemetery this afternoon, right?" she said, remarkably boldly under the circumstances.

"Right," agreed Carrie, equally emboldened. "Let's get on with it, if't were to be done, 'twere best done quickly."

"Done what?" queried Jane.

"Killing Duncan."

"Duncan who?" said Jane, still mystified.

"You know, Duncan. Shakespeare."

"Duncan Shakespeare? You haven't had a letter from him as well, have you?"

"Come on, dumbo, let's get going," said Carrie, laughing as she took her friend's arm as they left the coffee bar.

Thirteen

It was lunchtime before Carrie and Jane reached the cemetery. They paused at the wrought iron gates and read the plaque on the wall, *Overcrag Cemetery and Crematorium*. On their way here they had agreed on a plan. They would each take a parallel lane in the crematorium's garden of rest and, keeping each other in sight, an important condition this, would systematically study the inscriptions until they found the one they were searching for.

"They're all fairly recent ones on this side, Carrie," Jane called across the row, "1980, 1981."

"Yea, it's the same over here, as well, but let's keep to the plan and work our way round."

They met at the end of the aisle. "It's sad, isn't it?" said Carrie, quite moved by what she seen. "I mean, seeing all this bereavement carved into blocks of stone. Everyone of them meant such a lot of grief to someone; so much sadness, and especially the kids, them who never got the chance for a proper life. Look at that one on the end there, 'passed away 10th December 1982 aged 5 years.' Poor little bugger. God, 5 years old, how could you cope with something like that? If you were the mother it would change your whole life, wouldn't it?" Carrie's eyes filled with tears as she empathised with the bereaved mother.

Jane smiled sympathetically at her friend, "I know, it gets me the same way. Thank God, we've just been very lucky, haven't we? Which way do we go now?"

"Thank God?" queried Carrie. "You know me, Jane, devout atheist. If all the suffering and pain on earth, much of it in the name of some religion or other is an example of the Almighty's benevolence, then God help us when we get to Heaven is all I can say. Come on let's go along this one."

The friends separated and walked along the next aisle keeping more or less level with each other. They frequently glanced at each other for reassurance and to check on their respective searches but a shake of the head or a shrug of the shoulders indicated that nothing relevant had been found. Carrie reached the end of her row and glanced across at Jane. She could tell from her friend's body language that something was radically wrong.

She called across, "Jane, what is it?"

"Oh, God, Carrie," she cried in a tremulous voice, her body had stiffened into a rigid state of shock as she stared at the plaque on the wall. "Carrie! Carrie! Here, quick! I've found it, look at this. This is it." she pointed at the memorial as Carrie rushed round to join her friend. "Oh, my God," Jane muttered as she read the inscription.

Carrie, pale-faced and breathless, now stood behind Jane and read the inscription over her shoulder. Her voice faltered as she read aloud the words engraved on the stone:

In loving memory

JAMES PRESTON

1944 - 1969

by accident

R.I.P.

"Oh, God, by accident!" she exclaimed, holding her hand over her mouth. "It's the boy I knew at work, Jane. He's dead."

"That's not all, Carrie," Jane said solemnly. "Look underneath." She pointed to an inscription below the first and slowly read it aloud.

Also his beloved son

JIM PRESTON, aged 2 years.

1967-1969

In death

They were not divided

10th Oct.1969

The two friends stood in shocked silence as they tried to assimilate the information they were reading. Carrie glanced down at the base of the memorial wall and started violently at what she saw. She grasped Jane's arm so hard that the latter squealed in pain.

The small pot standing amongst the other flower containers was only too familiar.

"Oh, look there, Jane", Carrie said in a strangled voice. "Oh, my God, it's that bloody ginger pot." Her hands instinctively clasped her face as she bent down for a closer look. Jane bent down also and they studied the pot for a few seconds then Jane reached down and nervously picked it up.

"Are you sure it's the same one, Carrie?" Jane asked as she handed the pot to Carrie.

Carrie shuddered as she accepted it with some reluctance. "Ugh! It's the same one, all right, " she said with disgust, "there's that chip on the rim, look!" Carrie lifted the lid to show Jane but as she did she saw what was inside. She let out a piercing scream and dropped the ginger pot. It smashed into a thousand pieces on the path and scattered the contents on the ground. Carrie and Jane clutched each other in horror as they stared at the finely ground ashes around their feet. Their faces reflected the incredulous horror in their minds as they tried to make some sense of what they had just experienced.

Pass the Parcel

One

"Just pay the guy and let's go!" she said in her own inimitable way. She had a certain brusqueness of manner and an economy with words that was both arrogant and intensely annoying. As a consequence her friends were few. However, she more than made up for this deficiency in the number of male admirers she drew into her sphere. Her long blonde hair, exquisite features and a body, fulsome and buoyant where appropriate and slim and sensuous in the lower quarters, seemed to turn men's brains to malleable mush whenever she came within hormonal striking-distance. She could turn a man's head without entering the same room. Some seriously sexy bitch, the men thought: women usually passed on the 'sexy' aspect.

"Lou, will you just pay the guy, for God's sake?" she repeated impatiently.

Lou sighed and reached for his wallet. Two of the more frequent responses to Jade's demands. He sometimes wondered why the hell he put up with her, but then when he saw the envious glances from other guys he knew why. Their imagination fuelled his desire, although the bedroom delights fondly imagined and fantasized over in the viewers minds were seldom actually realized in practice. Jade's inherent selfishness and vanity precluded much in the way of giving anything of herself to another person, unless the rewards more than justified the exchange.

Lou peeled off a couple of notes from a substantial wad and handed them to the traffic warden with a knowing wink, engaged the gear and pulled away from the kerb. He'd been parked on a double yellow line for at least half an hour outside the manicure parlour. Jade's answer to all problems was quite simple – just pay them off and go! Traffic wardens, police, restaurateurs, politicians, officials of all persuasions, she couldn't care less. They had their price, Lou had the money, and she had the access; problems solved! If this particular supply of sweeteners dried up, Jade knew there were plenty of other gullible guys in the market who would be only too happy to take her on.

Jade and Lou had been together for nearly five years. Her first marriage had been a teenage mistake. She thought he was going places in the glamorous DJ disco world and she was going with him, but six months later she found out that half the bimbos in the town shared the same ambitions, so she split. Anyway, she found out later that he only got as far as Leeds, which information gave her a great deal of satisfaction.

Her second husband was also a big disappointment. Initially she had been attracted to his flash car, chunky sovereign rings and expensive gold bracelets and really unusual tattoos on his back and shoulders. He'd told her he was in the club trade but it wasn't until he been charged with GBH that she realized that the only connection with that trade was the front door and the club he'd used on some vulnerable drunk. Loyalty demanded that she stick around until he was sentenced then she was off. Another town another guy…and that turned out to be Lou.

They'd met at a singles bar some five years earlier, she'd been impressed by his big Mercedes and his obviously expensive designer gear. The fact that he was medallioned slightly on the wrong side of good taste only added to the attraction. She'd moved in with him almost immediately and they'd been together ever since, perhaps not in complete harmony but with sufficient measure of an accommodation to make it worthwhile for both of them.

Jade didn't really know what Lou did for a living. Frankly she didn't care; the fact that he was loaded was all the information she needed. He spent a lot of time at meetings, some quite late at night and he frequently went abroad on business trips but Jade never asked questions and Lou never proffered details so, on the business front at least, harmony prevailed.

On one occasion Lou had left his briefcase on the bed when he'd popped out to the local shop. Jade with the natural curiosity of her kind had flicked open the catches to reveal a case full of twenty pound notes. She quietly and thoughtfully snapped the case closed. The quick glance had been sufficient to satisfy her needs, the why and the wherefore were not important.

The house they now lived in had been built to her own specifications. Lou knew an architect and there was a plentiful supply of building labourers only too willing to work for cash in hand with no questions asked. Planning permission was only a formality if the right approaches were made to the right people. They had an indoor swimming pool, stables, adjacent paddock, loose boxes, garages, extensive landscaped gardens and the high wire security fences ensured almost complete privacy. Furthermore Lou had insisted on getting a sophisticated CCTV network fitted so that all approaches to the house could be monitored; just to make sure that Jade was safe whilst he was away on business, he'd told her. Originally the plaque on the gatepost had read LOUJADE VILLA, but to Lou's fury some bastard from the village had spray painted INS at the end, and so the sign now simply read LOUJADE.

"I'm flying out to Amsterdam tomorrow morning," Lou said over supper that night. "Got to see a guy about a deal I'm working on. Just be a couple o'days. Will you be all right?"

"Course I will. I'm riding tomorrow and I'm off to Martine's on Wednesday."

Martine's was the most expensive beauticians in the area and Jade a frequent visitor. For top-to-toe pampered self-indulgence Martine's was the place to be at, with its saunas, whirlpools, jacuzzis, pedicure, manicure, facials, coiffure, massage and skin-toning mud pools. One can imaging the degree of hardship Jade felt if she missed a week without visiting Martine's.

Later that night in bed Lou reached over and tried to pull Jade towards him. She twisted away, her body arching rigidly.

"No, get off! Not tonight!" She didn't amplify her reasons and Lou knew it was pointless to remonstrate. He'd experienced this reaction many times before. He cursed under his breath, turned over and settled himself to sleep. Amsterdam, he felt, would be far more convivial.

Lou was up and about early the following morning. He was showered, shaved and breakfasted well before nine.

"I'm going now, sweetheart. See you later."

There was a scarcely audible grunt form under the bedclothes. Lou paused for a second, shrugged, picked up his travelling bag and left.

Some hours later Jade peered at the clock on the bedside table: 10.30am. She stretched languorously, slipped out of bed and from the bedroom doorway called down to Maria, the housekeeper. "Maria! Run the bath.... five minutes! She strolled over to the window, drew back the curtains and looked over the garden towards the stable yard. She seemed satisfied that the weather was not too inclement to prevent her planned gallop over the moors.

Half an hour later she was sitting at the breakfast table eating the light breakfast Maria had prepared.

"Maria!" Jade called into the kitchen. "Tell Billy to saddle Juno. I'll be ready in about twenty minutes."

"Right miss. Will you be back for lunch?" Maria's voice was quietly submissive.

"I'll be back to change in an hour, but no lunch I'm dining out. Put that grey suit out, the one with the piping round the collar. You know the one...oh, and a white blouse!"

"Yes, miss."

She backed out of the room deferentially, if she'd curtsied at this stage it would not have seemed inappropriate to their relationship.

"Billy!" Maria called across the stable yard from the back door. "Billy!" she repeated. "Miss Jade wants you."

Billy's head shot round the side of the barn door. The mention of Miss Jade's name always had an electrifying effect on him. His rounded face with its ruddy outdoor complexion was full of expectation; if Miss Jade wanted something then he was the man to give it; anything! He was nineteen years of age, had lived all his life in the village and this was the first proper job he'd had and he loved it, and he thought the world of Miss Jade. To him she was the epitome of glamorous womanhood. He surreptitiously watched her whenever he could during the day and fantasized about her half the night.

Billy's eagerness quickly turned to disappointment when he realized that Jade wasn't actually there and his face did not disguise his feelings.

"Billy! Miss Jade wants you to get Juno ready now. She'll be out in half an hour."

Oh, right, that wasn't too bad then, he thought. He'd get to help her onto the horse. He always got a kick out of that process, figuratively speaking, of course. He could almost bite her gorgeous bum as he lifted her up with her foot in his hands. It crossed his mind every time he did it but the thought of Miss Jade's reaction and the terrible consequences were more than adequate controls. Still, it was the thought that counts and he hurried away to prepare the filly.

Exactly one hour later Jade entered the yard from the main door of the house. Immaculately dressed in tight jodhpurs, black riding jacket and matching helmet, she would not have looked out of place on the front cover of any glossy horse or fashion magazine. Billy ran out to meet her, he had been watching through a crack in the barn door for the past twenty minutes.

"Morning miss, Juno's ready; shall I bring her out now?" Billy's face was bright and eager and flushed at his dream-girl's proximity. Jade didn't even glance at the lad; servants were paid to serve and if they had a problem with that, they went!

"Of course I do! What do you think I'm dressed like this for? A fancy dress party. Get a move on!"

Billy scurried away, to return seconds later pulling Juno out by a bright blue lead rope. All too soon, for Billy's liking, Jade was in the saddle and cantering across the yard towards the gate. Billy ran in front, opened the gate, and watched her as she disappeared from view up the lane towards the open moor. His thoughts still dwelling on the tight buttocks which moments before had been within an inch of his teeth.

"Have a good ride, miss," he called after her, but Jade was away, blonde hair flowing behind her and if she heard him she certainly didn't acknowledge the fact.

As Billy turned away from the gate he saw Maria standing at the back door with a pot of tea in her hand. They never had had much to say to each other, but to some extent they shared the comradeship of paid lackeys and Maria often gave the lad a sandwich and something to drink when the mistress was away.

"Here you are, Billy. Come and get your tea. When you've had that we need some logs chopping for the kitchen fire. Miss Jade won't be back for an hour or so."

Billy was not stupid, although his speech and general demeanor may have given that impression. He was just basically uneducated and poorly socialised and this disguised an inherent native cunning which often surprised the many people who underestimated him.

Maria was of an indeterminate age, one would guess somewhere between fifty and sixty. She had been a live-in housekeeper for Lou and Jade for about a year. She did as she was told, earned her money and kept out of the way when she was not needed. She asked no questions; there were plenty worse jobs than this; she'd already done them! Anyway, in the silence of her attic bedroom, after the washing-up had been done, Maria had her own work to do. She'd been working on it for years. It was all contained in a collection of school exercise books. Every evening she meticulously pored over the minute and carefully written words with the aid of a plastic magnifying glass, often holding the book up the light to see more clearly.

Occasionally she would make an alteration or an amendment; these corrections were made almost reverentially and in the same neat hand as the original, as if they were part of some original holy script. However, these alterations were becoming less and less necessary as the work had been re-written so many times before. Hunched over her manuscript in rapt concentration in the dim light of the bedroom her pale face and smooth skin would take on a spectral quality as though she was not fully part of this world. She seemed to be almost in a state of transition between the real and the ethereal as the square-cut fingernail on her right index finger followed the words and her lips moved in silent synchronisation. No day was complete until she'd gone over her work and satisfied herself that it was all in order.

When Billy had finished his tea she went up to the master bedroom and laid out the clothes Jade had requested and then retired to her own room. Any spare time was always used constructively on her manuscripts. She could hear Billy chopping wood in the yard and she settled down with her magnifying glass to scan the pages for any inaccuracies.

Lou thought Maria was a weird old bird, but Jade liked her submissive and deferential attitude. It inflated her own sense of importance when she had someone to order around and have her commands obeyed without question.

Two

The hotel foyer was swarming with people when Lou walked through the hotel door. Full of suits he noted disdainfully; must be a conference on. Mind you it suited his needs, he was less conspicuous in a crowd, and as long as he didn't have to talk to them he didn't mind. Jobsworths on expense accounts, he thought, they'll drink as much as they can, tap up the local birds and go back home to the semi-detached wife, kids and dog at the weekend.

He checked in at reception and collected his key. The girl smiled her recognition and whispered. "Conference. Kitchen units," nodding towards the throng of identical suits.

Lou usually stayed at this hotel at least once a month. It was the contact point for his business connection and the system had become slick and efficient over the years, as well as highly profitable. His supplier, Hans, would make contact here, Lou would hand over the readies, and some unknown couriers would collect the gear and ferry it back to the receivers in England. A foolproof operation! The couriers received their instructions through a frequently changing mobile phone network with various middlemen. Contacts were restricted to the next level in the chain of command so that Hans and Lou negotiated the deal from a respectable distance, if respectable was the most appropriate word to use under the circumstances.

Lou strolled down to the hotel bar in the early evening; Hans never called before eight o'clock.

"Whisky, neat please."

Lou paid the barman and took his first sip.

"Hey! Hiya, Lou!" The voice was loud, confident and vaguely familiar.

Startled, Lou whirled round at this unexpected interruption. Walking towards him, hand outstretched in greeting was one of his neighbours from Leeds.

"Well, Lou, fancy seeing you here! Small world, eh?"

Lou summoned up a smile from some arctic region of his body and shook the guy's hand. He didn't know him particularly well, just a face in the avenue and a background figure in the local pub. It took him some time to even remember his name; Jeff, that was it! His composure recovered, Lou muttered, "Just a long weekend break, like. And you?"

"Same, came over with a few of the lads from work. One of 'em's stag party. Mucky weekend, you know."

The last thing Lou wanted was for some clown from home to see him around here. "I've just popped down for a quick one, before I get changed for dinner," he said raising his glass. He finished the whisky in one mouthful, grimaced slightly as the neat spirit hit the back of his throat. "Excuse me, will you? I might see you later on, eh?"

Lou didn't realise how prophetic those words were at the time and how he was going to live to regret this accidental meeting with a neighbour. Across the foyer two men in suits, indistinguishable from the kitchen unit reps, had been taking a keen interest in every person Jeff had met since he'd arrived in Rotterdam the day before. What, for the drug squad team had started as a routine watch on suspected couriers, now appeared to be developing into something much more worthwhile. Another link in the chain; perhaps a more important one?

Lou received the expected call from Hans about half an hour later. They arranged to meet at 9 o'clock in the Red Rose Café, a small intimate bistro-type place in the old part of town.

At 8.30 Lou left the hotel, briefcase in hand, waved up a cab from the nearby rank, climbed in and settled back comfortably. He didn't notice the two figures who had followed him out of the hotel or the car that picked them up and was now discreetly following him to the Red Rose. If he had spotted them he would certainly not have been feeling quite so smug as he did now at the prospect of a few hundred thousand grand profit coming his way. His mind toyed deliciously with what he would do with it. Enjoy life a bit more for a start, stash some of it offshore, no need to tell Jade about that. It could be his own little nest egg, perhaps a love-nest in Florida, or a yacht moored off St Tropez. Parties, girls, luxury in the sun, more girls. He sighed contentedly as the cab drew up outside the Red Rose.

"Hans, how are you?" Lou shook hands with the portly Dutchman at the bar. "Good to see you again," they'd worked together since they'd met in a bar two years ago. Their system was quite simple. Hans told Lou where the goods were, Lou phoned Paul, his second in command, who then checked the merchandise. If Paul was satisfied with the quality and the quantity he then gave the couriers their instructions to pick it up. When all was confirmed, usually about forty-five minutes later, Lou handed over the briefcase which was then passed to Han's minder, who had been waiting discreetly like a huge fridge-freezer at a corner table. The day's work over, the two men would then take a cab to a livelier hotel for an evening's drinking and some obliging female company.

Lou went to the doorway and stepped out into the street to use his mobile. "Paul? Lou. Eight o'clock, car park, corner of St Pauli and Kirche Strasse, know it? Right. Two Mercs, one silver, one light blue, second level. Forty kilos, top grade stuff, got that mate? Give me a call when it's sorted, yes? Right, see you later."

Lou raised his glass to Hans, "Here's to a successful business plan, pal."

"And many more of the same," agreed Hans.

The two men then settled down in the comfortable armchairs in the lounge to await confirmation of the deal. Neither was too worried about the outcome, they'd had no problems in the past and they had over the last couple of years developed, if not an absolute trust in each other, a certain respect for the other's business acumen. Neither wished to jeopardise such a lucrative enterprise by any dodgy dealing.

As expected Lou's mobile buzzed at a quarter to nine o'clock. Lou smiled in anticipation and thumbed the button. "Yeah?"

An unfamiliar voice queried, "Mr Louis Stretton?"

"Who wants to know?" snarled Lou aggressively, his eyes betraying his nervousness at this unexpected call. Without looking up he was aware that Hans was watching him closely.

"Detective Chief Inspector Wormald, Scotland Yard."

Lou's eyes flitted nervously around the foyer and the bar. The 'Fridge-freezer' in the corner had risen to his feet, he could tell the routine had been broken, and that usually meant trouble in his experience; things either went to plan or they didn't go at all.

Lou swallowed hard and tried his best to sound as casual and unperturbed as possible, " And what can I do for you Chief Inspector?" Out of the corner of his eye he saw Hans beckon his minder and both men hurried across the reception area towards the revolving door and the street exit.

"I'd like you stay just where you are Mr Stretton. My officers have control of the building and will be with you in a minute, sir."

Lou could see that Hans and his minder had never quite reached the exit, even as he looked they were being ushered away down a corridor by a group of men in suits who looked considerably more purposeful than any kitchen unit reps. Lou sat down and waited, he was still quietly confident that his fragmented operational system would not link him with whatever Inspector Plod was on about.

Men appeared from somewhere behind him and he heard himself being cautioned with the familiar words he'd often heard on some of his favourite television programmes, "Anything you might say may be used in evidence…". The phrase "dealing in illegal substances," worried him rather more, as did the scale of the operation and the cool confident way the arrests had been made.

He felt decidedly uncomfortable both mentally and physically, squashed as he was between two plain-clothes policemen in the back seat of a police car, racing through the streets of Amsterdam, blue light flashing and siren blaring as it carved a passage through the evening traffic.

Things did not improve for Lou once he'd been checked in at the police desk, when he caught a glimpse of Jeff, the neighbour he'd met in the bar earlier that evening, being led away from an interview room. Their eyes met briefly, and whilst Jeff's face registered complete surprise, Lou curtly nodded his recognition, he now knew only too well why he was here. In spite of all the careful planning that went into the operation it was just a stupid bloody accidental meeting in the bar with a guy, he now guessed, had been recruited as one of his couriers, that had connected him and Hans with the deal. Actually it wasn't entirely luck, although Lou didn't know that, that had led to his arrest. The couriers had been under close observation since they'd arrived in the country, their mobile phone numbers had been obtained whilst in their hotel, every call had been monitored, and the link to Paul quickly established. The squad would have got to Lou and Hans eventually if not this time, but Jeff's meeting with Lou just helped to short-circuit the investigation.

Three

The first hint Jade had that anything had gone wrong with Lou's trip was when she had a visit from Big Freddie, one of Lou's shady acquaintances. Jade had never liked the guy, he was scruffy, shifty and decidedly coarse. Jade had even forbidden Lou to have him in the house when she was around. "That Freddie friend of yours smells, if he comes here keep him outside."

That particular evening however she'd heard the dogs bark in the stables and a quick glance at the CCTV monitor in the kitchen had confirmed that someone was out there. Then she recognised Freddie's stooping figure and the peculiar way he walked, his head continually twisting to look over his shoulder. She hid the shotgun behind the potted plant and opened the door on the safety chain. There was no way he was coming in the house.

"Er," Big Freddie always started conversations in this way. "Er..... have you heard the news, Jade?"

"What news?"

"About Lou."

"Go on then, what?"

"'E's bin nicked in 'olland."

"Yer joking. Who says? I've heard nowt."

"Straight up, heard it from a mate in the force. Nicked the whole bloody lot of 'em last night, bang to rights." Freddie shuffled his feet nervously at this point and glanced quickly over his right shoulder. "I were wondering," he went on, "If Lou had left any cash for me. He owes me a couple of 'undred and he said if anything 'appened I was to see you about it...." His voice tailed off and for a brief instant their eyes met. From the steely glint in Jade's eyes and the fixed expression on her face Freddie knew that he had little hope of getting anything out of her.

"Sorry, he never said anything about it to me. Anyway he never leaves any cash here, you should know that." She started to close the door. She wanted rid of this dummy as soon as possible. If what he'd said was true she had a great deal to think about. She knew other people would be coming round soon, the police, customs and excise, Lou's 'friends' and various hangers-on who would seek to take advantage of her situation.

"Yer'll let me know if 'e says owt when you 'ear from 'im, won't yer?"

"Yea, 'course I will, see you later." With that Jade shut and bolted the door, picked up the shotgun and went into the kitchen to check that Freddie left the premises.

When the CCTV on the gate had shown him shuffling down the lane Jade hurried upstairs. The first thing she had to do was to find any ready cash. She checked under the bed where she had previously found a briefcase full of notes; nothing there. She'd not really expected to find anything, Lou had taken his briefcase with him to Holland and she guessed that it was now an important piece of the prosecution's evidence.

A search of the walk-in wardrobe was more profitable however. Under the carpeted floor she spotted a recent loosening of the floorboards. A quick lift under the edge with a table knife revealed a cosy little cavity containing a bulky sports hold-all. Jade smiled her satisfaction, hardly the place to conceal Lou's sweaty squash kit, she thought. Unzipping the bag on the bed she shuffled her fingers through the stacks of used ten and twenty pound notes. She retained the satisfying smile, it had all been worth it, her experienced eye assessed somewhere in the region of a hundred grand, give or take a few hundred.

The sound of the telephone ringing made her start with surprise. She froze, the bundles of notes still in her hands. Still clutching the money she moved nearer the phone; the answering machine would record in a minute. She heard Lou's pre-recorded message then an unfamiliar voice came on,

"Hello Jade.This is Jim McDonald, Lou's business partner, I need to speak to you urgently, please ring me as soon as possible on my mobile O9756 – 274334.

Well, she'd never heard of Jim McDonald for a start and she certainly wasn't going to get in touch with him. It did, however, confirm that what Big Freddie had told her was undoubtedly true. The vultures were gathering!

She hurriedly stuffed the money back into the sports-bag. She hadn't had time to count it as she would have wished, her main priority now was to check the house was secure, get an early night and make plans for her future. A hundred grand meant security, independence and a comfortable lifestyle for the time being, nor did she need to hang about waiting for Lou to sort himself out.

That night she slept with the bag alongside her in the bed, its proximity gave her far more satisfaction than she'd ever experienced with Lou.

It took Maria rather longer to get to sleep that night. She'd watched the coming and going of Freddie, she'd overheard some of the conversation and was bright enough to guess the rest. Her position was now in doubt and she needed to consider the best way forward for herself. She checked through her journal and that helped to settle her mind but it was long into the early hours before she slept.

Jade's first official information of Lou's arrest came next morning in a letter from the Foreign & Commonwealth Office in London. It briefly stated that her husband had been arrested in Holland and charged with conspiring to deal illegally with a large quantity of banned substances. He was temporarily being held in a remand prison on the outskirts of Amsterdam until the judge had heard all the evidence. Arrangements for visiting were also enclosed.

Jade put the letter down and sat down on the settee. She was not surprised by the content at all, she knew Lou was up to some shady dealing. There was no doubt in her mind that he was guilty. Her great, and only, worry was the effect it would have on her life. What if the police could take all his assets. She mentally ticked them off; the house, the land, the stables, the cabin cruiser and the big car were all in Lou's name; all she really owned when you got down to it were her car, her horse, and the contents of her wardrobe, in itself sufficiently large to stock a medium-sized department store, but not something that would see Jade secure for the rest of her life. She had the bag of ready cash and she needed to make that secure before she did anything else. She considered the various possibilities; bank safety deposit box? No fear, the police could get access to that when they checked the bank accounts. Left luggage box? Too dodgy, officials had keys. Hide it in the house? Certainly not, police search, possibility of a break-in. Hide it somewhere else, where? The stables, a possibility! Leave it with someone else? Who could she trust? No one sprang immediately to mind. What about Billy, he was simple enough and she knew he'd do anything for her. Give it some thought!

Unfortunately for Jade she didn't have that sort of time. A loud knock on the door heralded the arrival of an inspector and a sergeant both from the drug squad and a uniformed constable from the local nick.

"It's the police, miss," Maria whispered from the kitchen door.

Jade went into the hallway. The inspector introduced himself and his men and showed Jade a search warrant. Inspector Jim Metcalfe was a recent appointee to the area and has such had not realised that the local CID's power of deduction had been severely limited over a number of years by the influx of regular and unofficial payments at all levels of the force. For instance, the close proximity of a light aircraft landing zone to Lou's estate, the regular 4pm in-bound flights, and the subsequent arrival of a black-windowed 4x4 at the house were never investigated, or even regarded with suspicion. The extensive building extensions on the house, the paddock's encroachment into the 'green belt' to accommodate the horses, the luxury cars, and other ostentatious displays of wealth acquired without any apparent industry on the part of the owner, were noted by every local resident except the community constable.

"Do you mind if I get dressed first?" Jade snapped, indicating her dressing gown. "I wasn't expecting visitors so early."

"Yes, please do, we'll start down her."

"Right! Maria, put my clothes out while I shower!"

Jade flounced out of the hallway followed by Maria. As soon as the door was closed behind them, Jade grabbed Maria by the arm. "Listen carefully. This is important. Put any clothes out quickly and then go to the stables and tell Billy to come round the back of the house outside my bedroom window now! Got it? Move then!" She pushed Maria towards the bedroom whilst she went into the bathroom and switched on the shower.

Billy's face lit up with a mixture of delight and disbelief when Maria gave him Jade's message. His fantasies were about to be realised. Wow! Summoned to his mistress's bedroom first thing in a morning. Things didn't get much better than this! However, Maria's warning that the police were in the house somewhat dampened his enthusiasm, and fortunately, as it turned out, caused him to move with greater caution than he would have done otherwise.

Jade's ice-cool façade was nearing meltdown. She waited by her bedroom window tapping impatiently with her fingers on the sill, the sports bag at her feet. When Billy came round the corner of the house she furiously beckoned him towards her and opened the window. The lad came forward all eager-faced and smiling.

Billy," she hissed urgently. "Take this bag and hide it somewhere very carefully. Don't let anybody see you! It's very important." She handed the sports-bag out to him and then quietly closed the window.

When she went back into the lounge the inspector was staring out of the window into the garden. He turned as Jade entered. "Lovely place you've got here, Mrs Stretton."

"Johnson! And it's Ms," Jade responded curtly,

"Oh. I'm sorry," the inspector started apologetically.

"Don't be," interrupted Jade. "Just get on with what you've come for. I've a lot to do today."

"Right, Sergeant Robinson you check upstairs. Constable, the outbuildings and garage. I'll do down here. Let's get on with it. Excuse us, madam." He bustled off officiously leaving Jade alone in the lounge. She gave a hurried glance out of the window and saw with some relief that there was no sign of Billy. However, on the other side of the house the sight of the constable heading towards the stable block did nothing to relieve her anxiety.

Jade sat down on the settee, "Maria!" she called. "Coffee, for one," she added brusquely. It might be a good idea to mentally prepare her statement of innocence in case they found anything.

The search had lasted a good half-hour before the inspector and the sergeant returned to the lounge. "Well, Miss Johnson, thank you for your co-operation. We'll probably want to speak to you again in the near future."

Jade nodded curtly, secretly very relieved. It was obvious they'd not found anything incriminating. "Maria!" she shouted into the kitchen. "Show these gentlemen out."

Jade surreptitiously watched the two policemen through the window as they met the constable and stood talking in the courtyard. After a few minutes they moved away and Jade heard the their car crunch down the drive and out into the lane.

Jade gave them a good ten minutes to get well away. She wasn't daft. They were probably watching the house to see what reaction their visit had caused, but she desperately needed to find Billy to see what the young fool had done with the hold-all.

Unable to contain her impatience any longer she made her way to the stable yard in search of the lad. He was busy grooming one of the horses and didn't notice her approach. At the sound of her voice however he gave an embarrassed start and blushed deeply.

Jade moved close to him. "Billy, love," she murmured seductively. "Did you manage to do that little job for me?"

"Y...Yea," he stammered, completely overpowered by her proximity. "No problem, miss. I've put it ..."

"Shsh!" Jade interrupted, quickly putting her fingers over Billy's mouth. She looked around to see all was clear, "This is our little secret Billy. Nobody but you and me must know about this, right?" She gave his cheek a gentle stroke with the back of her hand. Billy felt his knees go weak, for a moment he thought he was going to faint.

"R...right, miss," he managed to blurt out. His wildest dreams becoming reality before his very eyes.

"You see, Billy. There are some people I don't trust; so-called friends of Lou's. You musn't say a word to any of 'em."

"Oh, I won't, miss. You can rely on me."

"I know I can, Billy. You and me have a special relationship. We'll keep quiet about today, but when things have quietened down you can show me your secret hiding place, right Billy?"

"Right, miss."

"And by the way, Billy. Stop calling me 'miss', can't you? Close friends call me Jade." With a gentle squeeze of his arm and a lingering look into his eyes Jade went back into the house.

Billy hardly knew how he got back into the stable. Once inside he took a deep breath and sat down on the bench, exhaled deeply to let out all the pent-up emotions and sat silently contemplating the opposite wall for the next half-hour.

Maria, watching from behind the net curtains in her first floor bedroom window had noticed the incident in the yard and she returned to her table with a wry smile on face, picked up her pen and painstakingly checked through a section of the minutely hand-written journal.

Four

Over the next few weeks, Maria, who noticed everything and said nothing, observed a radical change in Billy's attitude and behaviour, both towards Jade and particularly towards herself. He had developed a swaggering confidence; no longer did he play the part of the humble stable lad, he seemed to regard himself as on a social level with Jade and at a much higher level than herself. It was obvious to Maria that this change of attitude was not unconnected with the police search of the house and Billy's urgent summons to the bedroom window and the subsequent meeting in the yard. Ergo, to her acute mind, Billy was in possession of some kind of incriminating evidence and was using it to exert this influence over Jade. She would soon find out what it was all about. Billy might think he was flying high but he was still a simpleton at heart.

The opportunity arose one afternoon when she took his lunch to the stable.

"Here you are Billy, a pot of tea and a sandwich for you."

"Ooh ta, Maria! Just put it down over there, will you?" he said indicating an old packing case which served as a table. Billy was sitting on a bench lacing up a new pair of expensive training shoes.

"Nice trainers," Maria remarked casually. "Must have cost a bomb, those."

"Best yer can get," boasted Billy, almost swelling with pride, flattery was such a novel experience for him, and one guaranteed to produce results. "These are the very latest, only came out this month. Over a hundred quid a pair."

"Wow!" exclaimed Maria, not just to boost Billy's ego but actually shocked at the price.

"You won the lottery, then?"

"Naw, don't need to," Billy replied with a knowing wink.

Slowly and carefully, almost surgically, Maria teased out the whole story. She'd get him to reveal the actual whereabouts of the sports bag before long.

It was immediately apparent to Maria that Billy was not making the most of this opportunity, focused as he was solely on getting more of Jade's affection. He'd already had a taster, a little cuddle and a peck on the cheek, and in spite of the new training shoes his real aim was to get a much closer physical contact.

"You want to make a bit more out of this while you've got the chance, Billy," Maria suggested. "You don't get many opportunities like this in a lifetime, I'll tell you, " she added with some feeling, the bleakness of her own experience at the front of her mind. "You've got to make the most of it."

"Look, Maria, if you want some just help yourself." Billy's inherent generosity quickly rising to the surface. "Look, I'll show you where I keep it if you want," he went on, enjoying his bit of power and rather liking this unaccustomed centre-stage role. "I don't keep it in the stable, you know. I'm not stupid."

No, you little bugger, you're not, thought Maria. But you're a little bit too naïve for your own good.

Billy led Maria round the back of the stable block to a patch of waste ground at the edge of a small copse. The area was thickly overgrown with weeds, nettles and a tangled mass of brambles. Billy pushed aside the undergrowth with a large branch to reveal a rusty iron grate, the lid to the former septic tank which had not been used since the house was renovated.

Maria's nose wrinkled with disgust and her hand automatically shot to her nose and mouth as the foul smell rose out of the cesspit when Billy prised up the lid with the branch. He deftly swung the lid to the side with the piece of wood, and appearing to be completely unaware of the nauseatingly odious stench which hung like a cloud over the aperture, he flung himself down on his stomach and with his head and half his body inside the chamber he rooted about in the noxious pit. He emerged a few seconds later, a great big smile on his face and clutching a large plastic bag in his right hand. He held it up triumphantly, "Just look in here, Maria," he shouted gleefully, as he took out the sports- bag and unzipped it.

"Good God, Billy!" she gasped, partly as a result of rising nausea and partly in amazement. "How much is there in there?"

The bag was brimful of what appeared to be stacks of twenty pound notes, in bundles of what she guessed must be at least five hundred pounds. She just stared at it open-mouthed; the sight of it had completely numbed her brain.

It was Billy who spoke first, "I don't exactly know, Maria, but here take some. I've had a few, nobody'll notice."

I wouldn't be too sure about that, thought Maria. But, nevertheless, she gingerly helped herself to a bundle and slowly flipped through the wad, five hundred quid, as she'd guessed. "Thanks, Billy. But just remember, lad, we must keep this to ourselves, else we'll both be getting the sack, you know."

"Miss Jade'll see me all right," said Billy confidently. "Me and her have a special arrangement now."

Maria didn't share Billy's confidence at all but she didn't feel she could share this opinion with Billy just yet. Her trust in people had been considerably modified by her experience of human relationships. She'd met a lot of women like Jade, the only motivating factor in their lives being their own self interest.

Billy placed the sports-bag in the chamber and slid the grate back into position. He covered the entrance with brambles and brushwood and he and Maria walked back to the house together. "I'm going away soon," Billy said abruptly, just as they reached the stable. "Time I had a holiday, like."

"Oh, aye!" said Maria, unable to conceal the surprise in her voice. "And where you planning on going then?"

"Er, probably Spain or somewhere warm like that. Miss Jade's got a place out there."

Maria stole a quick sideways glance at Billy to see if he was joking, but the poor simple mutt appeared to be quite serious.

"Have you told your Mum and Dad about this trip yet, Billy?"

"Gunna tell 'em tonight."

"Well, just you be careful, lad. You never know with these foreign places."

"Oh, I'll be all right, don't you fret. I can look after meself now."

Jesus, a lamb to the slaughter, she thought, unaware at the time just how prescient a statement that was.

Five

"I'll be going away this weekend, Maria," Jade remarked sharply after breakfast that Friday morning. "Pack up some summer wear, bathing suits, cocktail dresses, you know what I like."

"Yes, miss," Maria said meekly, and thought to herself, I know what you like only too well, madam.

"Call a cab for eight o'clock tonight, use Ben if he's around."

"Right, miss."

Maria spent the next hour packing the three sizeable suitcases she knew Jade always took with her. Maria wondered if Billy knew about this trip. He couldn't possibly be going with her, she thought. They'd stand out like..... she couldn't think of anything remotely appropriate for some minutes, until she laughed out loud at the mental image of the couple walking arm in arm into some Riviera cocktail party looking like Snow White and Humpty Dumpty, or Beauty and the bloody Beast! Still, that wasn't her problem, Maria thought, but she was concerned about Billy. He wasn't a bad lad at heart and she'd grown rather fond of him, even though that was unusual for her to have feelings for anyone, but Billy had the sort of appeal one might find in a large friendly dog. She saw him as the labrador type; large, fat and amiable, eager to please, do anything for a kind word, a friendly pat and a biscuit. Not a lot up top, but a willing worker.

"Bags packed, miss," she called through into the lounge where Jade was lying on the settee glancing through a glossy fashion magazine. "And Ben's coming at eight."

Maria still couldn't get her head around the fact that Billy and Jade were going away at the same time, surely to God they couldn't be going together. "I hear Billy's going away on holiday," she said from the lounge doorway. She realised she was pushing her luck just by asking any question, not least one like that, but she was desperate to find out what was going on and she just hoped her question might produce some reaction which would give her a clue.

"I've given him the week off. He's probably going to Butlin's for a bit of culture," she said scathingly without looking up from the mag.

What would you know about culture, Maria thought. If it came up and bit you on the bum you wouldn't recognise it.

"Abigail from the village will be coming up to look after the horses," Jade added. "I'm going upstairs for a lie down now so I don't want disturbing."

Well, that little conversation didn't add much to the overall knowledge so Maria went out to the stables to look for Billy. He wasn't there, but Abigail was and she told her Billy had gone down to the village to see his parents.

After a late tea Maria retired to her room as Jade told her she was no longer needed that day. She spent an hour or so poring over her manuscript and making various minute alterations. She put down the magnifying glass, removed her glasses and wiped her eyes, reading the small print made her eyes very tired and sore. The sound of car tyres crunching on the gravel made her look up and move quickly and quietly to the window. She glanced at her watch, it couldn't be Ben already, it was only seven o'clock. She drew back a corner of the curtain, it was almost dark but she could make out the shape of a large 4x4 in the drive. Who the hell is that, then? Maria wondered. She crept out of her room and onto the landing. Jade's voice she recognised, but the other voice, deep and masculine, she didn't. Well, watch and wait, she thought, all will be revealed.

She went back to her room and carried on with her work. About three-quarters of an hour later she heard the sound of a car door slamming. She rushed across to the window just in time to see the 4x4, a dark-coloured Shogun type vehicle disappear down the drive, she couldn't see the registration number but it did seem quite a newish vehicle.

At eight o'clock, on the dot as usual, Ben arrived in his cab. She watched him load Jade's suitcases into the boot and then they both climbed in and away they went. Thank God for that, thought Maria with some relief. She hadn't taken the poor simple bugger with her.

Six

Billy's hands were shaking with nervous tension as he quietly opened the back door to the big house. In one hand he carried a canvas hold-all which he'd hastily packed that afternoon, spare jeans, a couple of t-shirts, flip-flops and his swimming trunks with his ASA bronze badge on the side. Jade had told him he wouldn't need very much where they were going. The all-important sports-bag was slung over his shoulder.

Jade had said come round about 7.15, but not before. He'd never been in this part of the house before and he was wondering whether he should take off his shoes when Jade called from the lounge, "Is that you Billy? Come in, would you like drink?"

Jade was stretched out on the settee, looking more beautiful than ever. Billy just gaped.

"Drink, Billy?" Jade repeated.

Billy could hardly talk, never mind drink. He somehow managed to stammer a refusal. "Nn..nno thank you, Miss Jade," he managed eventually.

Jade smiled, well aware of the effect she was having on him. "Well, I'm just going to get changed now and then we'll be off. Come into the bedroom and help me, will you?"

Billy's knees gave way at that and he clutched at the back of the leather settee for support. His head raced, he gulped for air, tried to speak but no words emerged.

"Come on Billy boy, show me what you've got," Jade murmured seductively. She reached out and took his hand and led him in a dreamlike state towards the bedroom door.

In a state of blissful anticipation Billy entered the bedroom, the first thing he saw was a large white decorators' sheet spread across the floor.

That was also the last thing on earth he saw. There was a crashing blow on his skull as the baseball bat was brought down with vicious and devastating force. Billy dropped senseless, and probably already lifeless, onto the sheet, twitched once or twice and then was still. A trickle of blood oozed out of the side of his mouth. The bulky figure of a man stepped out from behind the door, placed a plastic bag over Billy's head, tied it tightly round his neck and methodically folded the sheet over Billy's body and then rolled him up in the rest of it. He tied the pieces of rope, already prepared and in position, around the legs and neck. Within minutes of Billy entering the bedroom, he had been slaughtered and trussed up and was now ready for disposal. The big man wiped his brow and looked at his handiwork with some pride.

"You'll get your money when you've finished the job, "Jade said coolly.

"Yea, I know. Round the back. No problem, I've already sussed it out."

"Get on with it then, I want to get away at eight."

The man grunted as he hoisted the body on to his shoulder and went out of the back door into the night with his grim package of death and disappointment.

Seven

On the Saturday morning Abigail came up to the house to feed and groom the horses. Maria had been up early and gone through the house, everything seemed in order. She was, however, still curious about the mysterious seven o'clock visitor of the previous evening. She checked the stables, even looked in Billy's cupboard. That, surprisingly, seemed tidier than usual, no tea-stained mugs festering with mould on this occasion.

Maria had the whole weekend to systematically search the house. Abigail would only come into the kitchen for her snack so no interruptions were expected. However, the telephone rang at midday. It was Lou calling from prison.

"Maria, this is Lou. Is Jade there?"

"Sorry, sir. Miss Jade is away for the weekend."

"Where's she gone?"

"I'm sorry, sir. She didn't say. She said she'd be back on Tuesday."

"Oh, bloody hell. The stupid bitch. If she's living it up while I'm banged up in here I'll fucking well kill her when I get out!"

Charming, thought Maria, prison's done a lot for you. You must have been on the nick's social graces course.

"When she gets back Maria, tell her I need two hundred quid asap. She's to bring it over herself straight away. I'm now in Long Sutton. No pissing about. Have you got that, Maria, it's urgent, right?"

"Very good, sir, two hundred pounds straight away. I'll tell her"

"Don't forget." The phone was slammed down.

Maria gave the V sign to the handset. You'll be bloody lucky she thought, fondly remembering the five hundred quid she'd stashed away in the bank. This house was not a safe place for money; there were too many interested parties looking to get a share. Lou back in England already? Must have been some sort of fiddle, she thought, anybody else would still have been locked up in Holland.

Before it got dark that evening Maria prepared herself for the next task. Wellington boots, gardening gloves, a torch and a small wrecking bar she'd spotted earlier in Billy's corner of the stable. She wasn't looking forward to this little expedition, but it had to be done. She had little hope that the money would still be in the septic tank but she had to check to make certain.

Maria made her way round the back of the stable block and into the neglected area of the property. She forced her way through the banks of stinging nettles, past the vicious leg-snagging brambles and into the rosebay willow herb plantation. The grating over the septic tank was not as easy to find as she had imagined. She thrashed about a bit, not exactly in a state of panic but worrying doubts were beginning to form. The light was fading and this was not a particularly pleasant part of the estate. Fortunately she saw a gap in the undergrowth and close by leaning against a bush she spotted the large branch Billy had used to lift the grate. She pushed forward eagerly, keen to get on with the job and was soon standing above the metal plate.

The rusty manhole cover was very heavy and only by using a large stone and the crowbar as a lever was she able to raise it slightly and move it to one side. The rising stench was immediate; she'd been dreading this and even though expecting it, it still caused her to retch involuntarily. She slipped on her yellow marigolds and quickly pulled her scarf over her nose and mouth determined to get the job done as quickly as possible. Billy had simply dived in headfirst on her previous visit, impervious to the unsavoury nature of the situation. She had a more cautious approach, holding her nose with one hand and shining her torch into the fetid blackness with the other. Forcing herself to lie down on the edge of the aperture she leaned forward and poked about in the sludge and mud with the crowbar. She could feel something, something large, much larger than the sports-bag. She shone the torch downward and forced her head further into the opening. Something white, white material, God she was gagging with the stench. She poked about with the broken branch Billy had used and scraped away the mud from the object and traced its outline. She felt it give slightly as she poked it. The half-uttered shriek of horror was stifled by the vomit which retched from her stomach into her mouth as the white-wrapped body shape appeared in the beam of her torch, the expensive, very latest brand of training shoes poking out of the end. She jerked her head out of the cesspit and vomited violently into the willow herb. She lay on her back for some time in what must have been a state of catatonic shock. She was in no doubt whose body lay in that filthy tank. The bastards! Billy didn't deserve to die. And be dumped like this. Did anyone, in fact? Yes, she thought after a few seconds reflection; the evil bastards who did this.

It took her quite some time to recover her composure and it was now dark and decidedly eerie. She forced herself to get moving, slid back the cover, quite effortlessly now. She suddenly felt very vulnerable; suppose she had been seen? Suppose they were watching the house? What if Billy had told them about her and the money? In a state of panic she stumbled her way back to the house, locked and bolted all the doors, checked the windows and drew the curtains. Even under a hot shower she realised she was still shaking. Only sometime later now lying in a hot bathtub was she able to think logically about her future course of action.

She rejected the idea of telling the police. There wasn't any advantage to be gained in that, apart from the obvious revenge against Jade. Maria was quite interested in that aspect, of course. The sheer arrogance of the cold-blooded murder of the naïve youth had infuriated her and kindled a great desire to see that whoever was responsible got their due come-uppance. However, revenge apart, she was also aware that here was an opportunity to benefit in rather more financial terms. She decided to wait and see what happened next. She knew what was going on, she had the important knowledge, she knew where the body was. All she had to do was be patient and wait for the right moment for revenge and see what extra bonus she might gain for herself. The thoughts and options crowded into her mind and she only slept fitfully that night, starting at every slight noise in the yard outside. She was very relieved when the dawn light filtered through the curtains next morning.

Jade returned home late on Tuesday afternoon. When Maria told her about the phone call from Lou she just wrinkled her nose, muttered something unintelligible and disappeared into the bedroom, leaving her suitcase and jacket in the hall for Maria to pick up.

"Ignorant bitch," Maria muttered under her breath. She didn't see Jade again that day but during the evening she heard the phone ring. It was a short call but Maria could tell from the raised voice that there was an angry exchange of words. Listening as acutely as she could, however, she could not hear the actual content. Maria smiled, something not quite going according to plan; the thought gave her some momentary satisfaction as she returned to her manuscript with increased diligence.

Eight

The following Saturday afternoon Jade summoned Maria into the drawing room and told her to take the evening off; the offer was presented more as a command than as a suggestion and the element of choice did not appear to be an option. "Stay over somewhere for the night if you want," Jade added.

She must think I'm bloody thick, thought Maria, after such an unusual expression of generosity. How often has the bitch given me any time off? She's up to something all right. "Thank you, miss" she remarked brightly, "That's very kind of you, I'll go over to Dewsbury and see me mother."

"Oh, and by the way, in case I forget, Maria. I've arranged for a guy to come over next week and lay a patio and make a barbecue area over that old cesspit round the back. It needs tidying up a bit."

"Right, miss," said Maria meekly, her expression completely deadpan throughout the whole exchange.

At six o'clock that evening Maria was in the stable peeping out through a crack in the door from which she could observe the side and front of the house. After making a quick visit to Dewsbury in the afternoon she'd approached the house from the fields at the rear of the property and was now waiting expectantly for the evening's events to begin.

Seven o'clock came and went, she pulled up a stool and applied her eyes to the crack once again; still nothing happened and it was getting darker. She knew Jade was still in the house because she could see the light in her bedroom and had once seen her shadow move across the curtains. Maria's eyes were beginning to glaze over with boredom and fatigue, she had to force herself to stay awake. She glanced yet again at her watch, eight-thirty. For God's sake come on, she implored.

Half an hour later, or thereabouts, the sound of a car coming up the drive jerked her back into watchfulness. All alert, Maria leaned forward. A large dark 4x4 pulled up outside the front door, it could have been the same one that had come to the house the previous week, Maria wasn't be sure. A man got out went up to the door and was admitted straight away, Jade must have been waiting right behind the door. As the door closed there was a sharp crack. Maria stiffened, she was not sure what a gunshot sounded like, but it could easily have been one. She felt her herself sweating with nervous tension. What if the guy had shot Jade? Maria felt insecure, vulnerable and downright terrified. She grabbed the wrecking bar from the nearby bench and looked around desperately for a quick way out. Her immediate impulse was to run and get as far away as possible.

The house door opened, a shaft of light illuminated the front steps. Oh God, thought Maria, I should have made a dash for it when I could. She was frozen with fright and stared transfixed at the open doorway. A figure came out backwards, bent down and dragging, with some effort, what appeared to be a roll of carpet. Maria could feel herself shaking with terror, this horror-movie situation was far too real for her stomach to stomach. The figure turned and the light caught a flash of blonde hair. My God, it wasn't the guy who was doing the dragging, it was Jade! The guy was rolled up ready for disposal; Maria could guess where he would end up.

Jade closed the front door, looked around briefly and headed for the side of the house. Maria's eyes followed every movement. Seconds later Jade came back with the big wheelbarrow. Already prepared and waiting, noted Maria.

The carpet roll and its contents were lying on the top step; Jade seized the inert form with both hands and dragged it down onto the waiting barrow. It was obviously taking all her strength, Jade could hardly be said to be accustomed to manual work, other that of the manicuring variety, and she seldom did that for herself. Maria could hear her gasping and see the struggle she was having to lift and move the wheelbarrow. However, she did eventually get it moving and slowly made her way across the yard and round the back of the stables towards the cesspit.

Maria opened the stable door quietly, edged her way out and crept to the corner of the stable block. She still held the wrecking-bar in her hand and this gave her some feeling of assurance. It wasn't difficult to follow Jade, she was moving so slowly, there were frequent stops and much gasping, groaning and cursing. Angry as Maria was at Jade's callous indifference to human life Maria had to admire the tenacity and resolve Jade was displaying; this was so unlike anything the spoiled brat had ever done before.

It must have taken her a good twenty minutes to reach the disused cesspit. Maria watched from behind a nearby bush as Jade strained to move the grate aside and drag the body in its Axminster shroud to the aperture and unceremoniously tip it in. Jade stood up, hands on hips and looked down into the pit. To Maria she seemed to be gloating over the fact that she'd achieved what she'd set out to do. Jade bent down to pull the lid across the opening and Maria, acting instinctively and without any sort of premeditation, quickly stepped forward, raised the iron bar above her head and brought it crashing down on the back of Jade's skull with all the force she could manage. There was a horrible crack of splintering bone, a stifled gasp and Jade pitched forward face down across the opening. With hardly any thought or hesitation Maria pushed the still body into the hole and threw the bar in after it. She shuddered just once and then calmly and methodically dragged the grate over the opening.

Then she panicked. Her legs felt unable to support her. She looked around wildly. Not a sound, but suppose she'd been seen coming back to the house! What if someone else had been watching? She tried desperately to think logically, to calm down. Check the grate for bloodstains, all clear! Cover up the grate with branches, right! Move the wheelbarrow! She wheeled it back to the stable and put it in its usual place.

She hurried into the house and bolted the front door, then checked all the other doors and windows. Why had she done it? Something so alien to her beliefs. Was it just because the opportunity had presented itself? Was it the pent up fury of years of subservience, or revenge for Billy? A combination of all those factors she guessed.

She was still shaking even when standing under a hot shower and it was a good hour before she was able to think logically about her next course of action. She bundled up all the clothes she had been wearing earlier ready to destroy them, then she went downstairs, picked up the keys to the 4x4 from the hall table and pocketed the wad of banknotes which were lying beside them. Jade, the callous bitch, had obviously prepared everything quite meticulously, even to the extent of rifling the guy's wallet after she'd killed him. Maria recalled Jade once saying, when Maria had caught her going through Lou's pockets one evening, 'Just collecting the Lou's change' she had said with a brittle laugh.

What to do with 4x4 in the drive was now the big question, it was important to remove all traces of the guy's presence. She decided to act immediately and get the car out of the way whilst it was dark. She headed for the supermarket car-park in the town, waited until there was no-one around, parked the car in one corner close the building and pulling her anorak hood over her head and strolled nonchalantly away. It meant a good two mile walk back to the house but it was a quiet unlit lane and she met no one on the way.

Nine

Later that evening Maria went through Jade's handbag, smiled with delight at another roll of banknotes and put them in her anorak pocket. Jade's credit cards, her passport and cheque book she placed in the cardboard box she intended to destroy the following day. There must be nothing left in the house to suggest that Jade had not gone away.

Next morning Maria had the bonfire behind the stable block as planned. She carefully sifted through the ashes to make certain nothing identifiable remained then scattered the ashes into the long grass.

Maria did nothing for two whole days apart from working on her manuscript and her usual cleaning duties. Early in the morning on the third day after the traumatic night at the septic tank the local builder and his mate turned up with a wagon-load of hard core, sand and paving stones. They set up their cement mixer in the stable yard and got down to work straight away. Maria took out some pots of tea shortly after they'd started, primarily to see that nothing was being disturbed unnecessarily. She needn't have worried, these guys were master bodgers rather than master craftsmen. They 'd just cleared the bushes and weeds away, sealed off the grated area with cement and dumped the hardcore on top of it, spread it about, and were already levelling it off ready for the sand and paving stones.

It was going to make a very nice barbecue area, Maria thought, and would also serve as a garden of remembrance. 'Over my dead body' was one of Jade's favourite expressions and Maria couldn't help smiling to herself at the irony.

When the workmen had left, Maria went down to the new patio to check the result. It was basic rather than aesthetic, but it served its purpose, literally covering up a multitude of sins, and the brick-built barbecue fireplace added an extra permanent dimension to the place. Maria returned to the house with quiet satisfaction, so far everything was going extremely well.

Lou telephoned again that evening. Where the hell was Jade? Where was the money he'd asked for? Maria answered in the same vein as before; she'd passed on his message as instructed, sorry but Jade was still away, she didn't know where and she'd never mentioned the money. A short expletive and slammed-down phone ended the call.

The next day Lou's friend Jim called at the house. Maria had watched with some trepidation, the black BMW with the blacked-out windows come slowly up the drive. She answered the door to the short, thick-set middle-aged man in the large black puffer jacket.

"Lou sent me to collect some stuff," he said gruffly, and without waiting to be invited pushed passed Maria and into the hallway. He ignored, or didn't hear, Maria's quiet, "Please come in, sir," and went straight upstairs to Lou's study. This room was always kept locked, but Jim knew where the key was, as did Maria. If it was money he was after he wouldn't find any in there, both Jade and Maria in their turn, had been through it very thoroughly and the bulky hold-all was safely stashed away in Dewsbury.

Maria went back to the kitchen and pretended to busy herself with household chores but she listened intently as Jim moved about the upstairs rooms banging doors, slamming drawers, opening and shutting cupboards. She heard him go into her own bedroom which infuriated her even though she knew he would find nothing of importance, there wasn't more than fiver in the whole house and the holdall certainly wasn't here. She wasn't daft, this intrusion was not unexpected and it was actually better than she'd anticipated; a break-in during the night had been a constant fear.

After about half an hour Jim came down the stairs and into the kitchen. "I want to have a look round here now."

"Can I help you? "Maria asked politely, looking up from the sink. "Are you looking for anything in particular?"

The man looked at her keenly but she met his gaze with a calm and innocent expression.

"No, Lou sent me to get something for him."

"If it's clothes you want I can pack some up for you."

Jim looked at her again, not sure if she was taking the micky; decided against it and started going through the kitchen cabinets. Maria left him to it and started vacuuming the hallway.

Jim McDonald was there most of the afternoon. He'd been in every room in the house, in the outhouses, the garages, the stables and the greenhouse. He was not happy when he'd finished.

"Did Jade take anything with her when she left," he asked grumpily.

"Oh, yes sir. I packed up a trunk load of clothes for her and she had a big sports-bag and some hand luggage with her. Quite a weight there was sir, it took both of us to get it to the taxi."

"Taxi? Whose cab was that?

"I don't know, sir. I didn't fix it. I'd not seen the driver before. It was a black car though."

"Right, I'll be back later," he growled as he went out.

"Please yourself, you bastard," muttered Maria when the door had closed.

Ten

Maria now realised she had to get out of the house, and fairly quickly. She was not getting paid and it would look suspicious if she stayed on under the circumstances. Her main problem was how to recycle the cash. She'd already counted up her assets a couple of evenings before in her bedroom when the curtains were drawn and the doors locked. There was eighty seven thousand, seven hundred and sixty pounds in the sports-bag all in used twenties. She had discovered one thousand pounds cash in a make-up bag in Jade's suitcase, seven hundred and fifty pounds and forty-two pence and two thousand euros in Jade's handbag. She'd spread the whole lot out on her bed. With the five hundred pounds already in her bank Maria reckoned she had nearly a hundred grand to help her start a new life.

But where? That was the important question. Spain was too obvious, too many ex-pats, too many crooks, too many foreigners, language problem! America? Too much hassle getting in, too right wing, too simplistic a neo-born-again-Christian philosophy. Australia, New Zealand? Too far away from civilisation. She eventually settled on Canada as the place to make her new life. She got out her atlas, turned to North America covered up the United States, closed her eyes and stuck a pin in the map, that would be the place she would go to. She was a firm believer in predestination, if not in a supreme being, then at least in some guiding hand. She opened her eyes, the nearest town to the pin was Prince Rupert in British Columbia. She'd not previously known of its existence but that is where she decided to go; the fates had decreed.

The day after McDonald's visit when Abigail came to groom and exercise the horses Maria told her she was going away as she'd got another job in Manchester. There was enough feed in the stable to last a long time and after that Maria didn't much care. She knew horse-mad Abigail would see that the pair were well looked after.

It did not take Maria long to pack her bags. She'd moved too many times to be in any way sentimental about leaving a house. And anyway she was beginning to feel rather nervous about her situation. She'd seen suspicious-looking cars drive past the house, cars with darkened windows and low-slung body kits, they might just as well have 'Drug Dealers Inc' lettered on the side: a wonder the police hadn't copped on to the fact.

She left that afternoon. A brief call in Dewsbury, a taxi to the railway station and she was on the next train to London. It was important to distance herself from the area and disappear into the anonymity of the big city. She felt vulnerable with a bag full of cash in her hand but she was happy to be on the move and looking forward to her new life in Canada.

She booked into quite an expensive hotel near Victoria station, deposited the sports-bag in the hotel safe whilst she went out to book flights and change money. She still did not know what to do with the rest of the cash. Should she just chance it and hope Canadian customs didn't check? She assumed there would be a limit to the amount you could take in. Once she got it there she could pay for everything she needed by cash, changing it into Canadian dollars as and when she needed it.

To play safe and give herself a bit of reserve she deposited another two grand in her bank, and opened a further account with three grand in another international bank. That meant she had a reserve of over five grand in the bank if things went badly wrong.

What the hell, she thought, chance it! She was an elderly, apparently respectable, woman with one suitcase and a sports-bag full of cash. What did she have to worry about? She would chance it! And chance it she did. She labelled her bags with the name Sister Maria and wearing a white wimple-type headdress, which she'd made out of part of a bed-sheet, a crucifix at her throat and a rosary in her hand she reckoned even His Holiness the Pope would have difficulty not believing she was one of his flock. With cash spread all over her body and secreted in different sections of her luggage she sailed through customs like an overloaded Spanish treasure galleon, her bra full of fivers, tenners in her truss and her slacks lined with twenties. She rustled if she walked quickly so her progress was stately and deliberate but helped by leaning on her walking stick, also stuffed with notes. She received some additional help from the airline who insisted she be transported to and from the departure gates on one of their passenger vehicles for the disabled.

Eleven

Life was quiet in Prince Rupert, population just over 16,000. She'd rented a room overlooking the harbour and she spent much of her time at her desk by the window watching the fishing boats and working quietly on her manuscript. It was coming on very nicely and apart from a few alterations and adjustments it was almost completed. She was a little worried about that because she wondered how she would occupy her time when it was finished, as most of her adult life had been spent on its development. She need not have worried.

One evening a few weeks later her landlord knocked on the door of the room to find out why she had not paid her rent and when getting no reply had used his pass-key to enter. Maria was sitting by the window pen in hand, her lifeless eyes looking out over the darkened harbour. He glanced at the manuscript as he checked her pulse. The last words written in tiny meticulous letters were *'The End'*.

The post-mortem concluded that the unidentified female (aged approximately sixty years) had probably died as a result of deep vein thrombosis sustained on some recent long-haul flight. Severe compression of the leg joints seemed to indicate acute restriction of the blood flow, but no suspicious circumstances were noted and death by natural causes was the returned verdict.

Florence White had been a cleaner at the Harbour View Guest house for seven years, receiving in that time a paltry wage, never a tip and scarcely a 'thank you' for the hard and onerous work the job entailed.

When she turned the mattress over that Tuesday morning and discovered a couple of plastic shopping bags containing between them nearly eighty thousand pounds in English twenty pound notes she naturally assumed that the recently-deceased lady had remembered her in her final moments. She hurriedly finished her cleaning stint, stuffed the bags in her basket and cycled home to re-count, reflect and rejoice over her inherited windfall.

By careful and studied money exchange throughout the area over the next few months Florence realised her life-long ambition and bought the self-service laundrette and dry cleaning business in Norwood Street in Prince Rupert. She packed in her job as cleaner and general dogsbody at the guest house and enjoyed the rest of her working life chatting to her customers and generally sorting out the population's dirty laundry. Her motto pinned on the wall over the washers read – 'Get your whites whiter at White's.' Perhaps slightly over-stating the shop's raison d'être.

Somehow it seemed quite a fitting end for a bag of dirty money with an unpleasant and tragic history, but one wonders whether Lou still incarcerated in HMP Long Suffering and still trying to obtain money from the departed Jade and his elusive friends would fully appreciate the outcome. In accordance with the policy of sequestering the assets gained through criminal activities Loujade Villa was seized and sold, as were Lou's cars, the horses and the cabin cruiser.

Extensive enquiries failed to establish Jade's whereabouts so her assets were also liquidated and transferred along with Lou's to one of the government's contingency funds and put to good use for the many and varied consultancies employed by the government in health, education, transport, defence and welfare; as well as supporting the expensive army of accountants needed to advise on these and other PFI schemes. So it can happen that out of the evil machinations of men the political chicanery of governments can often be subsidised.

A Village Life

One Day

In R.P.Jackson's 'Guide to the villages of the Yorkshire Dales,' Ennydale is described as a typical picturesque Dales village. It has a population of five thousand and attractions listed include the pack-horse bridge over the beck, a 16th century church and a former coaching inn on the village green. We are also informed that it took second place in the regional final of the Best Kept Village Competition in 1992, and that the finest hotel accommodation is in the next large town, Farrington, some four miles away.

This July afternoon, pleasantly warm for the time of the year, saw the residents of Westpark Way busy with domestic and garden chores. Sandra Wilson pegging out a long line of sparkling white nappies. Elizabeth Simpson, her next door neighbour, kneeling in the front garden weeding amongst the rose bushes, and Jack Dolan, pensioner and local know-all, leaning forward over his walking stick offering Elizabeth his unsolicited horticultural advice.

"Nay, lass, you don't do it like that. You've got to get all the root out, they'll just grow again like that. Just take a look at my garden! There's not a weed in sight."

"Aye, an' I know why an' all, Jack. You bore the buggers to death, they're not gunna stick their heads up when you're there, your weeds come out at night, when you're in bed."

Sandra's laughter from the next garden drew their attention over the waist-high woven wood fence.

"And what might you be laughing at, young lady?" Elizabeth said in mock reproof, and then continued as Sandra smiled at the older woman. "You know, I've never seen anybody do as much washing as you...are you taking washing in for the whole village, or summat?"

The dark-haired young mother laughed engagingly again, "You'd think so, wouldn't you, Mrs Simpson? I've been at it all morning. Hello, Mr. Dolan," she called, waving to the elderly man. "Are you just going down to the bowling green?"

"What does she say?" Jack asked Elizabeth testily.

"She says, are you going to the bowling green?" Elizabeth repeated, raising her voice.

"Aye, eventually. I'll be calling at the post office first, though. In fact, I'd better get off now," pulling out a pocket watch by its chain from his waistcoat pocket and holding it up to see it properly. "Ten past two, exactly. You know this watch hasn't lost a minute in the last ten years. They gave it to me when I retired from Jackson's. Do you know Jackson's, Liz? Down by the old railway station."

"Course I know Jackson's, I used to work there with you." Elizabeth interrupted sharply. "Silly old bugger," she muttered under her breath. "You'd better get off for your pension, Jack. I heard they were running short of money down there this morning, there's too many pensioners in the country nowadays, they reckon."

"Oh, I'd better get off then, while there's some left, taraa." He moved away slowly along the pavement, peering into each garden as he passed, gently moving away a straggling frond with his walking stick when necessary. His neighbours usually suffered his criticism with quiet good humour, and those that couldn't, quickly sought the sanctuary of the garden shed whenever he appeared.

"He's a bugger, is yon," Elizabeth said to Sandra, when he was out of earshot. "You know that new chap over there," she nodded across the road. "The one with the untidy hedge, he daredn't come out when Jack's around. Jack's over like a shot telling him his garden's a disgrace, and what he should do about it. The chap can't get it done for keeping out o' Jack's way."

"He does very well for his age though, doesn't he? He certainly gets about a bit."

"Aye, but that's only so he doesn't miss owt. He's not that old really, he's probably about seventy now, just a couple of years older than me. Mind you, he's allus looked like that. Doris, that was his wife, she died the year afore last...grand woman she was," Elizabeth confided reflectively. "She used to say he stooped the way he does because his braces were too tight. He'd had 'em since he were a lad, like, and he were just too mean to buy anymore." Elizabeth laughed uninhibitedly at the recollection; Sandra joined in, laughing as much at the other woman's laughter as at the reason for it.

They were good friends, in spite of the age difference, and Elizabeth often amused the younger woman with anecdotes about the past. She was well known in the village for her ability to tell a good tale.

"By the way, Sandra, are you watching that new programme on t'telly? That one about that village family. You know, where the youngest daughter's pregnant. I'll bet it were that Italian cook, I don't trust him at all, he's too smarmy by half, in my opinion."

"Yes, you might be right there. Me and Mark watch every night. We get the young 'un to bed in time and settle down with a cup of ovaltine. You know, it's very life-like, in't it? I mean that family's just like any family in this street, and that landlord at the pub is the spitting image of Martin at The Olde Crown. Don't you think so?"

"I haven't been in for years, love. When Arthur was alive we used to pop in for the occasional drink on a Saturday night but I haven't been in since. Is it still as dead as it was?"

"Yes, but we like it like that. It's nice to be able to sit and talk, quiet-like, for a change. Mark's sister, Joanne, babysits for us and it's a nice break."

"How old is Ella now? She'll be getting on, won't she?"

"I'll say, a right little madam. She'll be five next. She starts school in September. Thank God for that, let the teachers sort her out a bit, it'll do her the world o' good."

"Aye, they soon grow up nowadays."

Sandra finished pegging out, put the prop under the line, smiled at Mrs. Simpson and went into the house. Elizabeth groaned to herself at the twinge of pain in her back as she knelt down again and resumed her weeding.

Ten minutes later Jack arrived at the Post Office and pushed open the door. The place was crowded with elderly people and one of the two glass fronted sections had a 'Position Closed' sign on it.

"Oh, bloody hell," groaned Jack when he saw the queue. The chattering stopped and the heads turned at Jack's outburst. This was obviously not an unusual occurrence because, after this cursory glance, they carried on talking as before.

"How yer doing, Jack?" asked the man immediately in front of him. "It's a right bloody faff is this every week, in't it?"

Ignoring any social niceties, Jack demanded loudly to everyone but no-one in particular, "Do you know why there's allus a bloody long queue in post offices?" Neither diplomacy nor discretion ever having figured prominently amongst his attributes. "It doesn't matter where the hell you go, half the positions are allus closed, aren't they?" The man in front nodded, and one or two others turned round with expressions of interest. "Well I'll tell thee. They do it so's they can listen to what you say, the Social Security, I mean. They've already got yer photograph, haven't they?" He went on, nodding towards the security camera in the corner of the ceiling, "and now they record everything what you say in that 'position closed' place, as well."

An uneasy silence had descended on the post office whilst Jack had been speaking, and some of the ladies were now eyeing the camera warily.

Even the young lady behind the counter was affected by the unaccustomed lack of bustle and a nervous edge crept into her voice.

One elderly matron eventually whispered to another, "He might well be right, you know. I've heard allsorts in this place and the Social's not daft, are they? You know that programme on telly? The one that's on every night, 'Village Life', or whatever it's called. That post office on there, have you noticed? They have a 'position closed' just like this, you watch tonight an' you'll see."

An old lady at the front of the queue turned round and confirmed this, "You're right, Alice," she whispered with her hand over her mouth. "I only said as much to our Tom. I said, look at that post office, Tom, it's just like ours in't village, I said." There was a murmur of agreement from the rest of the crowd, and those too intimidated to murmur, nodded their heads instead.

"Yer don't all watch that rubbish, do yer?" scoffed Jack from his position by the door. "By bloody hell, you must be short o' summat better to do. I can't stand stuff like that, yer might as well do yer own living, I say...instead o' watching somebody else pretend to do it on't telly"

The general consensus of opinion seemed disinclined to agree with Jack and the uneasy atmosphere remained in the shop as the queue slowly shuffled forward. Jack received his pension money in silence and carefully re-counted it in his hand and then held up each note to the light to check its authenticity.

"Oy, come on Jack. I've a bus to catch today," an elderly chap shouted from the back of the queue.

"Never mind come on, Keith," Jack retorted. They wouldn't take one of my fivers in't pub last night. And it were one I got from here, you know." He turned accusingly to the girl, "How often do you check 'em in here, eh? That's what I'd like to know." Not, however, giving the girl chance to answer, for which she was most grateful, he stormed on remorselessly. "Passing dud fivers to pensioners, that's no joke, it's against the law, you know. I'm thinking o' getting one of them little machines that light up the forgeries, and I'll bring it down here and check everybody's notes one morning." Jack shuffled out of the shop, to the visible relief of the counter assistant, and the general delight of the queue, which, because of the delay, now tailed out of the doorway and onto to the pavement.

"What's going on in theer, Jack? Why this bloody long queue?" the chap at the end asked.

"They're running outta proper money," Jack whispered to him confidentially, "and they've started passing dud 'uns. Yer want to check yours carefully when yer get in there."

The bowling green in the municipal park in Ennydale was a piece of hallowed ground to the veterans who played there. In the summer months, not only did they play there, they almost lived there. The imposing wooden pavilion, a Victorian relic, with its attractive open verandah, served many purposes and fulfilled many needs. It was a cosy tea room, a 'kalling' shop and a store room for woods and personal equipment. During inclement weather it served as a games room for dominoes, cards and draughts, and it had often provided a secure refuge at the height of many a marital storm.

There were only two foursomes on the green when Jack arrived. He nodded curtly to the players and stood on the green in one corner, examining a minute patch of worn turf.

"He hasn't done owt with this worn patch yet, has he? I told him about it two weeks ago. It wants raking out properly, then sanding and reseeding." He wasn't addressing anyone in particular, and the players were too absorbed in their games, or appeared to be, to notice his remarks, so he made his way down the edge of the green poking about with his stick in the gutter as he went along.

Jack settled himself on one of the wooden benches on the verandah; it was a peaceful spot, was this. The roses in the garden down the left-hand side of the green were in full bloom and the ivy cascaded down the high sheltering wall. That side had always been a sun trap and was the favourite place for spectators to sit during the summer afternoons. There were a few there this afternoon; one or two young mothers with prams, but mainly retired folk with either a newspaper or a dog, or both. An idyllic spot; peaceful, picturesque, sheltered and respected.

The clatter of wood on wood brought Jack back to the games in progress, one end of which was right in front of his position on the verandah.

"You should have come round finger bias, Sam. That were the onny way in," he shouted out by way of encouragement. He stood up and indicated which line Sam should take with his next wood, but although Sam's lips were moving in what seemed to be a response, he mustn't have heard him, because he came in thumb bias again. His second wood, travelling far too quickly, kept an almost straight line against the green's slope and crashed with a resounding smack into the wooden gutter.

"Nay, bloody hell, Sam! That were a wasted wood, were that. Yer length were all wrong for that bias. You should a' played it like I said in t'first place."

Jack watched a few more ends from his elevated position in the pavilion and, in his accustomed manner, proffered his critical analysis whenever he thought necessary. This was the only feature of Jack's life which never lacked generosity.

After some twenty minutes or so Jack stood up and stretched his legs. He was feeling decidedly energetic this afternoon, and he made his way round the back of the veteran's pavilion to the two public tennis courts. The groundsman obviously took great pride in his work because the lines were freshly marked out, and the red shale courts had been recently watered and dragged. A couple of young men in whites were playing on the first court and Jack stood watching for a minute, arms folded on his chest, head moving from side to side in time with the tennis ball. Jack had played a bit of tennis in his younger days, in fact he'd played two or three seasons with the team at one stage. There was a pause in the game as the ball rolled to the side netting near to where Jack was standing.

"You'd do better if you changed your grip a bit when you're serving," he advised the young man who came to collect the ball.

"What you need is a chopper grip, like this," and he demonstrated the hold on his walking stick, and he swung it back and over his head in, what he thought, was quite a reasonable attempt at the service action.

"Oh, thanks, I'll give it a try," the young chap smiled. "I haven't been playing long. I think he's a bit too good for me," he said, nodding across the court. He returned to the base line, carefully adjusted his grip in accordance with Jack's instructions and served. The edge of the racket struck the ball with a crack and it flew in a wide arc over the top of the surrounding netting and into the rhododendron bushes on the far side of the court. The young man looked sheepishly at Jack as his opponent bellowed with laughter.

"Don't you worry, lad," Jack sympathised. "That weren't too bad, you've just got to remember to flick the racket head round just before you hit the ball." He gave another, but less convincing, demonstration with his walking stick, but the young man had already served his second ball and the players were engrossed in the ensuing rally. Jack mumbled some further words of encouragement and ambled on towards the cafe which was adjacent to the tennis courts.

This cafe, a sturdily built wooden structure with large picture windows, affording views of the bowling greens to the rear and the tennis courts in front, had served the neighbourhood for as long as Jack could remember. His parents had first brought him into the cafe when he was a kid during the thirties and, apart from some of the staff, it hadn't changed much since then.

"I'll just have a pot o' tea, please, Mabel," he said to the buxom lady in the floral pinafore behind the counter.

"Right Jack, won't be a minute! How are you doing today?" She enquired pleasantly.

"Not too bad, lass. Me back's giving me a bit of trouble, especially of a morning..and me knees aren't what they used to be. I say, I've just been watching some lads playing tennis... they're not a patch on what we were like at their age."

"Well that's a long while ago, here you are then, Jack. Here's your tea, sugar's on the table."

"It's a bit weak is this, Mabel, in't it?" Jack queried looking disapprovingly into the beaker. "Do you use tea bags?" Mabel nodded her head and was about to speak but Jack was on one of his hobby horses and galloping madly away. "Haven't yer got any proper tea, like out of a caddy? They put dust in them tea bags, you know, not proper leaves. You can't see what's in 'em but I'll tell you what I do. I open 'em up and find out. I were telling that man in the new supermarket the other day, I said, 'if you're gunna sell me bags o'dust then you'll have to drop your price a fair bit'. I showed him the pile of tea dust I'd taken out of one of his bags. Look at that', I said, 'them's not tea leaves, there's bits o' stalk and God knows what in theer." He said he'd have a word with the rep when he came round. He gave me my money back, I'll say that for him, but they're not going to fiddle me, I'll tell thee."

Mabel shook her head and wiped her hands on her pinafore, the tolerant smile on her face indicating some degree of familiarity with Jack's forthright manner. She watched the old man take his tea over to a table by the window and sit down, and then busied herself wiping the counter and clearing the used crockery.

A couple of women at a table behind Jack were chattering away, mother and daughter Jack assumed, and baby grandchild in the pram. Jack adjusted the volume control on his hearing aid. Ah, that's better, he thought, as scarcely audible noise became recognizable speech.

"Did you watch it last night? Where that pony got stolen and it turned up in the vicar's barn? It were that Jason that did it, if you ask me. If you remember he was supposed to be going out with Kate er..whatsit, but he never turned up."

"Yea, you might be right, Mum. He's a bit of a creep, in't he? I bet you like the squire best, don't you? Sort of well-dressed toff in his tweeds like, with plenty of money and a nice sports car."

The mother laughed, "I must admit he's a bit of all right but I'm not sure I could trust him. Have you seen the way he looks at that lass in the stables?"

"I think that Shane Williams is really fit, don't you, Mum?" the daughter went on, her voice dripping with dreamy infatuation. "He's got such lovely dark eyes and when he looks at you and says. I'll see you when the lights go out, ooh," she squealed ecstatically, "it sends funny shivers down me back, dun't it you?"

Jack's snort of disgust interrupted the flow of conversation, and he got up and shuffled out muttering loudly to himself, "How in hell's name can he see you if the lights are out?"

The women gazed at each other in amazement and then at Mabel at the counter; their outraged feelings were mollified, however, when she shook her head again, implying certain undefined deficiencies in Jack's mental state.

Jack's further perambulations took him slowly around the duck pond. There is a variety of semi-wild species on the pond, mainly mallard, but some pochard, a pair of geese, a few waterhens and a couple of pairs of tufted duck. Jack was particularly fond of the latter; he would time the ducks as they dived and check when they surfaced; twenty seconds was the record up to now. He settled down on a wooden bench and took out his half-hunter pocket watch and prepared himself for a possible record attempt.

"What time is it, mister?" This from a scruffy little boy who had approached unseen from the shrubbery behind Jack.

Jack looked round in disgust, and eyed the boy up and down for a second before replying. "First of all, young man, haven't they taught you how to say 'please' yet? Secondly, you shouldn't be in those bushes in the first place, and when I tell the Head Gardener he'll skin you alive, and as for the time, it's time you wiped that filthy nose o'yours, it's disgusting." The boy hastily wiped his nose on his shirt sleeve and fled, his shirt flap fluttering behind him like a dirty dorsal fin. Jack watched him until he disappeared from view up one of the many tree-lined side paths which led to the pond. "Ummph! he snorted and turned his attention again to the watch in his hand.

A group which had previously been on the far side of the pond had now moved much closer to Jack. The mother was holding her small daughter by one hand and the lead of a large white dog by the other. The daughter, about five or six years old, was carrying a plastic carrier bag and pulling her mother in the general direction of a pair of mallard near the bank.

"Will you stop pulling, our Elaine?" the mother whined. "You'll have us all in t'pond, if you're not careful." The child freed her hand and produced half a loaf of bread from the bag. "Break it up first, silly," admonished her mother. "They can't eat big lumps like that."

At the first sign of food all the ducks on the pond headed in a vast armada across the lake towards the youngster and her mother Pigeons, not previously in evidence, now formed a fluttering, wheeling, diving squadron over their heads. Gulls, ever ready to gourmandise, hurriedly summoned by the noise had sped from their scavenging grounds on the household tip and swooped intimidatingly and screamed raucously over the now hysterical child and the snarling whirling dog.

"You shouldn't give bread to ducks, you know," Jack advised, in the middle of what was quickly turning into something like a scene from Hitchcock's "The Birds." The child was screaming with fright, the dog was at full stretch on its lead, barking furiously and attempting to get at the gulls, and the distraught mother was remonstrating with both the dog and the child alternately, and beating away pigeons and gulls from the half-loaf of bread.

"Excuse me!" shouted Jack. "I said, you shouldn't give bread to ducks. It swells up in their bellies and makes 'em sick. It doesn't help 'em to find their own food, an' all, it makes 'em depend on folk too much."

The woman glared at Jack in baleful bewilderment; she'd gained a little respite by hurling the loaf of bread into the centre of the pond, where it was currently being fought over by every species of wildlife in the area. The child was sniffling quietly now, in a state of semi-muted shock, and the mother, wild about the eyes was attempting to rearrange her hair and control the dog.

"Will you shut up, you bloody thing?" she shouted, yanking the dog towards her. "It's the last time I bring you two out together. Come here, will you? You fat useless lump."

"What sort o' dog is that, lass?" Jack enquired quietly.

The woman looked up at Jack, but surprisingly, under the circumstances, answered reasonably enough, with just a touch of pride in her voice, "It's a pedigree Pyrenean Mountain Dog, if you must know. It's registered at the Kennel Club." She paused to take a breath, as well as for effect, "Her full name is Serene Princess of the High Mountains."

Jack considered the dog with fresh interest, "There's a bit o' bull terrier in it though, in't there?" he enquired knowledgeably.

The woman stared at Jack in a speechless stupor, her mind struggling vainly to express her feelings, as she and her daughter were dragged away around the pond by Her Serene Princess, still eager to do battle with the scavenging hordes.

Jack got stiffly to his feet, he had decided to make his way home as he reckoned the pond life had been disturbed for the rest of the afternoon. Anyway, there was no way the tufted ducks were going to make any record-breaking dives today with all this lot going on.

Once at home he could do a spot of weeding in his garden, possibly have an early tea and then he might get chance to tackle that new chap across the street about his plot of land. It were no use all the rest of us keeping 'em neat and tidy when his was like a bloody rubbish dump. I could soon tell him how to sort it out! With these comforting thoughts in mind, and his plan for his neighbour's garden rapidly taking shape Jack strolled slowly back through the park.

He cut across the village green and had a few words with Jim Thompson, the village bobby who was waiting by the Belisha beacon for the kids to come out of school.

"Some o' them young 'uns cycle too fast down this road, you know Jim. They want telling before somebody gets hurt. I've all on to get across here sometimes."

Jim sympathised with him but there was no way he was getting involved in a long discussion with Jack about the younger generation. He'd heard it all before, many times, so when old Mrs Hudson appeared on the far pavement he moved gratefully into the centre of the street and halted the traffic for her to cross the road.

Jack wandered on and he was soon back in the little estate of semi-detached houses fronted by their small neat gardens, well, all except one.

Jack had his key in his lock when the quiet of the area was shatteringly disturbed by the strident tones of blaring pop music. This announced the arrival of the ice cream van which today, by some mischance, parked right outside Jack's house. Jack was off his step like a shot. Waving his stick in front of him in unsuppressed fury he rushed down his drive towards the Italianate gentleman in the white coat.

"Get this bloody van away from my house this minute!" he bellowed whilst still some yards away. "It's against the law to ring your bloody bell while you're driving, anyway. Get the hell out of here!"

The first of the crowd of children, to whom the bell was the signal to pester parents for money, were already assembling around Jack and the ice cream van.

"Stand back. He's going!" Jack shouted to the kids. "Bugger off and ring your damn bell outside somebody else's house!" he ranted to the driver. The man had taken a backward step into his cab at the sight of Jack's approach, and some of the kids had now begun to sniffle tearfully under the impression that they too were being admonished. The driver hurriedly slipped behind the steering wheel and inched the vehicle some yards up the street, followed Pied Piper-like by a stream of small children. Jack stood there at the end of his drive, red-faced and arms akimbo impervious to the anxious gaze of parents from their front room windows.

The Old Crown public house had overlooked the small triangular patch of grass known as The Green for close on three hundred years. Never in all its history could it have been quieter than it was on this particular evening in July. Even Martin Black, the landlord, wasn't in his usual corner of the bar; the place was deserted. Or so it appeared to Jack Dolan when he pushed open the door of the tap room at exactly 8.30 pm. He'd checked the time by the pub clock with his own reliable timepiece because Martin was in the habit of keeping the bar clock fast so he could call time five minutes early. Jack had not failed to inform him about this time discrepancy on previous occasions, very frequently, in fact.

Jack was a little later than usual because he'd been watching from his front window to see if that chap opposite, he of the untidy garden, came out. Not a sign of him. Honestly, Jack thought, some people just weren't bothered about keeping up standards. After waiting for more than an hour he set off for the pub, secure in the thought that he'd get him the next time he showed his face. If he didn't come out Jack would go and knock on his door; as self-delegated quality controller for the area Jack was not easily deflected from his duty.

"Hello? Shop?" Jack rattled his coins on the bar. "Anybody there?" A muffled voice from the private quarters behind the bar announced someone's marginal interest in his presence.

After a few minutes, the burly figure of the landlord filled the space behind the bar. His red face glistened in the fluorescent lighting and he wiped his handkerchief over his brow, as though he'd just come in from ploughing the fields. "Hello Jack, sorry to keep you waiting. A pint o'the usual is it?"

"Aye, please. Where is everybody? It's like the deserted village out there, apart from old Agnes Schofield on her bike, I didn't see a soul on the way down here."

Martin carried on talking, looking at Jack over the beer pumps like a brawny wicket keeper. "She'd be going to't church, she does t'flowers or summat on a Tuesday night."

"Aye, I know, she's been going theer for the last sixty years to my knowledge," Jack informed him curtly, not to be outdone on local history, "and three times on a Sunday."

"They'll all be watching that village programme on't telly," Martin continued unfazed by Jack's superior tone. "Me and t'wife were just watching ourselves. It's really good, you know. They've got village life off to a T. You could think it were based on Ennydale nearly. Here you are then, Jack. I'll top it up when it settles, just a bit lively yet. He picked up the exact amount that Jack had placed in a little pile on the bar, checked it quickly and rang it into the till. He reached over for Jack's pint glass and topped it carefully up to the rim. "There you are Jack, that's better. I say, would you excuse me for just a minute? I'll just catch the last bit of that programme, if you don't mind."

"Aye, you go on, Martin. Sam'll be in in a minute, I shouldn't wonder." As soon as Martin had disappeared into the back room, Jack moved over to the window and held up his glass to the light. Shaking his head slowly in despair he muttered quietly, "Bloody hell, he's been pulling pints for nigh on twenty years, and I don't think he's managed a good one yet." Jack sipped at his beer as though testing some particularly virulent toxic potion; his screwed up face as he placed the glass on the windowsill seemed to confirm the worst.

Jack looked out over the deserted village green, across to the weeping willow tree in the centre, and beyond to the herbaceous border which lined the green on the far side. He was not one to be moved to thoughts or expressions of beauty, but the silence and unexpected tranquillity of the evening, for a moment, completely took his mind off the taste of the beer. He could remember, as a kid, fifty odd years ago, God, was it so long ago? he thought struggling with the mental arithmetic. Aye, it was, at least that, unfortunately. He'd played round that same tree there with his sister, hiding from their mum at home time. Him and his dad had used it as a wicket to play cricket; he remembered with affection his dad bowling to him underarm with a tennis ball. Jack sighed, happy memories of times long past, it wasn't the same today. Bloody kids nowadays couldn't possibly have the same innocent childhood memories that his generation had. How could you get sentimental about a bloody computer game you played on your own, for God's sake?

Nostalgia became a thing of the past now that Jack's mind had locked on to one of his pet hates. He took a long draught of beer without thinking what he was doing. "Uugh, bloody hell," he said aloud, screwing up his face." Chip shop stuff, is this, he thought. He han't let it settle long enough in t'cellar. Present day landlords for you. They want to get into profit too quickly, they just can't bloody wait. Jack's thoughts were interrupted at that point by the door swinging open behind him.

"All right, Sam?"

"All right, Jack." Sam was roughly the same age as Jack; they'd been at the same primary school in the village and, apart from time spent away in the army during World War Two, their lives had revolved round this area and followed a fairly similar pattern.

Sam walked over to the bar and tapped on an ashtray with a coin, "Martin?" he called out.

Jack followed him over to the bar and whispered, "If I were you I'd shout for Lily. You might get a half-decent pint then. Martin pulls 'em too quick."

Sam's luck was in, because within seconds the petite figure of Lily Black appeared. "Good evening, gentlemen. What can I get you?" she said with a smile. She was a pleasant woman was Lily, always smiling and obliging. Whatever she saw in Martin, Jack couldn't imagine.

"A pint of bitter for me ,love. Er, do you want a half in there, Jack?"

"Aye, I wouldn't mind. It might settle it down a bit." Jack leaned forward over the bar towards Lily, "You know, Lily, that husband of yours swung on them pumps like Tarzan when he pulled my pint. He doesn't have your gentle touch at all."

"You don't have to tell me, Jack. He's always been ham-fisted and clumsy." She expertly filled their glasses as Sam and Jack watched in admiration. "Here you are, gentlemen, that'll be 1.84, Sam. Thank you."

Sam and Jack moved over to a table near the window and settled down. "Do you know where everybody is tonight, Sam?" Jack asked, and before Sam could even think of an answer, he added emphatically, "Watching bloody television."

"You don't have to tell me," retorted Sam. "There's the wife, the daughter, son-in-law, kid in t'pram and woman next door all gawping at the bloody set at our house. It's that sodding soap about village life. That's why I've come out, I can't stand it."

"You mean to tell me that all the adult population in t'village, are sitting like dumplings, watching people pretend to be living in a village."

"That's about it, Jack. I reckon."

"Well, they must be bloody barmy, that's all I can say." He called over to Lily at the bar, "What do you think about this village thing on telly, Lil? Have you seen much of it?"

"That Village Life, you mean. We watch it every night, Jack. Wouldn't miss it for the world. It's the best thing on t'box in my opinion. It's so realistic, you know."

"It's not more realistic than reality, is it, Lily?"

"What do you mean?" Then looking at him more suspiciously, "Hey, you're not trying to wind me up wi' one of your arguments, are you, Jack Dolan? You're not upsetting me like you do rest o't'village, so get on with you."

The men laughed and carried on with their conversation. "It might be quiet on the streets, Jack, but there's a hell of a row coming from the park. Bloody kids shouting and screaming and carrying on. Sounds as though they're wrecking the playground, if you ask me. Where's the local bobby? Or even the park ranger? Do you remember how we used to be terrified of him? He had black gaiters and a walking stick and he put the fear God into us kids," Sam laughed at the recollection. "And look at it now."

"I know," agreed Jack, "and it's getting worse, as well. Bloody parents have opted out. They've delegated their authority to the kids' peer group while they sit at home and watch telly, or go out boozing."

"The what group? Where the hell did you get all that from?"

"By mistake. I tuned into one o' them Radio 4 programmes on the wireless the other day. It were quite interesting, and they were right, you know. Parents let the kids do just what they want most of the time, as long as they're out o't way and not disturbing them. It's their pals and older kids who exert most influence on 'em. And where do you think that that lot get their ideas from? I'll tell thee, bloody television. And computer games, which are just as bad. There's some evil stuff on there as well, so I've heard. Mind you, to be honest, this professor chap said that most parents had no idea what their kids were up to, and if they did, they'd be horrified, and wouldn't want to know about it anyway."

"Well I'm glad I'm not a kid anymore. They don't have a proper childhood, do they? When they get to fourteen they think they know it all, certainly more than me and you. They're smoking and drinking, trying to get into clubs and pubs, they've got girlfriends, motor bikes, fancy clothes, ridiculous haircuts, the lot. Everything except their own money, and commonsense, o'course."

"And respect for other folk and other folk's property," Jack added. "The little buggers don't give a monkey's toss for anybody else."

"Is that what the chap on the radio said, then?"

"Well, not in so many words, Sam. I'm just translating it for you," Jack explained, grinning at his pal.

"Hey, I thought you were going off this week, Jack."

"I am, first thing in't morning! I'm off down south to my sister's, for a break. I'll be away for about a fortnight, I think I could do with a change."

"Right, I'll tell rest o't'village," Sam remarked drily. "They'll probably have a holiday as well while you're away,"

Jack glanced sideways at Sam, but the latter kept his face straight so he decided to let the comment pass unanswered while he thought about it. "Can you pull us two more pints Lily, please? Nice and gentle, mind."

The pub was filling up now, presumably because the programme on television had finished, Jack thought. He and Sam ran quickly through their usual agenda; the disgraceful performances of the English football team, the pathetic display of the cricket team in the latest Test series, the disastrous political state of the nation, and, one of their favourites, corruption in high places. Between them they had all the answers, from team selection to foreign policy, but would anyone listen to commonsense? Would they hellus-like.

Many of the conversations at the bar behind them were about what had happened in that evening's television episode. Sam, observed a familiar look of disgust and disbelief spreading across Jack's face, and not wishing to get involved in an acrimonious and prolonged discussion with some offended party, suggested, during a pause in their conversation, that they drink up and move on. He was really glad to get outside; he knew Jack well enough to spot the warning signs, and from past experience he knew what that could entail. Jack was a master at upsetting people; he'd upset St. Peter at the gates of Heaven, Sam mused to himself, trying to imagine the most extreme case. Jack standing there saying, "You could do with a drop of oil on them gates, if you ask me." Sam laughed to himself at the thought.

"What the hell are you smirking at now," Jack said, interrupting Sam's fantasy, as they walked slowly along the High Street together.

"Oh, nowt much. Did you hear them silly buggers in there? It's bad enough watching it, without spending rest o't night talking about it as well, in't it?"

"I know, I were just about to tell 'em, an' all."

Sam quietly congratulated himself on his foresight. They strolled slowly along the High Street, pausing occasionally to glance in the lighted shop windows and pass comment on the contents. It was a warm pleasant evening and both men felt the peaceful atmosphere of the silent village and the warmth of their companionship. So what if they did argue quite frequently? And what if most conversations threw up some major difference of opinion? Neither had ever convinced the other to change his mind, had they? Each continued to hold exactly the same opinion he had started with.

"Here we are then," he said, as they reached the end of Jack's road. "Have a good holiday, Jack. I'll see you when you get back." He knew Jack's sister from the old days and he suspected Jack might be back rather sooner than he expected.

"Aye, take care, Sam. I'll see you later."

Another Day

It was considerably longer than two weeks before Jack was able to return to Ennydale. Unfortunately, whilst on holiday at his sister's house Jack had had the misfortune to slip on a patch of mud and badly bruised his shoulder. He couldn't quite understand how this had happened because he was only showing some kids in the park the proper way to get on a roundabout. He'd somehow lost his footing and fallen awkwardly on his left shoulder. It was still a bit stiff but not really painful now, and he was glad, at long last, to be nearly home.

He wandered down the street looking in the gardens in his accustomed way; he saw immediately that the chap opposite had done absolutely nothing to his plot; it was like a bloody jungle now. He felt the anger rise up inside. Right, he thought, tomorrow that guy's going to get a reet earful. His own garden was a bit overgrown he noticed, and he'd spotted a weed or two, even from this distance. "Soon sort that out," he muttered to himself.

Jack's mind was busy with these thoughts right up to the time he reached his own gate. He'd just lifted the sneck when he noticed Elizabeth Simpson standing on her step next door. He knew instinctively, by her expression, that something was wrong, and his heart sank.

"Hello, Jack," she said, in a quiet voice, when he walked up the path. "I'm afraid I've got some very sad news for you, do you want to come in for a cup o' tea?"

"No thanks, lass. I'll get one when I get inside, you can have one here with me if you want."

She came across the gap between the two houses while Jack searched for his key. She rubbed her hands nervously on her pinafore whilst

Jack fumbled with the key in the lock and eventually opened the door, pushing the assorted pile of leaflets and letters on the floor back against the wall. She followed him in, the musty smell of the unlived-in house striking her nostrils forcibly as she entered. Jack left his single suitcase in the hallway and went straight into the kitchen, filled his kettle and switched it on, and put out two mugs for the tea.

Elizabeth had picked up the letters and preceding him into the lounge, had placed them on a table. "I've put your letters on the table, Jack" she said, glad in a way to be able to break the silence and lead into her painful disclosures.

"Come and sit down, Jack. I'll mash the tea for you in a minute." Her voice broke slightly.

"What is it, lass?" The unusual gentleness in Jack's voice reflecting the unease he was beginning to feel.

"It's everything, Jack," she blurted out. "I don't know where to begin," she took out a handkerchief from her apron pocket and began to blow her nose and wipe her eyes in some distress.

"Nay come on, lass; it can't be that bad." The sound of the kettle boiling drew Jack's attention and he got up and crossed to the kitchen. "It's you who needs a cup o' tea, lass. I won't be a minute, we'll soon sort it out then."

Elizabeth had a sip of tea, and she and Jack sat facing each other in the fireside chairs. She clasped the mug in both hands and glanced at him, then looked down again before speaking, her voice low and concerned, "First, Jack, I'm afraid your house was broken into, just last night."

"What?" exclaimed Jack, looking around the room. "It looks all right to me."

"They smashed your bedroom window, Jack, and got into the back rooms. I've had the window boarded up and I told the police, but I didn't have a key to get in and tidy up. Anyway, I knew from your postcard that you'd be back today, so I told the policeman that and he said he come back later on. Oh, I were worried sick, Jack." Elizabeth started sniffling again.

"Don't you get upset, love. It's not as though I've owt much to pinch, you know. I'll just go have a look round." He got to his feet and went into the bedroom, and after a second or two Elizabeth followed him.

"Bloody hell, the bastards!" Jack stood in the doorway looking at a scene of total confusion. It didn't look anything like his bedroom, it was as though somebody had tipped all his belongings in a great heap on the floor. Clothes, curtains, furniture, bed linen were scattered across the room; the bed had been overturned, the mattress ripped open, the pillows slashed, and feathers and stuffing were lying everywhere. The frenzy with which this destruction had been carried out, and the sheer wantonness of the action, left both Jack and Elizabeth speechless after Jack's initial outburst. Jack turned silently and opened the door of the spare bedroom; they'd been in there as well! "The thieving bastards!" he muttered grimly. "The sneaking, cowardly bastards. If you could only catch 'em at it, " his cold fury, his feeling of utter contempt for the villains, and his frustration at the lack of opportunity to respond satisfactorily, prohibited further coherent expression.

"Sit down and finish your tea, Jack. I'll give you a hand to tidy up in a minute." She covered her face with her hands and sighed, she couldn't bring herself to tell Jack the rest of the sad news at the moment. He'd had enough to be going on with.

"Hey, don't you worry lass. I'll soon get that straight," Jack said kindly, misinterpreting Elizabeth's sigh. "They won't have got owt, there were nowt much apart from a few of Doris's bits and pieces in't dresssing table."

"Look, Jack, you ring Bernard Mitchell and tell him you're back. I got him to put that wood in the window this morning, and I said I'd get you to ring him to put the glass in as soon as you got back. In the meantime I'll make a start on clearing up in there." She got to her feet in a business-like manner, better to be doing something useful at times like this, she thought. "We'll have this straight in no time," she said aloud. "I'll just go round home and get me dustpan and brush and then we can work on a room each."

"Right, thanks, lass. I'll get on to the police as well, in case they want to come round and check for fingerprints. So, in the meantime, try not to touch owt, like doors or t'windowsills, or t'drawer handles, and stuff like that."

"Right, I'll put me work gloves on. See you in a minute then, Jack."

For the next hour they worked separately in the bedrooms, straightening beds, replacing clothes in wardrobes, filling bin liners with flock and feathers, and generally getting things straight. That's the spare room, at least, just about done, thought Elizabeth, as she paused to consider her work, just the curtains to do. Why in God's name they should tear them down? I don't know; just malicious vandalism, she reckoned.

She was interrupted by the sound of the front door bell and she recognised Bernard Mitchell's voice when Jack answered the door. Bernard was the village's odd job man; there wasn't much Bernard couldn't tackle in the property repair line. She heard them go into the other bedroom and shortly afterwards heard the sound of the plywood being removed from the frame.

Elizabeth discovered she couldn't get the curtains to hang properly because the rail had been pulled out of the wall when they'd been yanked down; it would need re-plugging and fixing. Another job for Bernard whilst he was here, she thought. She pushed open the door of the main bedroom and went in, "Hello, Bernard, right do is this, in't it? They can't leave owt alone, can they?"

"Hello, Liz," Bernard answered brightly, he'd known her and her family for years. "This is nowt to what I've seen in 't village recently. I must be called out at least half a dozen times a week to summat like this. And they allus leave a right mess too, I'll tell you, bloody kids are running wild."

"What makes you think it's always kids, Bernard?" Elizabeth asked, "it could be anybody."

"Well, I don't think so. It's the way they just smash their way in, throw everything all over the place, take stupid things, like there was one two streets away, and do you know what they took?"

Bernard looked questioningly at them but neither Jack nor Elizabeth offered a response so he continued, "Three pork pies, a large bar of chocolate and two bottles of beer. Now I ask you, are they right in the bloody head, or what? And what a mess they left behind, for three pork pies," he repeated, shaking his head in bewilderment.

"I suppose t'police are looking for a thick little fat sod, puking up in some gutter?" Jack rasped vehemently.

"There's a few o' them about on a Friday and Saturday night when t'pub closes, I'll tell you," Bernard informed them knowingly.

"Would anyone like a cup of tea now?" Elizabeth offered. I'll just pop the kettle on if you like."

Both Jack and Bernard expressed a keen interest in the idea and Elizabeth bustled out, pleased to be able to fulfill, what she saw as her maternal role.

The door to the bedroom was slightly ajar and Elizabeth could hear the men talking without actually listening to what was being said. However, when she heard the name 'Sam' mentioned, her head whipped round and her hands, full of teabags, remained suspended over the teapot. She leaned towards the door and listened carefully. Bernard was speaking, but he had lowered his voice from its usual level and he no longer sounded his jovial self.

"You mean you haven't heard, Jack? I thought you knew? Sam had a nasty accident last week. He were coming home from the pub one night, last Wednesday I think it was. He were hit by a car, one o'them bloody joyriders, or so they're called, murdering bastards I call 'em." Elizabeth wasn't able to catch what Jack said, but Bernard's voice was much clearer, "I'm really sorry Jack, I knew he were a good friend of yours. Funeral were on Monday, church were packed out, everybody in't village were there. He were a very popular chap, a real gentleman."

Tears welled up in Elizabeth's eyes; her feelings were for Jack, cantankerous old bugger that he was, it was a terrible shock for him to come home to such bad news, and his house broken into as well. She was glad Bernard had been here and broken the news to him, it was something she hadn't been able to do. She composed herself, wiped her eyes on her pinafore and busied herself making the tea. When she entered the bedroom with the pots of tea on a tray Jack was sitting on the edge of the bed with his head in his hands. Bernard was leaning against the windowsill looking down at him, a sombre look on his face. He looked up with a wan smile when he saw Elizabeth, "I've just told him about Sam," he explained. "I didn't know he hadn't heard?" he ended lamely.

Elizabeth nodded her head sympathetically and put the tray on the dressing table.

"Here you Jack, love. Cup o' tea here for you, this'll do you good."

Jack raised his head, all the spirit seemed to have drained out of him and he looked like a very tired old man.

"Oh, thanks, Liz," he said gratefully, "Just what I need. He took the mug from Elizabeth and sipped the tea. "It were a bit of a shock, were that, Bernard. I mean he were as right as rain when I left him. We grew up together, me and Sam, I've known him all his life. Aye, it's a bad job is that." He was silent for a few minutes and then he added, "Did they get who did it?"

"No, not up to press," Bernard replied." It were a stolen car, full o'kids, old John Pritchard said. He saw it speeding up t'street a few minutes before. It took that bend near 't fish shop far too fast and skidded across t' road and on to t'pavement at t'other side where Sam was walking down. They never stopped, just left him lying there, the bastards. They set the car on fire afterwards, near the edge of the woods; then I'll bet they ran away. That's what they always do, have you noticed? They're so bloody brave, aren't they? Yet someone is allus seen running away from the scene of the crime." He stressed the words 'running away' to make his point. "If they do cop 'em, you can bet they'll either get let off or sent to some bloody holiday camp...unless they're really bad uns, that is. Them buggers'll be sent on some foreign trip for a bit of character building. Yer can't credit it, can yer?"

It was another hour or so before they'd finished getting the house straight and Bernard had fixed the window and the curtain rails. A young policeman had called just after six o'clock and Jack had been able to give him a list of the things that were missing. Not a valuable haul by any means, but items of great sentimental value to Jack, his late wife's engagement ring, her wedding ring, and a gold wristlet watch he had bought her in Morecambe on their honeymoon. The fingerprint man would come round later, the constable said as he was leaving, as he was busy with another job at the moment.

Next morning Jack was up and about very early; the sadness of the previous evening still hung over him, but he had things to do and these thoughts activated him. His pension to collect from the post office and his garden to weed were the duties foremost in his mind as he locked his door, and went round the back to check the windows and the garage. This routine satisfactorily completed, he made his way down the street, his familiar stooped shape observed covertly from behind at least half-a-dozen net curtains long before he'd reached the main road.

Jack pushed the door of the post office and was surprised to find it locked. "What the bloody hell...!" he muttered. Then he saw the printed notice on the door.

With effect from 1ˢᵗ August this Sub-Post Office will close.

All pensions and benefits will be paid directly into bank accounts

or may be drawn in the usual way from the main Post Office

in Farrington

Jack was speechless and stood gazing at the notice unable to take in the information.

"Bloody criminal, in't it?" a voice said behind him.

"What the hell is going on, Fred?" Jack spluttered when he recognised the man who had spoken. "Farrington's bloody miles away. What were up with this place?"

"It were after that robbery the other week," Fred started to explain.

"What robbery? I were in t'other week and it were all right then."

"Where've you been, Jack? It were in all t'papers. Two lads in balaclava masks threatened the girl with a shotgun and stole thousands o'pounds. She's been off work ever since, poor lass."

"Did they get them who did it?"

"Not yet, but the police reckon it were locals what did it."

They chatted for a few more minutes and then Jack headed for the park. He noticed a few other changes as he walked down the High Street. Those concrete pillars, for instance, in front of Ramsdens, the Jewellers. They were not there the last time he passed. Those steel roller shutters on the shop windows were new. He remembered then that he and Sam had looked in those very windows as they'd walked home from the pub together the other week; neither knew then it was for the last time. Jack's sorrow welled up inside him at the thought and he looked around him despairingly.

A man with a newspaper under his arm came out of the newsagent's next to the jewellers and greeted Jack cheerfully, "How do Jack. How're yer doing? Haven't seen you for ages."

"Nar, I've been away on holiday and I've had a bit o'trouble wi' me shoulder, so I haven't been around much, Billy. Here, what's all this bloody lot in aid of?" Jack pointed to the concrete posts in front of the window.

"Them's to stop ram raiders, Jack, them is. They got done a couple o'weeks ago. Took all t' stock outta window, every bit of it."

Jack's first thought was of sheep rustlers but that didn't quite tie-in with Ennydale's main street so he queried it with Billy.

"Ram raiders, Billy? What the hell's them, for God's sake?"

"These cheeky bastards nowadays, they nick a car or a van and just ram it into t'shop window, pile the stuff in and drive off."

"That's why these steel shutters are up as well, eh?"

"Aye, most o' these shops have been done at one time or another in t'last few weeks. Council didn't like the idea of shutters up though; they said they didn't look suitable in a village street. Shopkeepers said it were either shutters up or shut up shop; so they put 'em up and t'Council backed down."

"Hey, Bill, I don't know what things are coming to. I'm just going to have a stroll down t'bowling green, so I'll get on. I say, old Jim Thompson seems to have put a bit o'weight on since I last saw him," Jack said, looking across at the policeman on the other side of the street.

Bill laughed, "That's 'is bullet proof vest, yer dozy sod. They can all wear 'em now if they want."

"What, to see the kids across the street?" Jack snapped in disbelief.

"Aye, well you never know nowadays, Jack. What wi' drugs in t'schools and pensioners getting mugged in t'street you've got to watch out. anyway take care, Jack, I'll see you later."

The first things that Jack noticed, his angle of vision naturally inclined downwards, were the marks on the surface of the bowling green. He was so used to seeing a perfectly smooth billiard table finish that he initially thought there was something the matter with his glasses. Across his field of vision, were two deeply scored parallel grooves, it almost appeared as though a heavy tractor had skidded right across from one side to the other. Jack cleaned his glasses and then gazed around in horror.

Noticing a group of veterans near the pavilion, he headed towards them as fast as he could, his stick tapping out his anger on the path as he went. Muttering imprecations to himself as he went, cursing the groundsman as an incompetent fool and the Bowling Committee for dereliction of duty, he stopped abruptly at what faced him. His mouth fell open with shock; he couldn't take in what he was seeing. The ornate wooden pavilion with its elegant covered verandah was no longer there. In its place was a square concrete blockhouse with sheet metal plates over the windows and what looked, to Jack, like an armour-plated door. It closely resembled one of those large containers one finds on any dockside, but probably not quite as aesthetically pleasing. He looked around in bewilderment, believing, for a moment, that his sense of direction had failed him and that the pavilion was on the other side of the green. No, somehow, this coarse monstrosity had taken the pavilion's place.

"What the bloody hell's going on here?" he shouted to the group desperately, feeling as though his world was disintegrating around him.

The men looked round at the sound of his voice and one of them, Walter Stevens, a committee man, answered him. "How do, Jack? Have you been away?"

"Aye, but not that long. Where the hell's the pavilion gone? What are they doing to us?" He appealed to the group, raising his arms pleadingly.

"Pavilion were being vandalised every night. We just couldn't keep up to it; they were breaking in and stealing all our stuff and wrecking the place," Walter explained despairingly.

"Aye, that's right Jack. We all lost summat," interjected another member of the group. " I had me trainers and me woods nicked. Fred, here, lost 'is shoes and 'is best trousers, didn't you, Fred." The unfortunate Fred nodded in agreement, and Jack, in spite of his anger, couldn't help but notice with interest, Fred's bright green flared bell-bottoms. Obviously he listened to Jack's frequently propounded philosophy, "Never throw owt away, you never know when it might come in handy."

"Well, who's been doing it? Why not just stop 'em doing it instead of rebuilding the whole bloody world?" Jack retorted heatedly.

"The police say it's kids," Walt went on, "but none of them have been caught; we don't have a park ranger full-time nowadays. They do it in the evenings when no one's about. Look at the green. They did that last night, driving motor bikes across it, bloody disgusting. It makes me sick."

"The bastards want shooting," snarled Fred savagely, his trouser bottoms catching the slight breeze and billowing out round his legs.

"Anyway the committee had to make a quick decision and the Council offered to help, so here we are. At least our stuff's safe now."

"Well I'm not leaving owt o'mine in theer again, I'll tell you," Fred said emphatically.

"Well, you haven't got nowt left, have you?" One of the group remarked unkindly.

"Just look at it though, it's disgraceful," Jack pursued his point relentlessly, "it's as though somebody's dumped one o' them massive containers you see on t'back o' them big wagons, or those disgusting portercrap toilets you get at fairgrounds. Fred's right, you should have told me, I'd a' sat here at night with a loaded shotgun and blasted one or two of 'em. T'others wouldn't 'a' been so keen to come back night after, would they?"

"Nay, yer can't do that in a civilised society, Jack. Talk sense man." Walt reasoned.

"What's civilised about this society, Walt, I ask you? When stupid louts can decide what the place is going to look like? Look at that wall there." He pointed at the new concrete wall which was already marred with the inane scrawl of juvenile grafitti, the words 'Shit' and 'fuck off' prominent examples of the genre.

"If nobody stops 'em, if nobody says 'no', they'll turn the whole bloody world into a wasteland," Jack persisted.

Jack's tirade had silenced the group momentarily. Fred nodded his head, he felt certain he agreed with what Jack had said, although he wasn't entirely sure what he'd meant; he'd caught the bit about the shotgun, however, and he quite liked that idea.

Jack left the group in disgust and stomped round the back of the hut to the tennis courts. "Oh God, look at this mess," he groaned. The courts were in a state of total neglect, the nets were torn and hanging untidily from the posts, the remnants of the line-tapes were dirty and frayed, the wire mesh of the surrounding netting had gaping holes in it, the only bright feature about the scene was the crop of rosebay willow herb flourishing along the edges. Two youths, in jeans and black training boots, were desultorily hitting a ball at each other across the sagging net. Jack only gave them a contemptuous glance; as far as he could see their 'rallies' consisted of one wild shot, a prolonged search in the undergrowth and a long stream of invective.

The first things he noticed about the cafe were the new windows. Well, not actually windows, more steel shutters.

"A cup of tea, please. Strong if you don't mind," he said to the young girl behind the counter. "Mabel not here today?"

"She's left," answered the girl shortly.

"How do you mean, left?" Jack enquired, not to be denied the facts by some slip of a girl. "Mabel's been here for twenty odd years."

"Well, she's not here now. Have a look round if you don't believe me? She left, after the last burgulary," she added reluctantly.

What burglary?" Jack's thirst for knowledge not easily quenched by a cup of weak lukewarm tea and dismissive comments from a jumped-up little madam like this one.

"The burgulary. That's all I know." was her short-tempered reply, she didn't have much time for these doddering old pensioners; they took all afternoon over a cup of tea and were always full of questions, or complaints. Or like this guy, both.

"You'll have to see the boss and ask him," and she busied herself ostentatiously with some washing up.

"Who's the boss, then?" Jack knew his insistence was getting on the girl's nerves, and this encouraged him to keep nagging away.

"Mr. Smith, he only comes in on a Saturday, so you'll have to wait till then," she smirked maliciously and flounced away into the kitchen area.

Jack finished off his tea and left the pot on the counter,

"Thanks for your help," he called out sarcastically as he headed for the door. Last bloody time I'm going in here, he thought to himself. The end of cafe life in the park, the end of a way of life, he sadly concluded.

Jack's sense of disillusionment stayed with him as he wandered down to the duck pond. He would sit by the pond and think things out; it must be possible to do something about this decline in standards.

It was unnaturally quiet by the pond; there were usually two or three of the regular duck feeders there at this time. He couldn't see a bench anywhere so he strolled along the edge looking over the fetid water. His spirits rose at the sight of a pair of swans in the distance near one of the islands; as he got nearer, however, he was disappointed to discover that they were not swans but only white plastic bags floating on the surface. He was also horrified to see, now that he'd got closer, what a disgusting state the pond was in. There was all sorts of rubbish floating in it, and bending down more closely to look at something which had caught his eye, he could just make out the shape of one of the park benches and some of the larger stones from the wall nearby.

Jack headed for the conservatory, another one of his favourite havens; they always had a nice display of geraniums at this time of the year. It was with some relief that he saw it was still there as he made his way up the slight slope towards the arched doorway. One of the park gardeners was just coming out of the greenhouse as Jack approached. He nodded to Jack and smiled.

"Where's all t'ducks gone, lad?" Jack enquired.

"Oh, they took 'em all off t'other week. Somebody was having a go at 'em with an air rifle. They shot a few one night and then they came back night after and got a few more so t'boss had 'em taken away. They're on a protected reserve in Leeds now, I think."

"Well, that's bloody disgraceful," Jack retorted. "We're Council ratepayers, we pay for all this park and you're telling me all our ducks have to be looked after in Leeds. Do you mean to tell me we can't bloody well look after them ourselves? We have to send 'em to Leeds for protection?"

"Aye, I know, but that's how it is. I know what I'd do with the bastards if I caught 'em. Here, just come in here a minute and have a look at this." He led Jack into the conservatory and pointed to some broken panes of glass, "Now, they were all right when I went home last night, 'cos I closed them windows next to 'em. They've smashed them three and taken them pots of geraniums out." Jack could see from the marks in the dust where the pots had been. "Do you know what they did with 'em?" the gardener asked, looking Jack straight in the eyes. "What do you think? With half a dozen pots of' geraniums. What would you do with 'em, eh?"

The man's direct gaze and insistent manner forced Jack to reply. "Er, I'd take 'em home, I suppose, or perhaps sell 'em in a car boot sale."

"Right, that'd be more like normal behaviour, wouldn't it? You know what these stupid buggers did?" Again, he looked at Jack for a reply, who this time only shook his head negatively. "They threw 'em all in the duck pond. Can you believe it? They must be out of their bloody minds, that's all I can think. They were all there floating in t'duck pond when I came on this morning. And not only that, the night before some bastards threw all t'benches in t'pond, and they were not lightweight, I'll tell yer. It couldn't a' been easy, they'd have had to really work at it, it bloody beats me. T'other day we found an old bike in't pond. Turned out it belonged to that old dear who helps out at the church."

"Mrs Schofield, you mean?"

"Aye, that's her. They'd nicked her bike from outside t'church and threw it in 'ere. I can't understand it, can you?"

They shook their heads in disbelief and Jack wandered off home. There were lots of things wrong with the old days, as Jack had always been quick to point out, but this present state of affairs was totally beyond his comprehension. He couldn't understand it either.

That evening Jack went down to the Old Crown. It was his first visit since his return and he was looking forward to a decent pint for a change. He'd make damn sure it was Lily that took his order, he thought, as he strolled down. As he got near the public house he was disturbed by the amount of noise coming from that direction.

"There's a hell of a lot of noise coming from in there," he grumbled to himself, "sounds like some jazz festival or summat." If the noise outside was loud, when Jack opened the door, it was deafening. Even for Jack with his hearing aid turned down, it was like walking into a solid wall of sound. Jack was halted on the mat, both by the noise and by the milling mass of bodies. He couldn't see the bar; he couldn't see anything past the people blocking the entrance. They were all youngsters he noted disapprovingly. Standing on his toes at the entrance he could only just see the ceiling through the haze of tobacco smoke that was now swirling out of the open door behind him.

"Are you coming through, grandad?" remarked a sneering youth to Jack as he moved marginally to one side to create a tiny gap in the throng.

Jack edged his way through with a look of disdain on his face.

"Miserable old bugger," Jack heard the lad comment, in spite of the thunderous noise, but he was far too absorbed in his struggle to get through the massed ranks to the bar to make any stinging retort; he'd get him on the way back if he remembered.

Jack was sweating, out of breath, dishevelled and decidedly disgruntled when he finally forced his way through to the bar. There he was faced with, not the familiar and welcoming face of Lily, nor even the less-welcome face of Martin, but a young barmaid. One of three, he realised, when he'd wiped the steam from his glasses. He took a second glance, they were all chewing gum and moving their bodies rhythmically in time to the thudding beat of the music. The sound reverberated from the walls and was absorbed into the corporate body on the floor, amongst which there was a constant swell of movement. Jack, in immediate danger of being swept away by this human tide, hung grimly on to the bar with one hand whilst attempting to turn off his hearing aid with the other. He feared for his survival if the blast from the speakers blew the batteries in his jacket pocket. Normal conversation was impossible under these circumstances and Jack found even ordering a drink almost beyond his capability.

When he eventually got both hands on the bar and felt himself more or less secure, he straightened his glasses over his eyes and looked up to see one of the barmaids mouthing at him. At first he wasn't sure whether she was still chewing gum or actually saying something, so he stared closely at her lips for a while, his face rapt with concentration. After a few moments of this scrutiny the girl raised her eyes to the ceiling, looked despairingly at one of her colleagues and hip-swung her body over to the other side of the bar. The other barmaid came across to Jack, flashed her teeth at him in a wide smile; her lips framed some unheard words and her face looked at him questioningly.

Jack mouthed, "A pint of best bitter, please." The girl obviously queried the order because she raised her eyebrows and lifted her head. Jack re-mimed his request, and this time the barmaid shook her head and said something. Jack shook his head to indicate his lack of understanding, and the girl bent down under the bar and came up with a pencil and a drip pad. She wrote in capital letters on the underside of the pad and turned it round for Jack to see; "NO BEER ONLY LAGER". Jack raised his eyes in disgust, after all this. No bloody beer? What a dump. Well, he thought, I might as well have drink while I'm here, and he wrote on the pad; 1 PINT LAGER PLEASE. The girl smiled, highly delighted with her success in dealing with this senile geriatric and reached up for a pint glass.

In the meantime Jack was having trouble getting his purse out of his back pocket as he was being crushed against the bar by drinkers eager to refill their glasses, and impatient at the delay Jack was causing. He eventually managed it and sorted the correct amount out on the bar; he was always punctilious about this because he'd once been wrongly changed, and he wasn't going to give them another chance. The barmaid put his pint in front of him on the bar and Jack handed her his one pound 28 pence. She turned to the till to cash it in but when she saw the amount in her hand immediately whirled round to face him. He could tell from her expression that something was not quite right. Jack watched the rapid movement of her lips intently but could not distinguish any individual words. He shook his head to express his lack of comprehension at which the girl angrily reached for the pad and scribbled a message and passed it across to him.

The baying demands of the waiting drinkers had reached a crescendo now and a tall, dark-suited young man, long hair smoothed and oiled down flat had appeared behind the bar. He was now looking at Jack with some disdain. Jack's temper, less than mellow at the best of times, had been boiling up for the last fifteen minutes; he hadn't yet had a drink, he'd been deafened into a state of shock, crushed flat against the bar, treated like an idiot by some gum-chewing floozie and now, to cap it all, was being subjected to nasty looks by a jumped-up jerk in a shiny suit. If he could have been heard, he would have told them what to do with their bloody beer; and if he could have moved, he would have been out of there like a shot. As it was he fumed internally like a volcano, until the build-up of internal pressure threatened to endanger the safety of those packed around him. His red face, incoherent speech, bulging eyeballs and perspiring brow were indication enough, one would have thought, to prepare people for the resultant explosion. But in that level of noise and in that density of crowd, apopleptic fits could easily pass unnoticed, indeed, could almost be taken to be an accepted part of the general scene.

The final rein of Jack's control finally snapped when he caught sight of the amount the girl had written on the drip pad; it said in the same bold letters: LAGER 2-50 A PINT.

That was it. Jack's face contorted even more grotesquely, he frothed at the mouth in impotent fury, gesticulated wildly and even shook a clenched fist at the man in the shiny suit. The young man stepped back a pace in alarm and pressed a concealed buzzer under the bar. There was a sudden flurry and the massed ranks behind Jack divided as two enormous gentlemen, wearing suits which had obviously been made for much smaller men, ploughed through the heaving mass like destroyers through a stormy sea responding to some urgent 'mayday' call. Their joint bow wave of humanity eventually reached Jack and the pressure from behind forced him bodily off the floor and up on to the bar like some improbable figurehead of a spanish galleon. The girls behind the bar shrieked with terror and they, and the bar manager, recoiled instinctively against the far wall; if the white shark in 'Jaws' had smashed its way up through the floorboards and reared up over the bar with its teeth snapping they would not have reacted with such alacrity.

The large gentlemen cruised up to Jack, seized him, one under each armpit, lifted him off the bar and carried him backwards shoulder high through the crowded room. The furrow their passage created was just as quickly filled again by the swirling mob which closed behind them. The music didn't miss a beat and no-one gave the trio a second glance, apart from the lad who was still standing with the group blocking the doorway. "G'night, grandad. Not staying?" he called familiarly, as Jack cruised effortlessly past.

The bouncers dumped Jack on the step outside, "We don't want to see troublemakers like you in here again, sir," one of them grunted, "so bugger off home!" he added viciously.

Jack straightened his jacket, adjusted his glasses and wiped his face with his handkerchief. "Plonkers!" he muttered under his breath as he walked across the street and onto the green.

The moon had just lifted itself over the horizon in the south-east, abnormally large and very bright. It shone through the branches of the willow tree like a benevolent smiling face. The sight did wonders for Jack's stressful condition and he strolled, slightly more at ease now, across the grass towards the tree in the centre. Natural beauty, he thought to himself, feeling decidedly poetical, but struggling to express his feelings adequately, that's what life's really about, he finished lamely. His peace of mind, however, only lasted a few seconds. The rusty burnt-out shell of a motor car was smashed into the trunk on the far side of the willow tree; bits of wire, fragments of glass and assorted auto-debris littered the grass for yards around. The bench at the foot of the tree had been smashed to pieces by the impact. Forcing his eyes away from this scene of devastation on the ground, Jack looked up, but his eyes found no relief there; the fire had blackened the trunk and burned off the bark, scorched the branches and completely stripped the leaves from one side of the willow tree. Tears welled up in the old man's eyes, precipitated by this latest outrage, but more probably the cumulative result of all that had happened over the last couple of days.

"God, it only seems like the other day and look how things have changed. What are things coming to?" He looked up again at the tree, "You didn't deserve this," he sobbed, "a friend to generations of villagers, you didn't deserve this. Bastards!" he shouted, as anger replaced sentiment. "Mindless, ignorant, stupid, bastards!" he went on, enunciating each word carefully.

With one long last look behind him Jack turned and headed for the High Street. He glanced over his shoulder to look once again at the moon before he turned the corner by the pub. "You've seen it all haven't you, old pal? You were here before I came, and you'll still be watching when I've gone," he reflected. "Same moon, same people, just different faces, different values."

He sighed to himself as he walked along the High Street. The orange glare from the sodium street lamps reflected eerily from the steel shuttered windows and created a harsh metallic impersonal atmosphere which Jack found disturbing. He was glad when he smelled the appetizing aroma from the fish shop at the end of the row; he could just do with a cake and chips for his supper. It hadn't been what you could call 'a reet good neet out' so far, and a good chip supper would improve things no end.

Three teenage boys were at the counter when Jack went in, but they'd already been served and were just putting salt and vinegar on their chips.

"'Evening, Jack," Eric called from behind the chromium range of pans. "How did your holiday go? Good weather?"

"Aye, weather weren't so bad, Eric," Jack answered. "It were a change I suppose. A cake and a portion please, love," he said to the assistant, in response to her questioning look. "Oh, and a few scraps on, if you don't mind."

"Bad news about Sam, wasn't it?" Eric said as he shook the fat out of a wire scoop of hot chips. " We heard the crash, me and the missus. Came down the High Street like bloody maniacs they did. They've got nobody for it yet neither, trouble is, when they do, they'll only get a caution or summat stupid like that."

Jack was inclined to agree but he didn't fancy a long discussion just now when his chips were going cold.

"Aye, I don't know what things are coming to. Thanks, love," he nodded to the girl and tucked the warm parcel under his arm, wished them goodnight and stepped out into the street.

The youths who had been in the fish shop before Jack were sitting on the window sill of the shop next door. Around their feet were screwed-up newspapers and empty chip packets and the boys were sniggering and completely engrossed in what they were scrawling on the metal shutter.

"Hey, what do you think you're doing?" Jack stormed. "Bloody well leave other folk's property alone!" As the youths made no attempt to move Jack added, "Get off there, get off home! Look at this bloody mess you've left, as well?" The lads had backed off nervously at Jack's approach but immediately adopted a more truculent attitude when they saw he was elderly, and alone.

"What's it to you, you old goat? one of them retorted nastily. "If you don't like the mess you can pick it up." The others guffawed loudly at this witty riposte.

"I'll give you a thick ear, you cheeky young bugger! It's time you learned some respect," Jack shouted furiously.

The youth was about to continue with his banter but the figures of Eric and his assistant had appeared in the doorway behind Jack, and in the face of such overwhelming odds the three youths turned away and ambled down the street, hands in pockets kicking an empty lemonade can in front of them.

"They're a bloody nuisance, that lot," said Eric coming up to Jack. "They're always up to summat, I don't know what the parents are thinking of, I don't really." He picked up the discarded paper and bags as he spoke, "You'd better get off home, Jack. Your chips'll be getting cold."

Jack sat at the kitchen table and ate his supper. Eric was right, the chips were cold, and there were a load of black ones amongst them. Honestly, the number of times Jack had told him about that.

Jack went round the house following the nightly routine he'd done for years. He checked that all the plugs and switches were off, that the plugs in the bath and sink were in, that the doors were locked and bolted, and all the windows securely fastened. He put out the light and drew the kitchen curtain back and peered through the window to check the garage door. Satisfied that all was secure for the night he undressed and got into bed, gently wiped his glasses on the sheet and put them carefully on the bedside cabinet. His last job was to wind-up his reliable pocket watch and prop it up in its usual place; when he was satisfied that the angle was just right for seeing it from the bed, he turned off the light.

Three score and ten's not a bad old total, he mused when he was lying comfortably. I'll bet some o' them English cricketers wish they could do as well. This in't my world now though, it's a new order, and there's no future in it for me. They've made the world the way it is, and it's up to them to sort it out. Jack was not feeling sorry for himself but simply expressing what he believed was an objective opinion. He pulled the covers over his head and snuggled down cosy and warm; he smiled to himself contentedly as he thought how easy it was to escape from the world's problems in a warm bed.

Elizabeth Simpson was out in the garden next morning pegging out her washing when Sandra appeared from around the corner of her house. She was lugging a massive laundry basket. "Never ending, is it?" said the younger woman cheerfully.

"No, you've got your hands full with that lot," Elizabeth acknowledged. "By the way, Sandra," and her voice became grave with concern. "You haven't seen owt of Jack this morning, have you, by any chance?"

Sandra shook her head, "No, but I've been busy in the kitchen so I might not have noticed if he'd gone past. Is everything all right?"

"I don't know, love, it's just that his milk's still on the doorstep, and the blinds are still drawn, and that's not like Jack at all ..."

The author lives in West Yorkshire close to the Yorkshire Dales National Park and within easy reach of the Pennines. He is a keen on most sports, fell-walking and cycling and has a great affection for the natural world and is very keen on its conservation. He has travelled extensively throughout the world, often in remote and mountainous regions, but always enjoys coming home, meeting friends in the local, listening to classical music and spending time with the family.

By the same author.

The Three Men of Gragareth

The Dogmatists

The Golfing Society

All available at http://www.normanharrison.co.uk